SEA CHANGES

Kay Stephens

This first world edition published in Great Britain 2003 by
SEVERN HOUSE PUBLISHERS LTD of
9–15 High Street, Sutton, Surrey SM1 1DF.
This first world edition published in the USA 2004 by
SEVERN HOUSE PUBLISHERS INC of
595 Madison Avenue, New York, N.Y. 10022.

British Library Cataloguing in Publication Data

Stephens, Kay
Sea changes
1. World War, 1939-1945 - England - Yorkshire - Fiction
2. World War, 1939-1945 - Participation, Norwegian - Fiction
3. Love stories
I. Title
823.9'14 [F]

ISBN 0-7278-5995-1

Typeset by Palimpsest Book Production Ltd.,
Polmont, Stirlingshire, Scotland.
Printed and bound in Great Britain by
MPG Books Ltd., Bodmin, Cornwall.

Author's Note

Studying *The Shetland Bus* by David Howarth has provided me with some of the background material for this novel. I dedicate my work to all those who lived and died to maintain this dangerous World War II operation.

One

Hamish was smiling, brown eyes approving all that she had achieved; Rachel could never have guessed that the news he brought would shock her so terribly.

'Glad to see this place will soon be up and running.' Glancing all around him, he came striding into the panelled entrance hall of Keld House, the mansion they were converting into a military hospital.

'I've a nasty feeling we'll be even more necessary now,' Hamish continued. 'When Norway is occupied, our troops are unlikely to hold out against the Germans. I'm afraid we must anticipate that there'll be Allied casualties.'

'Occupied? But Norway is neutral . . .' Rachel felt sickened.

'*For the present*, perhaps. Word is that our navy witnessed flotillas of German warships escorting their troopships, all heading towards the fjords.'

'There must be some mistake. I'd have known.'

Hamish Wilson was giving her a curious look. Rachel realized that he had no knowledge of her family connection with Norway. And she had been isolated here for days during this spring in 1940. As the only doctor on site, she'd been too busy to give much thought to whatever might be happening beyond these Yorkshire hills.

'Sorry to generate alarm,' said Hamish, his eyes sympathetic.

Rachel tried to smile. She had liked this military surgeon instantly when he had first interviewed her in the Leeds hospital where she'd worked since qualifying, but she would need more than their rapport to ease her increasing anxiety.

'You couldn't know – my mother's half-Norwegian, her mother Hedda lives in the hills overlooking Bergen. And we've other relatives over there.'

'I see. I suppose this explains your glorious fair hair.' Hamish wanted to know more; during these weeks of working together his longing to learn all about Dr Rachel Skelton had grown.

She shrugged. 'I'm not sure about that. Just so long as you understand why this news shakes me up, and will forgive me if I'm a bit quiet. Couldn't bear to face losing anyone else, ever.'

Hamish nodded, took a step towards Rachel and grasped her by both shoulders. His expression was grave. 'Loss, I do understand, Rachel. My fiancée was on the *Athenia* when it was sunk by a U-boat last September. The . . . the gap in your life doesn't go away, but work does help, don't you think?'

She nodded, forced herself to smile again as his hands slid away. She had always used her career to help obliterate that dreadful sense of having someone missing. Some part of her.

'As you can see through there, most of the beds have arrived now,' Rachel told him, indicating the former reception room which already looked more like a ward.

'And the theatres – are they equipped yet?' Setting aside his suitcase and an armful of files, Hamish began walking through the large, still elegant entrance hall.

Crossing the tiled floor beside him, Rachel's expression was rueful. 'One is, although still waiting for the plumbing-in of the area where we'll scrub up. I'm afraid the principal theatre's not ready, though. The builders hit problems meeting your requirements for lighting, the sterilization unit . . . you name it, they encountered snags. Evidently the previous owner didn't believe in servicing the upper rooms with electricity. All were lit by gas. A team of electricians is due in tomorrow.'

'Sounds like you've done your best.'

'With help from the admin side. Jock McGrath kept on at them while I was occupied seeing in beds and lockers and stuff, and setting up sluice rooms.'

'So this ward is operational then?'

'Virtually. Not much good, though, until the theatres are.'

Hamish grinned. 'Oh, I don't know. We could take men who need medical attention almost straight away. I hope you don't consider me one of those surgeons who forget the rest of their training, only to come alive in theatre!'

Rachel laughed, and wondered how long it was since she had done so. Challenging though the work here was, she had found it lonely with mostly workmen on site, and many of them prepared to believe she was there just to criticize.

With Hamish absent, she had frequently felt rather out of her depth, and it was during such times that she always experienced the sense of being incomplete. Reasoning told her, as it had so often over the years, that if Richard had lived there would have been many situations to face without him. But reason, even for a down-to-earth Yorkshirewoman, did not supply the answer. Steeling herself to tackle everything head-on – and alone – seemed a kind of solution. Albeit one which was subject to misunderstanding.

No man she'd ever met had appeared able to discover the true Rachel behind that instinctive reserve. Since meeting Hamish she was beginning to wish that she could somehow become more *approachable*.

He had taken her out for a meal shortly after they began work at Keld House, and a few visits to the cinema had followed. Tall, with dark wavy hair and those keen brown eyes, he couldn't have been more attractive.

And Rachel *was* attracted. He had kissed her tentatively in the back row of the pictures, and she'd had to engage considerable will power to resist the impulse to respond quite fervently. Wanting him wasn't enough, she mustn't mislead him into believing this physical need was all that mattered to her. Hamish had perturbed her recently. Before going off to this course in reconstructive surgery, he'd assured Rachel that he felt more than mere desire for her.

She had been unable to reciprocate. Today, already wondering if he was curious about the cause of her sudden silence, she began detailing her chosen layout of the ward they had reached.

'I thought the nurses' desks should be in the middle there – and we'll have space for your desk in the tiny office where we're stacking medical supplies and so on. Not much more than a cubbyhole, I'm afraid, but we might find you somewhere better when upstairs is completed.'

'This'll be fine, don't worry. You're doing a grand job. And I anticipate spending most of my time on the wards, or in theatre.'

'We're just beginning to get the second ward equipped,' Rachel continued. 'The lockers are due next week, and the beds are here now, but no mattresses or linen as yet.'

Hamish was smiling. 'You've done far more than I expected. This is great.'

'How did the course go, was it as useful as you hoped?'

'I suppose it was – if only to convince me where I shall need to draw the line. There's so much – especially regarding facial surgery – where only the true experts will do any real good. Still, I should be able to assess many of the patients sent our way, if only to offer primary care before pointing them in the right direction.'

The enthusiasm in his voice revealed Hamish's eagerness to make a start. Rachel caught herself experiencing again the longing to be striving to heal people alongside him. She'd had enough of all this preparatory work.

'We've been promised a few Red Cross volunteers, as soon as we're open.'

'That's good, Rachel, it'll free us to tackle stuff we're trained for. What's the latest on recruiting nurses?'

'Haven't had a firm answer on that one, it seems to depend on having a definite date for receiving our first patients.'

He took a quick glance around the second ground floor ward, nodding approval over the beds installed there.

'Tomorrow we'll chase up those lockers and the linen. Did you say some supplies of dressings and medication are already here?'

After showing Hamish the items stacked on shelves, Rachel

noticed how tired he looked and, remembering his long journey that day, asked what else he needed to check.

'Nothing tonight, I'm satisfied the rest can be left till morning. I'll just dump my stuff upstairs, then I'm off for a bite to eat. Why don't you join me?'

Rachel hesitated. She'd been intending to use some of her meagre petrol allowance and head for the coast. If her parents knew of the imminent invasion of Norway, she must try to find some means of reassuring them. Asta Skelton had always been so close to her own mother. Even before this wretched war started, Asta had been unhappy about Hedda Davidson living so far away across the North Sea.

Rachel glanced at her watch and sighed. It would be late evening before she reached their home in the outskirts of Scarborough, not the best time to set her mother worrying about absent family.

'I could use your company,' Hamish told her.

Remembering then how he'd confided that his fiancée had died six months previously, Rachel decided she might be of some use as a friend.

'Why not then, thanks,' she said with a smile. 'I just hope you're not planning on going anywhere posh.' She was too tired for more than a hasty wash.

Hamish laughed. 'The local pub, if that suits you? I believe you know what it's like.'

They had both sampled the quite plain cooking over there, sometimes with Jock McGrath or others of the admin staff, if they hadn't eaten there together.

Rachel grinned. 'It's the only pub I'd dare go into on my own.'

'What – and you from a seaside town, where there's a bar on every corner!'

'And me the daughter of a trawlerman? Have you seen some of the places fisherfolk frequent?'

Their banter continued throughout the walk to the pub, and until they were served with pies containing dubious quantities of meat, which were accompanied by massive dollops of mashed potato.

'How is your father?' Hamish enquired eventually.

'When I phoned through the other day, he was still at sea. Mum didn't know much, beyond the fact that his fleet was struggling to operate. Despite regulations, and the perpetual need to remain on constant lookout for E-boats and enemy aircraft . . . Mum didn't say, but I suspect Dad's minesweeping whenever he goes out. He let slip to me that his own trawler's equipped with gear for that – I could certainly see an anti-aircraft gun on the foredeck.'

'You must be extremely worried for his safety.'

'I try not to let that take over; if you surrender to anxiety you can't do your job.'

'And now there's the news I brought with me today. I am sorry, Rachel. Just wish there was some way I could lighten the load for you.'

'Yes – well, that's purely circumstances, isn't it? Part of this damned war, and a part of our lives. My mother relied on Grandmother Hedda so greatly when . . . when we went through a dreadful time many years ago.'

Hamish was mystified, but sensed that Rachel was no more likely now than ever in the past to enlighten him about what had happened. About her loss. Perhaps, however, he ought to make one further attempt to persuade her to talk things through . . .

'Do you want to tell me?'

She shook her head emphatically. 'No, no. I can't. Sorry. Please don't ask.'

And I truly am sorry, she thought. If anyone could understand, it might be Hamish. Only that would help no one. She would go to pieces, as she only ever had with Hedda Davidson. Her relationship with this fine surgeon was professional and must remain so, and that depended upon her keeping her emotions severely under control.

Conscious of Rachel's need to relax, Hamish spoke lightly of his recent course in the reconstructive surgery so unfamiliar to him, dredging up incidents that bestowed a small degree of levity on the grave subject.

'I was thankful there were others who'd as little knowledge

of such procedures as myself,' he said finally as they settled the bill and headed back to their rooms at Keld House.

'I can't imagine you ever seeming less than well informed on any aspect of your work,' Rachel observed.

He laughed. 'I hope I don't have occasion to remind you of that touching faith in my abilities once we get down to treating people.'

For several days they were both fully occupied, overseeing the building work and checking in further supplies of medical and surgical equipment, along with bedding, plus everything needed to fit out the big hospital kitchen.

Whenever Rachel found time from somewhere to catch the BBC news, she waited in vain for futher details of the possibility that Norway was being invaded.

By the evening when she finally managed to drive over to see her parents, she was convincing herself that all Hamish had heard was just a rumour. Even though normally well informed by those in authority, who indicated any areas from where they might expect an influx of casualties, nobody was infallible.

Welcoming her into the warm living room, Asta Skelton was smiling so cheerfully that Rachel immediately felt reassured. She knew her mother, and knew those silver-grey eyes, so like her own, which were never any good at concealing emotions.

'Your dad's due home an' all, any time now!' Asta exclaimed, releasing her daughter from a hug. 'You couldn't have timed this better. I hope you can stop the night? It's that long since we've seen you.'

'If I set off back at the proverbial crack of dawn,' Rachel replied. 'Hamish is interviewing the first batch of nurses tomorrow, and wants me in on that.'

'We'll make the most of these few hours then.'

'You're looking well, Mum,' Rachel remarked, following through into the kitchen when Asta insisted she must make a pot of tea.

'It does me good every time I hear your father's on his way

back. Don't mind admitting it isn't easy when he's away for a long stretch.'

'Has this been a long trip then?'

'Aye. But we won't dwell on that. He sent word an hour since that he's put in. All he'd got to do then was take a look at any paperwork and stuff in the office.'

Andrew Skelton came from a long line of fishermen, and was the first to own a substantial fleet of vessels. He wouldn't readily permit this war to diminish his running of the business.

Rachel and Asta were sitting companionably at the kitchen table when Andrew came stomping in.

'My two favourite women!' he exclaimed, his hazel eyes lighting up.

He kissed each of them before turning to discard his sea boots beside the door. 'So, Rachel love, how's that hospital coming along? Fully equipped now?'

'All but, Dad, though we're still having difficulty kitting out the larger surgery. It's been a long haul, but the last of the building contractors have gone now, and the cleaners have almost finished.'

'That surgeon pal of yours will be glad when you can get down to business.'

'He's not the only one. I was beginning to think we'd never have the place ready. Did I tell you most of the upstairs still had gas lighting? Unfortunately, that was the only area suitable for surgeries, hence a lot more work to be done.'

Washing his hands at the sink, Andrew turned to glance at them over his shoulder. 'Something smells good, Asta. I expect that means you've supper in the oven?'

His wife smiled. 'I have been saving our ration of meat until you were in port again.' She glanced towards Rachel. 'There's plenty for the three of us, don't start fussing.'

'Right. That's good, Mum. But I've brought you a few things, anyway. I'll just get them out of the car before I forget.'

Since rationing was introduced, few people visited family or friends without contributing something to help eke out the weekly allowance of those foods in short supply.

They ate their simple meal at the kitchen table, reminding

Rachel that since the outbreak of war her mother used the dining room hardly at all, in order to economise on the fuel required for heating the good, solid Victorian house.

Andrew Skelton said little about his latest trip, something which they now accepted as usual; he had no wish to alarm them by stories of the hazards to be encountered in the North Sea. Instead, Asta began telling them of the work she was doing ashore. She had joined the Red Cross, and was learning first aid as well as helping to organize other women determined to do all they could to assist the war effort.

'My father had a good laugh when I told him about the first aid classes, but he's coming to accept that I might prove useful one day!'

'How is Granddad?' Rachel asked.

Her father laughed. 'If I know Bernard Davidson, he'll be in his element now that doctors his age are needed to replace younger men.'

Asta gave her husband a look. 'And what is wrong with that?' she asked, a certain asperity revealing in her accent her half-Norwegian ancestry. 'He always has been an exemplary member of his profession, and one who doubtless will still be curing patients however long he may live.'

'I'm sure you're right, Mum.' Rachel didn't wish any differences to mar the family evening.

But Andrew was just as keen to maintain a calm atmosphere. He winked at his wife. 'You know I could never have wished for a more genial father-in-law, even if I can't resist making you rise to his defence. And we all know how genuinely delighted he is to have our Rachel here follow in his footsteps.'

Asta nodded agreement, although she remained serious. 'It is only that we have to remember that practising as a doctor cannot always have been easy, since he has lived alone all these years.'

'He still has his housekeeper, surely?' asked Rachel.

Asta's smile was rueful. 'Mrs Hardaker is eighty now, don't forget. I do wonder at times who is caring for whom in that household!'

'But it suits them both,' her husband suggested.

Rachel watched her mother's expressive shrug. They all knew that Dr Bernard Davidson would have had a far happier life if his wife had not felt too homesick to remain in Yorkshire.

Eventually, Asta sighed. 'It is too late to argue the rights and wrongs of what has happened so long ago – and to undo anything. I only give thanks that my mother's homeland is neutral territory . . .'

Rachel glanced towards her father when a sudden silence revealed his unease.

'Er . . . actually, Asta love, I'm afraid that may be changing,' Andrew began, running a hand over his red hair. His eyes darkened. 'You have not listened to the news on the radio?'

'I never do, you know that well enough. When something bad occurs, I do not wish to hear of it.'

With her husband working the North Sea, Asta had ceased following the BBC reports weeks ago as they so often carried news of Allied vessels being sunk by U-boats or those terrible magnetic mines.

Andrew reached across the table to grasp her hand. 'Just the other day reports came through that the Germans have landed out there. Swastikas are being flown over Oslo.'

His wife did not wish to accept that this signalled the end of Norwegian freedom. 'We must be fighting back, surely? Norwegian armies and the British too. No one will let Hitler overrun the country completely.'

'Our navy has tried. I heard that British destroyers dashed through a snowstorm to catch a German flotilla near the entrance to one of the fjords.'

'Did they drive the Germans away, Dad?' asked Rachel.

'Not quite, there were losses on both sides. However, since then some of our forces, together with the French, have landed.'

'Where? Where exactly?' his wife demanded, her face ashen.

'Andalsnes was one spot, and the Lofoten Islands.'

Asta gave a wan smile. 'Then you will see – with Norway's

men to one side and the British to seaward, the Germans will be squeezed out.'

A few days later Asta's words seemed over-optimistic as news came through that Hitler's armies were forcing the Allies out of Lillehammer.

By the beginning of May, Rachel and Hamish were working harder than ever to have the hospital ready for use. They had been warned to expect some casualties to be transferred to them from the south of England, which seemed more vulnerable to German attack.

Preparing their principal theatre had taken even longer than expected, making Hamish frustrated because of his determination to practise surgery instead of chasing up suppliers, who in turn perpetually struggled against shortages of specialist equipment. On several occasions he had travelled some distance to operate elsewhere, satisfying the need for surgeons and his own longing to make more of a difference.

During these weeks Rachel had made one further visit home, only to learn from a neighbour that her mother was attending a Red Cross course. Rather than try to track down Asta, she'd continued on to call on her grandfather.

Dr Bernard Davidson had seemed in good spirits, which was more than Rachel could say of herself. She had set out cheerfully enough, thinking as she headed over the hills towards the coast that the quiet there was very different from the reality of the hazards out in the North Sea. Moments later she had paused en route, her attention caught by a 'Danger of Invasion' notice which she felt compelled to study.

'Eh, Rachel lass, you mustn't let that alarm you,' the elderly doctor reassured her when she explained her frown. 'They're putting them up as a precaution, that's all, in lots of the coastal towns.'

'If you say so, Granddad. I don't want to go upsetting you.'

'It'd take more nor that, love. During the last lot I had to learn to accept that Germany's capable of all sorts of attacks. Nobody's immune – although I'll admit I do take comfort now in knowing you're based further inland.'

Rachel smiled, if a little uncomfortably. Dr Bernard Davidson had always had a soft spot for her, but should he be especially concerned for *her* safety? What had she done to deserve that?

'You're the one who'll maintain the tradition,' he reminded her when he read the thoughts behind her eloquent eyes. 'It's the future that counts, and you know very well that if my father had lived, he too would have been thrilled to have another doctor in the family.'

'Even one who's not yet allowed enough opportunity for healing folk?'

'There'll be more than sufficient opportunity in another few weeks, I'll warrant. And times when you and Hamish Wilson will look back longingly on this period when you're setting up that hospital.'

'You reckon? When we both feel this is not what we were trained to do?'

'Who else but medical folk would understand what's necessary there?' The silver-grey eyes she and her mother had inherited were smiling.

'I hope you're right, Granddad. We certainly aim to have one of the best equipped military hospitals around. Even despite difficulties in getting supplies through.'

'And how have you yourself been, love? Are you . . . are you beginning to feel any happier?'

Rachel sighed, toyed with the prospect of sparing her grandfather the trouble that had plagued her throughout the majority of her life. She recalled then how rarely she and Bernard Davidson were alone together, and how she always felt she ought not to speak of the family loss whenever her mother was present.

'I'm all right, most of the time.'

'When you're fully occupied, eh? And maybe when Hamish Wilson is around. By all accounts, he's a good man.'

'And sympathetic, if only I could let him be. The problem is, I can never find the words for explaining how . . . strangely *lost* I often feel, without Richard.'

The elderly man nodded. 'Twins always are special, you

must know that, love. Nine months together in the womb, then coming into this world with each other as the only truly familiar beings they could see. Or touch.'

'No one's ever put it that way before.'

'Happen nobody's ever been given the chance? Have you ever really talked through what you felt, since Richard died when you were less than a year old?'

'Not properly, a little perhaps with Grandmother Hedda.'

'Aye, well, there's been gallons of water flowed under the bridge since she took herself too far away to do much good. You'd better bear in mind that I'm still here for you, Rachel love – and unlikely now to go to pieces at mention of the bairn that died.'

Rachel could believe that this large, bear-like man would always be reassuring.

She soon felt better for her grandfather's words, and better still when she and Hamish began in earnest to utilize their hospital to the full. The last few items of equipment for the operating theatres were delivered, and nursing and auxiliary staff brought in with something of a rush.

The German armies advancing across Europe were trapping the Allied forces in a strip of land along the coasts of Holland, Belgium and France – a strip which was narrowing at an alarming rate.

Readying Keld House for its first influx of patients, Rachel scarcely had the time to dwell on news that Allied forces had been obliged to withdraw from Norway. On the same day that she found a map and identified Narvik, which had been evacuated, Hamish received information of another, massive evacuation that had to begin: the immense effort to rescue the British Expeditionary Forces from the beaches of western Europe.

The men arrived in varying degrees of distress, and with a monstrous assortment of injuries. Admitted for immediate assessment by their strong team of nurses, soldiers seemed to fill the waiting beds so swiftly that Rachel was soon pressing their admin staff to order in more beds to occupy spaces that already appeared too generous.

Many suffering burns, gunshot wounds or the loss of limbs were processed through the two theatres in a depressingly constant stream, making Hamish declare that he would have begged for some respite were not the need for his skill so evident.

Exhausted by the end of every day, he was turning to Rachel for his only comfort – all too frequently no more than a chat over a hasty snack which they were generally all but too tired to eat.

'You're the one who gives me strength to keep going,' he told her one night, with a sudden hug as they parted to go to their rooms. 'I expected our lives here to become frenetic, but not quite this much!' And the trauma was the worst, he reflected silently, reluctant to infect her with his hatred of this daily evidence of human suffering.

Rachel grinned, raised exhausted eyes to meet his gaze. 'It is daunting, I agree, but we're turning into a good team, aren't we? It should get better when we're more accustomed to all the different injuries.'

Experience should help, shouldn't it? All she knew was that, for her, working so hard, and at Hamish's side, was finally providing an escape from the loss that had always haunted her life.

Rachel's worst days came a few weeks later. Arriving by special ambulance came a man who had been blinded, a man who had spent nights adrift in a tiny boat, a sailor who'd been picked up following the battle for Norway.

Seb Taylor had been brought ashore on some island to the north of Scotland where, after basic medical attention, he'd been flown south by the RAF. Sadly, nothing could be done to restore his sight, but he required further treatment of superficial injuries sustained during and after battle, plus general care to help restore his depleted strength.

Someone en route to them had begin to help Seb adapt to being blind, but although he was able to feed himself and wash and dress, he would need practice to adjust further and learn to use his time.

Rachel took to Seb immediately, warming to the determination with which the lad, who was only twenty, was facing the future. Checking with nurses and auxiliaries that he was receiving all the good food he needed, she made it her own task to ensure that he developed his remaining skills.

At first, rather at a loss to know where to turn for expert advice, she telephoned Bernard Davidson who instantly recommended someone who could teach him Braille. The old doctor had enlisted similar help for one of his own patients.

Until Seb became au fait with Braille, Rachel volunteered to maintain contact with his family. She quickly learned that Seb's mother was running the family farm in the Wye Valley and, although naturally perturbed by her son's injuries, couldn't immediately find someone to take over in order for her to visit him. A sailor like himself, Seb's father was on active service.

To Rachel's surprise, the lad wasn't unduly distressed about his mother's remaining at home. 'She has her job, Dad and I chose ours,' he said philosophically. Rachel wondered if Seb had a strong desire to increase his ability to cope before his mother saw him.

She seemed to be proved right when she saw the effort he was putting into preparing himself for his different way of life. In the meantime, another of her tasks was to help him overcome the nightmares resulting from his battle history.

Speaking with her, Seb soon revealed that he had not been wholeheartedly in favour of fighting on behalf of Norway. 'Some of the crew on board would have it that the Norwegians had always had some sort of pact with Germany. They used to say parts of certain cities there were German already.'

'Oh, I don't think so,' Rachel quickly reassured him, but the thought was one which remained to trouble her even long after Seb had been transferred to a rehabilitation centre further south.

Wouldn't she have known if such an allegiance had existed? she wondered. But she continued to worry in case Grandmother Hedda could be under some kind of threat from among the inhabitants of her own country.

Two

For weeks after Seb Taylor had been transferred elsewhere, Rachel was too busy to begin to find out if there was any truth to the rumoured old allegiance between some Norwegians and the Germans. She felt so awful just thinking about it that she wouldn't mention it to Hamish, and she saw no one outside the hospital except her own mother.

With Asta Skelton's concern for Hedda only too evident, Rachel had no intention of worsening her anxiety by bringing the matter into their conversations. Instead, she related stories of the men they were healing, something which her mother's new-found interest in first aid seemed to render fascinating.

Although often harrowing, Rachel was finding her own work satisfying, especially whenever she assisted Hamish in one of the theatres. The theatre sisters they had taken on were efficient enough, but with only two of them to hand, emergency surgery often took place while neither was on duty.

In what little time he had available, Hamish was teaching other nurses operating theatre routine, but such time was rare. A few days after the evacuation of Dunkirk, news reached them that Italy had joined the war against the Allies. To make everything seem worse, France had capitulated to the German armies, and the Channel Islands were occupied by enemy forces.

The pressure on them increased as demands to admit more wounded men threatened to overwhelm their small hospital. Rachel was surprised by how swiftly another month passed. She noticed the date only when news bulletins brought word that the Luftwaffe was attacking merchant shipping in the

English Channel. According to Hitler, this was only the beginning – he was intent on invading England.

Nearer to home in that July of 1940, Spitfires from Catterick and Hurricanes from Church Fenton often flew overhead to intercept enemy aircraft – one Junkers Ju88 was brought down somewhere off Scarborough.

Such events inland in the area were unusual. Even when raids by the Luftwaffe became horrendous further south, amid the moors of Yorkshire they quite often spent their days and nights in relative peace.

Naturally, provision had been made for offering protection from air attack, and every bed could be wheeled along to lifts which provided access to the specially strengthened cellars. Nevertheless, moving all their patients was a long process, and not one that was relished by any of the staff.

More often than not the men themselves protested they should be left where they were in the comfort of their wards; insisting that they had suffered far worse hazards already. But those confined to bed were not in a position to make such a decision for themselves, and both Hamish and Rachel viewed their responsibilities very seriously.

On one night when the sirens sounded, they and the rest of the staff had manhandled beds into and out of lifts, and settled men into the chill cellars. Almost immediately they heard the 'all clear' sounding and were obliged to begin to reverse the entire process.

It was five in the morning, and the sky over towards Ravenscar was already bright with dawn light when Hamish and Rachel looked ruefully at each other.

'Poor wee lass,' he exclaimed, smiling down at her. 'You're exhausted, aren't you? Better grab an hour's sleep.'

'And what about you – you look no better. What time's the first operation scheduled?'

'Seven, I believe. I'll not go to bed, that'd only make me feel worse. I'll rest for a while in the room we use on call.'

Rachel could tell no one afterwards why she went with him into that room, or what reasoning could have prompted her to accompany him to the narrow bed. Some impulse perhaps, never before acknowledged, just to remain with Hamish when life seemed especially tough.

He didn't remark on her decision, or ask one question while he meticulously set the alarm clock to rouse him in time for theatre.

They had worn casual clothing and sweaters for facing the cold cellars that night, and now discarded only the woollens before lying together on the bed. Hamish kissed her at once, affection making his mouth linger over hers while he settled his long limbs to accommodate her more comfortably. Overhead RAF aircraft droned past on their way home to their stations.

They kissed twice more, pressing close and relishing that closeness which seemed to convey reassurance without demand. When Hamish slept, Rachel smiled drowsily, pleased about the relaxation that she suspected she had generated.

She herself did not sleep, but felt refreshed nevertheless when the strident alarm wakened him. From that day, she would always remember their special night, enhanced by their rare closeness.

Those few shared hours seemed to induce a new familiarity between them, making even easier their co-operation in running the hospital. Anything that facilitated their working was necessary: German bomber attacks on British cities, as well as airfields and coastal defences, were generating ever more casualties.

To date, though, the expected invasion had not come and, having learned what German forces had done elsewhere in Europe, they were all thankful.

Week by week, patients were being discharged – some to return to their units, vessels and squadrons, others to specialist hospitals. The course that Hamish had taken earlier in the war enabled him to assess which patients would benefit from the skill of Archibald McIndoe and the maxillo-facial unit in East Grinstead.

Rachel was often deeply moved by the extent of the facial injuries suffered by some of their men, and was extremely thankful when they could offer them a degree of hope by referring them to Archie McIndoe.

During those months of late summer and autumn in 1940, the bombing of London and other cities continued relentlessly, filling civilian hospitals and making the need for any like Keld House ever more imperative. And the air raids were reaching further north – Birmingham was badly hit during October, followed by Coventry in November when the cathedral was struck, and then Sheffield was damaged in December.

Allied forces were valiantly fighting back, with RAF planes seeing off the Luftwaffe as well as conducting bombing raids over Germany; but whilst this seemed to have deterred Hitler from invading Britain, he was receiving support elsewhere. On other fronts the Italians were invading Greece, then they were drawing the Allies to help withstand their attacks on Egypt.

This lead-up to Christmas was doing nothing to generate a festive mood. Spurred on by reports of fighting, many Keld House patients were desperate to be fit enough to return to active service. Men were urging Rachel and Hamish to discharge them, even before they were fully fit.

'I'm running out of reasons they will listen to,' she admitted to him one night when they were drinking cocoa together as usual after lights out. 'I've been reminding them that unless they're truly better they could be more of a liability than anything when they reach the front.'

Hamish gave a tired smile. 'I know, I'm having the devil's own job trying to prevent them from discharging themselves, sometimes even before their operation wounds have healed.'

'I suppose we've got to admire their spirit, even when it creates problems for us. They did join up to fight, after all. It *is* what they're about.'

He nodded. 'Perhaps those who are obliged to remain here over Christmas will improve radically and be nearer reasonable dates for leaving afterwards.'

'And how are we going to give them a good time over the

festivities? We ought to do something, but I'm sure I don't know what. This wretched rationing doesn't help, does it?'

'We'll have to rely on something other than feasting. Suppose I should have been racking my brains before this . . .'

'You're always too busy. I could ask the vicar if his choir would come in and sing carols.' Rachel had attended the local church a few times when she had had free time on Sundays.

'Or failing that the Salvation Army – one of our nurses is a regular with them.'

Rachel approached both, and was delighted that the Salvation Army band offered to play and sing carols on Christmas Eve. The church choir would give them a firm date for a visit after they had met again to practise. More than that, they had a concert party which put on shows for nursing homes and council-run children's houses: they would be glad to perform for the military hospital.

Being able to arrange something to entertain their men cheered Rachel, and she soon found she was looking forward to having a break from their normal routine. Hamish had been informed that, as long as there was no major crisis, new admissions would be suspended during Christmas.

'Maybe you'll actually do a bit less work,' Rachel suggested. Even without her medical training, she couldn't have failed to notice his exhaustion.

When Christmas came and she did indeed watch Hamish taking part alongside their patients in the entertainment, she was thankful. He looked to be relaxing at last, enjoying the fun.

Rachel couldn't know that he was enjoying most of all the opportunity to share something other than work with *her*. During all the months since they first began to set up the hospital at Keld House, his affection for Rachel Skelton had been growing – and it was more than affection. Tired and preoccupied as they so often were, he rarely experienced more than a brief reminder of the desire she aroused in him, but that desire did exist.

When Boxing Day came and they promised to have far

less work demanding their attention, Hamish had to engage considerable will over his own feelings and suggest that she should seize the opportunity and drive off to visit her family.

'Are you sure? You're the one more in need of a change . . .'

One of the nursing sisters overheard and smiled at them both. 'We're not admitting today, are we? Everyone's medication is to hand, and there are no operations listed. There's nothing to stop the two of you taking leave, if only for a few hours.'

'No point for me,' Hamish demurred. 'Scotland's too far to make, there and back.'

'Then come home with me, you'd be more than welcome,' said Rachel quickly. 'Mum's always saying she doesn't know enough about my work here, and if Dad happens to be at sea she'll be desperate for company.'

'Even mine!' Hamish's expression was wry.

'I didn't mean that. And, in any case, Granddad Davidson is likely to be there – he'd love to see you. He might be one of the old school of doctors, but he relishes hearing about all the modern stuff that's going on.'

Happier than he would have admitted, Hamish accepted and began planning when they might set out. He ought to complete his ward rounds that morning but the rest of the day was theirs.

Rachel wasn't surprised that he insisted on taking his own car, she couldn't imagine him being a man who relished being driven. She wasn't sorry to save a little of her own petrol ration, and nor did she regret having him at the wheel.

Suggesting that Hamish go home with her had been impulsive and, whilst not having second thoughts about the invitation, she was hoping that her mother wouldn't read too much into the fact of his being there.

Over the years Rachel would have had to be blind as well as deaf to have remained oblivious to Asta Skelton's longing to have her daughter meet someone she might marry. And while Rachel herself felt that Richard's death left an abyss in her life that never would heal, her mother seemed to believe his loss was a major reason why the girl must be found a partner.

Concern about Asta's possible reaction had made Rachel phone ahead, but it appeared when they arrived at the house that she need not have worried.

'Our Rachel tells me you hadn't a chance of getting home to Scotland. I hope we can compensate for that, love,' Asta welcomed him.

Hamish smiled as he thanked her. 'You'll do more than that, I'm sure. We Scots are better at celebrating the new year, anyway. We haven't learned all your skills yet for putting on a good Christmas.'

As Rachel had anticipated, Bernard Davidson was spending a few days with his daughter and son-in-law. He was soon chatting with the young surgeon and to Rachel's embarrassment, emphasising his delight that *she* had taken up medicine.

'My own father was a doctor too, you know, over in Whitby. He'd have been thrilled that Rachel decided to go in for it as well. And maybe not all that astonished. He was married to a lass who had a lot about her – ran her own business at one time, carving jet.'

'I understand that was mined along the Yorkshire coast here,' said Hamish. He would not let on, but he had discovered quite a lot about Rachel's family history.

Catching up on her mother's news, Rachel was barely conscious of what the two men were discussing. If she had known, she might have been perturbed by the interest Hamish had taken in her already. As things were, she was more concerned that her father was out at sea. Minesweeping didn't take time off even for holidays like Christmas, she supposed. At least her mother was expecting him home before nightfall.

'I don't believe you'll have had any word from Grandmother Hedda this Christmas?' Rachel said.

Asta's silvery eyes filled with tears, but she tried to smile. 'I wasn't expecting to hear. I dare say the only letters allowed out of there have to be censored. I keep telling myself no news is good news. We'd have had to be told if anything had happened to her.'

Determined not to spoil the day for either Hamish or Rachel, Asta took charge of her own emotions and began setting lunch out on the table.

'We're only having a bit of a snack for now; when your dad's home tonight we're going to have our proper dinner. I'm hoping he'll be in tomorrow, that'll give us something to celebrate.'

When Andrew Skelton arrived and was introduced to Hamish, he seemed to have brought more to celebrate than notice of a day's holiday.

'I've got something that'll make your eyes light up, love,' he told his wife, taking from an inner pocket a crumpled envelope. 'I don't mind anybody here knowing as this has come by quite a circuitous route. Handed from one seaman to another, all secret like. From Bergen.'

'And you've resisted the urge to open it,' Asta remarked, her eyes brimming full of tears. She glanced at the name on the envelope. 'But it's not my mother's writing.'

Tearing it open, Asta dropped the envelope from shaking fingers while she smoothed the single sheet of notepaper. 'Oh, it's from Olav Larsen.' She looked towards Hamish. 'Olav's a sort of half-cousin.'

Andrew had been gazing across at his wife since her voice lowered dejectedly. 'I hope it's not bad news, love?'

'I can't really make out. Olav says my mother is well, except for the diabetes, of course. Only . . . well, you know how he's always kept an eye on her? He says he's not going to be able to do that any longer.'

Bernard Davidson sighed. 'If I know young men, he'll be after a bit of excitement. Wouldn't surprise me if he's joined the resistance fighters over there.'

'Olav?' Rachel asked, astonished. When she had met Olav Larsen during holidays there he had been a fat schoolboy, terribly lazy.

Her mother was offering the note for Andrew to read. 'Just see if I've got this right. His writing isn't very good, and my

Norwegian's rusty now. But I think he's advising us to try and get my mother away from there.'

'Out of Norway?' Bernard demanded. 'Never in this world. You'll not get her to leave there, ever.'

'Are you sure, Father?' asked Asta. 'It is dangerous there, isn't it, since the occupation?'

The elderly doctor shrugged. 'Knowing Hedda as I do, no hardship would be worse than quitting her homeland. In any case, the civilian population are unlikely to face any real threat so long as they don't engage in subversion.'

'Unless . . . well, isn't there a proportion of inhabitants of Bergen who're of German descent – aren't they a potential threat?' asked Rachel.

Her father smiled reassuringly. 'You mean descendants of old Hanseatic families?'

Frowning, Rachel shook her head. 'Not really sure, Dad. I only know that a patient we had was talking about a pro-German section of the local people.'

Pushing his red hair off his face, Andrew continued to smile. 'And talk is likely to be what most of this amounts to. It's centuries since the Hanseatic League was operating. It's likely this war is arousing feelings against anything German, and that's understandable. I dare say any such potential cause of unease is being exaggerated.'

'From what I recall, it was only one area of the city where there were families with German roots,' Asta put in. 'And I know my mother had friends among them. I can't imagine them upsetting her.'

'Quite,' her husband agreed. 'I don't think we need to consider they might present problems for her. However, it is disturbing to think that Olav won't be visiting her so often to check that she is all right.'

'It's her diabetes that worries me,' said Rachel. 'She's never been very good at regulating her medication, has she? How many times has she had to stay in hospital to be stabilized?'

'Don't remind me!' Asta exclaimed. 'Not when there's nothing we can do from here.'

'Perhaps she has become more accustomed to the insulin – her dosage and so on,' Hamish suggested. 'If her doctor is good, your mother may be better able to cope than she was.'

Asta smiled. 'That's what I'm going to believe. Got to, haven't we? No matter what Olav says, there is no way that we can bring her over here.'

'Even if Hedda would consider coming back,' Bernard added heavily.

Throughout the rest of the day, including their evening meal, their thoughts returned repeatedly to the problem of Hedda Davidson's living in Norway. By the time Rachel and Hamish were leaving, the general consensus was that nothing they could do from Yorkshire would be of any use.

As Andrew Skelton was seeing them off at the door, however, Rachel turned to him again to ask one final question. 'How exactly did that letter reach us, Dad? It wasn't simply posted in Norway was it?'

'Anything but, love. It was passed on to me by somebody who fishes out of Aberdeen.'

'Aberdeen? But what on earth has that got to do with Norway?'

Andrew smiled. 'That's only one half of the story – you wouldn't believe the contact there is between folk over there and parts of Scotland. Particularly with the Shetland Islands.'

'Really?'

'You must have heard about their king and the government getting away – they weren't the only ones. There's been a constant stream of folk coming over. And it's mainly the Norwegian fishermen who are managing to help refugees make it across the North Sea.'

'I'd never heard a word about this.'

'No – well, it's not something that's broadcast very much. But I know you'll understand that the existence of such a . . . such a scheme has to be kept quiet.'

'Did you hear all that?' Rachel asked Hamish who was waiting beside his car.

He shook his head as he opened the passenger door for her. 'Not really. Was it connected with what your family were discussing?'

'In a way. I wanted to know how that letter had reached us.'

As Hamish drove off Rachel told him about the sea route to and from the Shetlands. When he spoke after hearing her out there was a smile in his voice. 'I was aware something of that nature existed. My understanding is that the Scottish end of the operation is run by British officers. Although all the boats are manned by Norwegians.'

'Dad seemed to believe the crew are all civilians as well.'

'I imagine they would have to be to pass in and out of harbours over there.'

'At least my mother knows that Grandmother was all right when Olav Larsen wrote. Happen we'll have news from time to time in that way.'

Even as she spoke, though, Rachel sensed that none of the family would ever feel easy about Hedda Davidson remaining where she was.

Pleased though Hamish had been to be invited to join Rachel's people that day, he wished that the occasion had not been marred by such anxiety. She had needed to relax just as much as he had, and he saw as she sat tensely beside him that she was not easily relinquishing her worries.

When they reached Keld House he was thankful that the nursing staff reported all was well. Satisfying himself and Rachel with a quick tour of the wards, he decided they had earned a little more time to themselves. Time in which to take her mind off the problems gnawing into her.

'We're going to have a nightcap,' he told her, leading the way into the rarely used sitting room adjoining his own room.

'I'm not sure I want anything,' Rachel protested. 'I was going straight to bed.'

'And would you sleep?'

'I hardly ever sleep properly when I've been home. All the conversations are always running back and forth in my head.'

'Quite.' Hamish beckoned to her. 'Come here.'

His arms felt welcoming and his chest warm as he drew her close, and she could not prevent her own arms from sliding around him. For a long time they held each other, motionless, quiet.

His breath stirred her hair when he spoke, softly, gently. 'I owe you one, you know, for that night when you held me while I slept. We're good partners, you and I, you must let me near, even if that happens all too rarely. There's not much ease in this life of ours, God knows. Surely things can only improve if we rely a little on each other?'

Hamish kissed her then, tenderly on her forehead, convincing Rachel that he understood the limits of her feelings towards him. Releasing her, he went to pour brandy into glasses, then indicated the sofa.

Seated, the room felt cold, its only heat permeating from the rooms below. Rachel shivered and Hamish smiled before rising from the sofa.

'Won't be a second.'

He returned from his own room with a thick tartan car rug. 'If you'd lived north of the border you'd know what cold is!' Sitting beside her again, he tucked the rug across both their knees and pulled it up around her shoulders.

The brandy she was sipping had quelled the shivers and seemed also to be stilling the worries that were plaguing her. As Hamish's arm came round her, he was drawing her closer, comforting with his nearness. He kissed her tenderly, full on her mouth, then turned slightly away to sip from his glass. The next kiss was moist with the brandy, suddenly so exciting that Rachel yearned for more. Aware of her response, Hamish drank from his glass again, found her mouth with his lips and fed her more brandy.

Exhilarated, Rachel savoured his lips with her tongue, tested his teeth, and thrilled to feel them parting. Her tongue sought the brandy taste, she felt longing surge right through her, and went on and on kissing. Hamish pulled her nearer still, crushing her breasts against his powerful chest while his mouth again found hers, his tongue urging her teeth to admit him. Desire was pulsing through every vein, willing him to seek release with this woman who was becoming all the world to him. The only world he wanted.

For Rachel, too, the months of denial had generated a need more fierce than she'd believed existed within her. Pressing her body to his, she sought some kind of ease for the yearning that fast was growing insatiable.

'Kiss me again,' she cried, heard the moan in her own voice, and stirred in desperation.

'Steady now. Rachel, my love, you're a doctor, you must know what you're doing. Where this will lead . . .'

'No, no. Just hold me, kiss me. I can't stop now.'

And nor can I, thought Hamish, but he hadn't the heart to change anything. His hand was tracing her breast, the cloth of her dress was no disguise for her arousal. Her reaction fuelled his own urgency.

Rachel was kissing him, the rhythm of her lips echoing the insistence of his own pulses. He knew she must refuse the ultimate act of loving, but he knew himself his inability to withhold completely.

'We'll have to stop,' he said. 'We really must. You are making me so . . . uncomfortable. Do you understand?'

She understood far more than he'd anticipated, had been a student for years among other healthy students, and knew that curtailing love-making needn't mean total denial. Hamish was surprised by her smile. 'This should help,' she said.

No longer anxious about the effect she was having upon him, he let his kisses grow more passionate, his caresses more insistent. Rachel sighed dreamily. She had never wanted any man so much. When they finally agreed they should part in order to sleep, she was no less reluctant than Hamish himself.

Morning carried in with it an unease as sombre as the wintry clouds hanging just above the bleak moorland. No matter how she tried, Rachel could not resurrect the bliss she had found in her intimacy with Hamish. She was uncomfortable and, even well aware that they had not made love completely, she felt that her body no longer belonged solely to her.

Coming to bed, she'd been full of regret that their being the only doctors at Keld House would prevent them from taking much time off together. Today, on the other hand, she could only be thankful that such a reason *did* exist for refusing to see Hamish alone outside the hospital. Last night she'd made a bad mistake: she had allowed desire to motivate her.

Hamish's brilliant smile and the warming of his brown eyes when she joined him for ward rounds increased Rachel's concern.

'And how are you this morning?' he enquired afterwards when they went to his tiny office for their customary discussion about their patients.

'All right, thank you,' Rachel said very quickly. 'Busy, of course, because of taking yesterday off.'

'That wasn't what I meant,' Hamish began gently. 'I just wanted to assure you of how much I care, how greatly I need you to understand that last night wasn't just a one-off. I don't do that. We'll have to find some means of ensuring some more free time for ourselves.'

'When we take on another doctor perhaps, otherwise I don't see . . .'

'That'll be taken care of, I hope,' he told her. 'I'm about to begin interviewing again for a third doctor, preferably someone with surgical experience as well as medical.'

'We'll have to see, *if* that happens,' said Rachel. 'Do you need me for anything further?' she added hastily.

'Work-wise, not at the moment. But you shouldn't need to ask about my personal feelings.'

She made an excuse and bolted. Hamish had shaken her by emphasizing his reliance upon the attraction between them. She'd been accustomed to similar remarks from medical students. From him, she expected more originality.

As the hours passed, she reflected on his reaction. With mundane tasks engaging her, Rachel began to realize that hoping Hamish would just dismiss the personal aspect of their relationship was unrealistic. Mature or not, experienced or otherwise, he was living this limited existence that placed him in a similar situation to life in medical school, where cravings abounded.

Unless he was drawn to one of the nurses – and most of those were either middle-aged or extremely young – there seemed no real alternative to herself as a focus for his attention. But even believing she understood, Rachel did not feel any happier about Hamish's expectations regarding their relationship.

Later that day, when they bumped into each other giving the wards a final visit before settling everyone for the night, he manoeuvred her into his tiny office again.

'I've been thinking all day, Rachel, and we ought to talk. If only for a short while now, just to know where we stand.' He was waiting for her to say something. When she remained silent he gave a little shrug and continued. 'Surely you're aware that such intimacy isn't a habit of mine with someone I'm not particularly fond of? I thought you were beginning to feel the same way. All I want is for us to make time for each other, regularly.'

'Not like this, not here,' she said, glancing towards the glass panels of the door.

Rachel should have anticipated that he would interpret 'here' as meaning his box of an office, and insist on their going upstairs. Entering the room where they had come so close to making love was another mistake, for her. The place felt charged with their passion, while her emotions were raw with regrets.

She had never allowed anyone as near to her as that. Or at least not for what now felt like a lifetime. Rachel steeled herself to explain. 'I'm sorry, Hamish, I really am. It's not you – it's me that's at fault. Ever since I lost—'

'Lost,' he echoed, interrupting. 'Ah – so that is it. But I told you, love – I do understand. I've had to come to terms with losing my fiancée.'

'This wasn't like that. It was more . . . special. Richard was always there, further back than I can remember. He was my twin, you see.'

Pensively, Hamish nodded to himself. 'And you grew up together, that would be a bond.'

'Actually, no,' said Rachel wretchedly. 'Richard didn't grow, or hardly at all. He was only a year old when he died.'

Hamish said nothing, didn't know *what to* say. That she ought to be over losing her twin, after all this time? How could a baby of less than a year have developed memories – memories that bound her forever to another infant? He could not imagine it being possible.

This lovely woman, this woman he was learning to love, could not seriously have committed herself to her poor dead brother?

'My grandfather understands, he said so not long ago. He recognizes that Richard and I grew accustomed to being so very close.' Before we were born, she added inside her own head.

Hamish's laugh was harsh. 'Grandfather? That's all right then. But your grandfather isn't the one involved. Maybe he doesn't really appreciate that you are the one who is alive – passionately alive – and keeping everyone out.'

'It's not something I enjoy.' Rachel saw his eyebrows rush towards his dark hair, and wondered how he could misjudge her so utterly.

Eventually Hamish shrugged. 'If you can't see it, I'll never persuade you. I only hope you're not using this . . . this twin as a barrier, simply to avoid living.'

Three

At the end of December there was a terrible air raid on the city of London when many civilians were injured, and along with them several soldiers who had been helping the fire services to extinguish the inferno.

A number of the army personnel were transferred to Keld House where it was hoped they might be treated in relative safety. Rachel was thankful for the additional work – anything that prevented her from reflecting for too long on Hamish Wilson's forthright opinions.

He had done nothing further about taking on a third doctor, yet she was not certain this indicated that he no longer wished them to be together. Her emotions were in turmoil: despite originally wanting to avoid occasions when passion might surge, she was compelled to admit that her own body was driving her to seek Hamish's kisses. And his caresses.

Determined to steel herself to ignore all such emotions, Rachel drove off home as soon as she had a few hours free. It was a Sunday afternoon and she wasn't due back on duty until late that night. Finding her father at home was a bonus Rachel hadn't dared to expect, and she was glad to be able to ask him more about the message he had received all the way from Bergen.

'You did say it came by a roundabout route, didn't you, via Scotland? I've got this right, haven't I – some Norwegians have made it across by boat?'

'That's it, love.'

Asta sighed. 'I wondered if some of them could be persuaded to bring my mother with them, but your dad didn't see how we could arrange something like that.'

'From what I've gathered, these voyages are undertaken specially now – not like in the early days when it was more a matter of their fishermen bringing refugees over, then being persuaded to make another trip back,' Andrew explained. 'Word has it – and this is highly confidential, mind – that we're sending agents across to help their saboteurs, some say as we're helping arm them an' all.'

'Any road, we've talked this over, and we both think it'd be unwise for my mother to even set off. It'd be different if she was really fit. But reading between the lines of that note from Olav . . .'

'Where is that note, Mum? I'd like to read it for myself.' Rachel needed to know how Hedda Davidson really was.

Translating slowly, as it seemed years since she had either spoken or read any Norwegian, Rachel sensed how frail Grandmother Hedda was becoming. Had she aged so seriously? Olav Larsen certainly seemed to doubt that the elderly lady would be able to cope alone in her own house.

'Did Olav live nearby, do you remember, Mum?' Rachel asked. The address he gave was care of some post office. 'Did he have to visit every day to check that she had the diabetes under control?'

'Eh, don't ask me, love. Since they've had the Germans there, I haven't been hearing from them, have I? Before then, knowing Norway was neutral, I wasn't this bothered about her. Can't say where I put any of her old letters.'

Rachel could see that Asta had become gravely concerned now – a concern that was showing in shadows under her eyes and grey hairs in among the blond ones.

She turned to her father. 'Tell me again, Dad, how does anybody get to the north of Scotland, these days? As the first stage of trying to cross the North Sea?'

'Whatever have you got in mind, love?' Andrew Skelton was frowning.

'I just wondered.'

'I've not been told, not specifically. I'm only surmising. It must be by sea, happen in a succession of different vessels that work the coast. It has to be by folk that know what they're about, so much offshore is blockaded.'

'Didn't you say the trips across to Norway had to be in wintertime?' Asta checked with her husband. She wasn't going to have him attempt that crossing. His work was dangerous enough already.

'Aye – it's t'only way they will succeed. They need the darkness for cover. Don't forget how light it is at night most of the year that far north.'

Asta was shaking her head. 'My mother would never survive a crossing like that, least of all in winter.'

'Certainly it would be very risky, especially if she were to be seasick,' said Rachel. 'That would ruin her control on her diabetes.'

'What're you thinking now?' her father enquired. 'I hope you're not contemplating . . .'

'Rachel, you wouldn't do owt daft, would you?' Asta interrupted, appalled.

'I don't think you've any real idea of what you'd be up against,' Andrew protested.

'I'd find out first, wouldn't I? I'm not stupid, you know.'

'No. Don't even think about it! I couldn't let you,' Asta insisted. 'I'm not going to lose another of you. Don't expect that of me.'

Rachel sprang to her feet and went to hug her. 'Don't, Mum. It's all right. Nothing's going to happen to me.' But if there was some means of rescuing Grandmother Hedda, she wanted to have a go.

When she returned to her chair, her father continued speaking. 'Be practical, Rachel love, you're no sailor, are you? Even crossing on a steamer from Newcastle, you were always sick long before you reached the other side. You'd be miserable in fishing boats no bigger nor mine.'

She smiled ruefully. 'I might not be as bad now. In any case, there are things being developed to ward off sickness.'

'I don't want to hear any more about it, do you hear?' Asta protested. 'I wouldn't have an easy minute all the time you were away.'

Rachel said nothing. Living away from home as she did, she was not obliged to tell her parents if she were to set out . . .

'I'm sure your mum's glad that you've even thought of such a thing, but I'm equally sure that when you work it out properly you'll realize the idea isn't practicable,' Andrew said, his tone of voice indicating that as final.

Resolving to think the whole business through, in private, Rachel left the subject for the present. Her parents would naturally be anxious if she embarked on such a journey; until she had a definite plan there was no point in worrying them further.

Avoiding the matter that was preoccupying her so thoroughly was far from easy, but Rachel soon found that her mother had become adept at providing a distraction. Asta glanced at the clock, then turned to her daughter. 'You don't mind if we have the wireless on, do you? It's one of my favourite programmes.'

Listening to anything was a welcome alternative, permitting Rachel to shelve her half-formed plans while she made an effort to provide her parents with the change of company that was her original intention.

When Andrew Skelton had to prepare for putting out to sea again, Rachel wondered what on earth she was doing to even contemplate risking her own life while he constantly faced the hazards of the sea. Could she do that to her mother who already had so much to worry her?

As soon as mother and daughter were alone, Asta demonstrated afresh her reliance upon keeping her mind occupied in order to obliterate anxiety. 'I've been thinking a lot recently about how your dad has made good. That couldn't have been easy at first, not when most of the Skeltons were lacking in ambition.'

'They were always fisherfolk though, weren't they, years ago?'

'Aye – all the men were, but having the sea in your veins weren't always sufficient. According to my father, the Skeltons had big families; often enough, shoes and clothing didn't quite go round. His father before him was their family doctor, and used to tell tales of the children sharing six to a bed.'

'I can just picture that, sleeping both ends – two rows of little redheads.'

Asta laughed. 'Brighter than your dad's hair even – his has toned down a bit since I first knew him. I have to confess I were a bit relieved when your hair turned out to be the same colour as mine.'

'Tell me more about the Skeltons. What was Dad's father like?'

'Eh, love – I couldn't say for certain now. He died young, you know – lost at sea. And that finished his mother an' all. Never got over it, did she, never!'

'But Dad has brothers, hasn't he?'

'Oh, aye. Over in Whitby, but they might as well be on the moon. Nobody's really said, but I reckon they were envious of how your father's made something of his life. So far as I know, he's not set eyes on them since they made out he was getting above himself. Establishing his own fleet of trawlers. Nowt much was said, but I gather none of them aspired to owning more than one vessel.'

'Perhaps if they continued to have large families they couldn't put more money into the business.'

'And perhaps they drank the profits away. I've always been thankful that was one family trait my Andrew didn't inherit!'

'There was a lot of heavy drinking, wasn't there, even going back to Victorian times?'

'So my grandfather used to tell, and doctors would see what was going on, if anybody did. I dare say lots of poor folk were only to be pitied. They didn't have much to come home to when their work was done. I was a long time realizing that, because of my father and grandfather being doctors – folk that were better off.'

'And with a decent education. Wasn't that how Granddad Davidson came to meet grandmother?'

'In a way, yes. My grandfather was a great believer in

widening experience, for himself as well as his family. When he decided to visit St Jorgens, the leprosy hospital where some man called Hansen worked—'

'Armauer Hansen – who identified the leprosy bacillus, you mean?'

'I suppose it must have been the same. Any road, when Grandfather arranged to go over to Bergen, he took his son Bernard with him.'

'Was my granddad already training as a doctor then?'

'If he was, he was less keen on research into leprosy than his father was. Or perhaps the older man spent longer with the experts than anticipated. Bernard was more eager to see something of the country – after all, very few people travelled so far from home in those days.'

'Didn't he once say he went off on his own somewhere?'

'Not quite alone, as it turned out. Bernard had always loved old ecclesiastical buildings – Fountains Abbey and the one near his old home in Whitby and so on. The man they were staying with in Bergen was interested in their Yorkshire connection because he'd seen nearby Lysekloster, which was founded by the Cistercians and linked to Fountains Abbey.'

'Naturally, Granddad had to visit it.'

'And Hedda Larsen went on the outing too.'

'Didn't they get married quite quickly after meeting like that?'

'That's right, love. I think we'd say today that they became besotted with each other. And of course, travelling back and forth between here and Norway would have been far from easy then.'

'Like lots of couples separated by distance they had to make up their minds as to what they really wanted.'

'Aye. Later on it began to look as though they ought to have made sure there was more than an interest in ruins to hold them together,' said Asta dourly.

'But they were happy for a long time, weren't they, while you were growing up?'

Her mother sighed, shrugged. 'They didn't seem miserable, certainly. Or at least not until during the last war.'

'Wasn't it after 1918, though, that Grandmother Hedda went back there?'

'Oh, yes. Because Norway had been neutral throughout the Great War, Hedda didn't think us British fighting was right, no matter how just the cause. I can't help wondering what she thinks about that now – neutrality only seemed to leave them wide open to Nazi invasion this time around.'

They were back on the subject of war again – not the best of topics on which to leave, but Rachel was nevertheless compelled to set out again for Keld House.

She had thought Hamish would have finished his shift, but was surprised to meet him emerging from the wards as she returned.

'Long day?' she enquired, noticing how exhausted he appeared, yet again.

Hamish smiled. 'Not too bad, and I've some news for you. I've engaged a locum surgeon who'll be very useful for cover.'

'That's good,' said Rachel, although she wondered if Hamish had fixed this in order to press her to spend more time with him. 'What's he like?'

'*She*,' he corrected her with a grin. 'And immediately available; she's here now. Like you, she's not long out of training, was doing her stint of theatre work after qualifying – unfortunately, in one of the hospitals hit during the Blitz.'

'At least while she's here you'll be able to delegate a bit.'

'And so will you, we mustn't overlook her general medical training either. And you haven't taken a real break since we began setting up Keld House.'

'Are you offering me the chance of leave?'

'It's high time you took it, Rachel. You might wish to spend time with your mother while Andrew's constantly at sea.'

'If you could spare me for a while, there is something I want to do. But I need to find out what it would entail.'

Hamish frowned. 'Don't tell me! You'll not be satisfied

until you make an attempt to get your grandmother out of Norway.'

'Wouldn't you feel the same, if she was your relative? You don't have to tell me it'll be anything but easy. Only, can't you see? If I do it, I'll be able to keep a close eye on her diabetes, have all the necessary medication to hand.'

'I'm not disputing that, love. But I don't believe you really understand how damned dangerous it would be.'

'You sound just like my dad.'

Because Rachel was due on duty she was still standing near the entrance to the wards. Hamish glanced up at the wall clock and sighed. 'No time to discuss anything properly just now. Will you promise me you'll give this a lot of careful thought before you leap in?'

'I'll have to, anyway. If I go ahead I can't rely on my dad to arrange the initial stages of the journey – as far as Shetland. I won't worry either of them.'

No, thought Hamish as he left her to remove her coat and go through to the wards, but Rachel had no idea how greatly the prospect of her undertaking such a trip would worry him!

Introducing herself to Shirley Trent, their locum surgeon, Rachel smiled privately despite her preoccupation. She could see why Hamish Wilson had engaged the girl so instantly.

Even though Shirley must have been at least her own age to have qualified in surgery as well as on the medical side, she looked about twenty, and had warm brown eyes and glossy hair to match. Her slender figure was ill concealed by her white coat, and the legs beneath would do justice to any pre-war advertisement for silk stockings.

As soon as Shirley spoke, Rachel recognized that her cultured voice owed more to an expensive education than to years in medical school anywhere. 'You have a pleasant little hospital here,' Shirley enthused, smiling. 'And Mr Wilson tells me you were involved from the start, setting the outfit up.'

'That's right, we were kept busy, and I had to shoulder a lot of responsibility when Hamish went on a special course.'

'What course was that?'

'Oh, to do with plastic surgery, reconstructive work and so on. Not that we handle the worst cases here.'

'They go to East Grinstead, don't they? I went to take a look there. I was working in the south, you see.'

'Well, I hope you settle in here,' said Rachel. 'Where are you staying? Do you have a room on site?'

'I shall have. Mr Wilson is going to have it fixed for me. Until then I've got a room in the local hotel, quite a quaint place.'

Shirley had evidently finished whatever she'd been doing on the wards. They said goodnight, and Rachel added that she looked forward to working with her.

Alone, and beginning her nightly routine of checking with the ward sister about any difficult cases, Rachel wondered how much she and the new doctor would work in tandem. Would Shirley's arrival mean that she herself would now have fewer opportunities for assisting with the surgery that she so enjoyed?

When Hamish was waiting for Rachel as she came off duty the following morning, she was afraid he was about to explain that her involvement in surgery was going to be curtailed. He certainly appeared very serious when he strode towards her from the foot of the main staircase.

'Have you a minute, Rachel? I know you're just going off, but this won't take long.' He paused, making her wonder why he was so reluctant to set out the fresh regime. 'I've been giving this some consideration,' he continued eventually. 'There is a way in which I might help, if you are determined to attempt to make it across to Norway. I'm sure you don't need me to tell you that at this time of year sea trips will be diabolical. However, there is a means by which you'd avoid some of that, and would also take far less time over the journeys.'

'Really? I don't see how.'

'By flying north to Shetland with the RAF. Through our work here, I'm in regular contact with Fighter Command, know one or two of their chaps. If you have thought it through and are determined to go, I could arrange a flight for you.' I just don't want you to go, he thought. You'll never know how greatly I do not wish you to even have a shot at this!

'That would be marvellous. Of course I'll go ahead. As soon as you tell me you can manage here for however long it would take – and the trip certainly should be quicker if you could arrange for me to fly up there.'

'We'll talk again. There'll be an hour tonight before you go on duty, and after I've finished for the day. Subject to there being no major crisis, naturally. Come up to our sitting room at – what time shall we say?'

After arranging to discuss plans for the first stage of her journey to Norway, Rachel could not sleep. She found adjusting to shift work difficult enough normally; with so much to contemplate now her brain was far too active. She would need to work out what additional clothing she must have for the sea crossing, then there would be supplies of medicines – for seasickness as well as Grandmother Hedda's diabetes. Consulting Hamish about the latter would be wise, she ought to ensure that someone approved what she would carry with her.

Seeing her grandmother again would be wonderful, although for the present any such emotion was outweighed by anxiety concerning the old lady's health.

Trying to ignore the daylight that even the blackout curtains did not entirely obliterate, Rachel willed herself to sleep. Otherwise, she would only dwell on her dread that attempting such a route could prove too much for Hedda Davidson. And all too swiftly a further difficulty occurred to her, one which might prove insuperable.

The idea of her grandmother leaving occupied Norway had been Olav Larsen's, there was nothing to say that the lady herself would be willing to come to England. Rachel ought to try and contact Olav to discover how much much Grandmother Hedda knew about his suggestion. Suspecting that any mail in and out of Norway would be censored, she wondered how on earth getting in touch with Olav might be possible.

Her sleeplessness did nothing to help Rachel prepare for discussing plans with Hamish. Her mind seemed to be running on only a quarter of full power when she went through to the sitting room. He was there already, and looking brighter than she felt, despite his having worked a full day.

'Are you all right?' he enquired, brown eyes searching her wan face.

'Never have been great at sleeping during the day.'

'And plotting trips across the water doesn't help.'

They laughed together and Hamish indicated one of the easy chairs. 'I've made some coffee, looks like you need some if you're to stay awake on shift.'

'I'm sorry, don't know what's come over me. I don't usually let other things jeopardise my ability to work.'

'I know that,' said Hamish, handing a mug to her. 'Here's hoping you have a quiet night. Shirley's doing a split shift, anyway – came on three hours ago, so you won't be the only doctor who's on for the first half.'

'You don't have to make concessions on my account.'

Hamish laughed again. 'I know – I could be entirely selfish and have her backing me up full-time. However, you are permitted a little human anxiety about the prospect of a voyage like that. This way we're covered until you're back into gear.'

Sipping from his own mug, Hamish settled into the chair across the hearth from her own. 'I take it that since you have come here you're going ahead?'

'I was, but I'm up against a hurdle that I hadn't even anticipated a few hours ago. It isn't Hedda's idea that she should leave. I need to get in touch with Olav somehow to learn if she agrees, but posting a letter is altogether too risky.'

'There might be a way round that. If you really are set on going.'

'I said, very much so. And whatever happens, I can't thank you enough for thinking of a way for me to avoid some of the sea voyage.'

'No trouble. I've had a word with one of the RAF chaps,

and he's suggested we go over to the station some evening when you and I are both off duty. Someone there will talk you through the drill, discuss tentative dates and so on. They have to remain tentative until the last minute, often become operational at short notice.' Hamish had gathered that the missions they flew to Shetland were covert.

Rachel grinned. 'Better that way for me, I'd only become more keyed up in anticipation. The only thing is, this still leaves uncertainty about whether Hedda would be willing to come here.'

'You have this Olav's address, though? He got a hand-delivered note to your father.'

'Trouble is, I don't want Dad to be worried by this.'

'I know that, just listen – write Olav a message and we'll see if the RAF chaps can get it to a boat leaving for Bergen. One of their tasks is filtering stuff into occupied territory. Before you set anything in motion, though, just remember no one would think any worse of you for opting out.'

'I wouldn't quit.' Her heart was set on providing hope of a better life for her grandmother.

'Well, work-wise for us, this could be as good a time as any. With a lot of the action focused in North Africa and around the Mediterranean it could be some while before many freshly wounded troops arrive over here for treatment.'

Rachel nodded. 'I gather Malta has been bombarded though.'

'I hadn't heard that.'

'It was on the news while I was getting dressed.'

Hamish promised to liaise with the RAF station again and fix free evenings for them both in order to go over there. When Rachel went on duty she felt more content that the trip really would go ahead, and was thankful that she would first be going to the air base to learn more about that flight to the Shetland Islands.

Rachel had had little time to do more than discuss with Hamish the medication that she should carry with her for the trip overseas. The visit to the RAF station was set up within the week, and Hamish was soon driving off into the cold January evening with a nervous Rachel Skelton beside him.

'God knows what I'll be like when it comes to the event itself,' she remarked ruefully.

He slid his hand from the wheel briefly to squeeze her fingers. 'You'll be fine, I'm sure. You know how it is when you're tackling something fresh, once you start out the problems recede.'

'I hope so.'

'I'll help you draw up lists of stuff you'll need, make sure you cover all eventualities.' It was the least he could do, while all the time he was aching to be able to go over to Norway with her.

The noise from the mess where they were meeting up was something she hadn't anticipated. Someone was thumping out one of the latest popular tunes on a piano. Masses of voices were singing along, accompanied by a shuffling sound which, once through the entrance, Rachel identified as dancing.

A squadron leader signalled to Hamish with a raised hand and manoeuvred a route through the dancing couples to join them.

'Glad you made it tonight,' he exclaimed after introducing himself to Rachel as Will Henderson. 'You're catching us in off duty mode. If we make our way through to the bar, I'll fill you in on the gen while we down a few glasses.'

After setting them up with beers, Will smiled towards Rachel. 'Later on I'll see you meet two or three of the chaps, with luck one of them will be the pilot taking you out to Shetland. In any case, *whoever* it is will know the routine. This won't be the first occasion they've flown someone there for the Shetland Bus.'

'*Bus*?' she enquired.

Will laughed, turned slightly to include Hamish. 'That's the name the scheme is acquiring. Regrettably, they can't function to any timetable, but I gather from the folk we met at their base they're already causing the Germans quite a headache in Norway.'

Rachel wasn't sure she fully understood, but was glad that

he took her note for Olav. A note written on silk, as Hamish suggested, to be concealed in clothing.

'How's that?' she asked the officer. 'I thought their object was to ship refugees out of there?'

'As they do, but they don't take empty vessels over from this side.' Will glanced all around them. Even on an RAF station discretion should be paramount. He lowered his voice. 'You'll find out. Let's say it isn't only refugees who consider crossing the North Sea desirable.'

'He meant agents, didn't he?' she whispered to Hamish when the squadron leader excused himself to locate a couple of pilot officers.

'I think we may assume that,' said Hamish gravely, while his brown eyes gleamed.

'The real war,' Rachel remarked, now even more in awe of the nature of her expedition.

The pilots to whom she was introduced looked far too young to be handling anything more advanced than a bicycle, and Rachel willed herself not to comment on their youth while struggling to master her own increasing apprehension.

One of the men had red hair which reminded her of her father, but there the resemblance ceased. His manner seemed overconfident, and his assessment of her overtly sexual.

'Care for a dance?' he invited, while virtually ignoring Hamish, to whom Will was still introducing him.

Rachel was saved from responding by the other pilot who was an altogether different person. From his softly waving golden hair to his immaculately pressed uniform, Frank Smith was so well presented that the word coming to her mind was beautiful. His manners, too, appeared well groomed: unlike his colleague, there was no lingering of his hand on hers, and no masculine challenge in his eyes when he met her gaze.

Will was speaking again, suggesting possible dates for her departure, indicating how long the flight would be, and assuring her that contact would be maintained with the Shetland Bus in order to try and arrange her homeward flight.

'And it'll be all right that I'll be bringing somebody home with me?'

He smiled. 'Hamish has explained. And that the lady could be feeling rather "fragile". If you should need to rest up on Shetland, you've only to keep us in the picture. Our chaps who fly out of there work with them quite often, searching for missi—' The officer's voice trailed off abruptly.

'He was going to say missing vessels, wasn't he?' Rachel said when she and Hamish were left alone together.

'I don't suppose he knows your father trawls the North Sea, that you go into this with your eyes fully open.'

When Hamish asked her to dance, Rachel was thankful to feel his arms steadying her against him. Reminders of the hazards did come hard, even while she had refused to close her mind to their existence.

The dance was a quickstep, and Hamish proved himself proficient. Determined she wouldn't make a fool of herself, Rachel concentrated on their steps and the music. The pianist had been replaced by a gramophone, providing a greater emphasis on the beat and somehow cajoling from her feet something approaching a sense of rhythm.

The next dance was a foxtrot. The floor was so crowded that there wasn't really room for anything more elaborate than a smooch around the room. While the pace felt quite leisurely, Rachel's emotions remained heightened by the purpose of their visit to the air base. Emotions that were generating a keen awareness.

Despite shortages, Hamish seemed to have maintained a stock of some soap whose scent provided a welcome change from the antiseptic stuff in general use around their hospital. Each time Rachel inhaled she took in the pleasing fragrance which urged her to move closer. And they were close already, surrounded as they were by masses of other couples, while the music willed them on with increasing sensuality.

Relieved that, for this short while, dancing diverted her mind from the mission that lay ahead, Rachel was happy to surrender future anxieties. But the awareness didn't disappear and she grew steadily more conscious of the blissful co-ordination of her partner's steps with hers, and the pressure of his lean body.

'We make a good team, you and I,' Hamish murmured, and kissed her forehead. 'Good like this, as much as at Keld House.'

There could be no mistaking the tenderness in his voice, any more than ignoring his attraction. And now Rachel owed him a great deal for helping to organise that difficult journey, there was no way that she could turn cold and warn him off. Even without the part of her that was willing on this rising wave of passion.

Every dance appeared only to lead on to the next, allowing no time in which to draw apart and find reasons for leaving the floor. If she had gazed around Rachel might have seen there were no reasons, while men and women held on, clinging as they did to a moment's surety in a night shadowed by tomorrow's hazards.

The night was dark, cold with snow carried on the north wind, when they finally left their hosts and ran to Hamish's car. He kissed her then, deeply on the mouth, before switching on the ignition.

They kissed again, more lingeringly when he parked outside the hospital. 'My wonderful partner,' he exclaimed. 'So well attuned. Better even than I imagined.'

Distantly, way beyond conscious thinking, Rachel felt concern stirring. Was it right to accept that Hamish allowed himself such imaginings? But his kisses were real enough, too passionate to permit her attention to stray from the force that was surging between them. His hand was on her breast, willing her to comply, and her own fingers felt alive with the urge to caress.

It was Hamish who drew back at last, turning aside to open the car door. He faced her one more time, his voice serious. 'Just be sure to come back safely, I need you so much. I would spend the rest of my life ensuring that we overcome any barriers that your past losses have created. You're dear to me already, Rachel, don't you forget that.'

As if she could! The night had generated so many feelings, and now among them all was the one that threatened to supercede even her immense longing to belong. She and

Hamish were close, and might become closer still, but only if time could miraculously alter her completely. She had wanted to be loved, had wanted him so fiercely, but that craving still could not feel *right*.

There was no escaping her own alarm, the alarm that grew out of each of her senses, reminding her that this intimacy with Hamish was too new, really quite strange, and almost foreign to her.

Four

The call to fly up to the Shetland Islands came swiftly, so quickly that Rachel felt relieved more than frightened by any potential dangers. She needed to get away and stand back from her friendship with Hamish which, for her, had grown uneasy after dancing together had led to such passionate attraction.

To herself, Rachel admitted that he might be justified in thinking she had encouraged him to expect more than kisses. 'Leading him on' was the expression her mother would have used, and Rachel hated to believe that she'd let desire carry her on its tide. She was becoming too fond of Hamish not to worry about treating him unfairly.

Recognising that she was ready for love-making while she knew something was missing from her feelings towards Hamish was disturbing. His conclusion that she was forging a barrier out of her twin's death might be correct, but she must check this situation before it went any further.

While packing for the journey, Rachel decided that she had to make Hamish understand. He'd been open about his feelings for her, he didn't deserve somebody who could neither explain nor commit herself. She must come back to Yorkshire prepared to convey how it really felt to spend most of her life seeking the other half of herself, someone who would make her feel complete.

When Hamish arranged free time in which to see her off from Keld House, Rachel's heart began strumming agitatedly. She was torn – couldn't help being delighted that he cared, but worried that he was caring too greatly. He pulled her to him in a powerful hug, and kissed her fiercely, kisses that demanded a response.

'God, but I'm going to miss you! Mind you come home safely . . .'

Home, thought Rachel, driving away, and wished that she could feel home was wherever Hamish might be.

The route to the RAF station over the wind-battered moors demanded her full attention. Snow lay in crevices and on the higher points had frozen on to the tarmac, and she was glad to dismiss all her emotions and give her mind over to keeping the car on the road. Dusk had fallen before she left Keld House, and overhead hung a half-moon, small assistance for her heavily shaded headlights. She continued to feel relief that driving was not so easy as to permit her thoughts to wander.

Arriving at the air base, Rachel sensed that her heart rate had quieted from the earlier agitation and she was breathing more easily. If she engaged a little effort she might convince the pilot who was flying her north that she possessed a small fraction of composure.

Rachel had instructions on where to report, just as she'd been told how much – actually, how *little* – to bring with her. Her admiration for the organisation on site soared when she learned everything was virtually ready. There were just a few checks to be made, among them that she was not carrying documents which might identify her as British. Alarming at first, this stipulation became reasonable with reminders that, after leaving harbour on Shetland, she must seem to be Norwegian.

Rachel had been told that her grounding in that language had impressed the officers running the Shetland Bus, strengthening her case for making the journey to Bergen. Given more time, she would have swotted up on her half-forgotten vocabulary, but she owed the hospital her full concentration – all the more so because of consent for this absence. She hoped that once aboard with Norwegian crews, additional phrases would come back to her.

This evening, meanwhile, she needed to listen intently to

the briefing for her flight and be ready to clamber aboard, fulfilling all instructions so that she would create as little nuisance as humanly possible.

The hope that everything might have been smoothed by meeting the squadron leader again came to nothing. Even before she realized just how imminent her departure was, Rachel was being led out on to the airstrip by a young man whose overalls identified him as an engineer.

'This way,' he had said, his way with words evidently strict economy.

If any snow had lingered on the airfield it had long since been cleared away, no hint of white aided visibility as she struggled to make out more than a massive dark shape somewhere just ahead, which she assumed could only be their aeroplane.

They were almost near enough to touch the fuselage before Rachel's companion spoke again. 'He's up front already, I'll give him a shout.'

Finding her pilot was to be Frank Smith was a bonus, and Rachel smiled widely when he emerged from the cockpit and came near enough for her to recognize him.

'All set then?' he asked, and nodded approvingly at her small amount of baggage. 'That'll stow under your seat. I'll show you.'

With Frank's 'Thanks, mate', the engineer was already departing, and soon became barely visible as he strode through the darkness.

Her eyes adjusting to the gloom, Rachel could tell that Frank was smiling encouragingly. 'We'll get you kitted out, then I'll help you aboard. You haven't flown before, have you?'

'Afraid not. I trust you'll not have cause to be ashamed of me. Sailing's more my line. My father has a fleet of trawlers.'

'Oh, yes? My old man's a bit of a landlubber. Sporting type – played cricket for his county, that sort of stuff. Now he's a golf professional. Pre-war, anyway, I understand he's putting in a lot of time training men in the Home Guard.'

Something in Frank's tone made Rachel sense that there wasn't any great affinity between his father's chosen life and his own. But he was speaking again, indicating the parachute into which she must harness herself after donning the flying suit.

When she had struggled into all the gear, Frank slipped a helmet on her head. 'That's all, I promise,' he told her, grinning. 'And you will be able to breathe, just about. In fact, you'll be thankful for insulation from the intense cold aloft.'

Rachel hadn't doubted that Frank knew the truth of what he was telling her, and it was proved right soon after take-off.

The actual ascent hadn't been quite so awful as she'd expected, it was the immediate coldness that seized her more swiftly than any fright. And Frank began speaking again through the intercom when his initial checks were completed. 'You can relax for a while now we're airborne, and if I think there'll be turbulence ahead I'll try and give you a bit of a warning. As you'll guess, where we fly over the sea we've to bear in mind how far north we're travelling – not that we're guaranteed much better when it's land we're above. But perhaps you're accustomed to northern climes? Where are you from?'

'Oh, I'm Yorkshire through and through . . .'

'Excepting the Norwegian bit?' Frank teased.

'That's just a quarter of me. And where is your home?'

'I've lived near Oxford since university, but originally south Wales.'

'And have you had to leave your wife behind?'

His laugh down the intercom startled her. 'Wife? I don't have a wife.'

'You must have a girlfriend then.'

Again Frank laughed, sounding hugely amused. 'Must I?' But he was so very attractive, the most beautiful man she'd ever met! 'Don't tell me you've led such a sheltered life,' he said.

Rachel felt colour rush to her face, was thankful in the darkness that he couldn't notice it. She supposed her life must have been to some degree sheltered. Except for during her medical training she'd not heard a great deal about people who weren't heterosexual. Certainly, so far as she was aware, she didn't know any man who didn't fancy women.

'You're not going quiet on me now, I hope?' Frank enquired into her silence.

'No. No, why should I? Might be a bit of a relief, for once, not to . . .' Her words trailed off mid-sentence. She hardly knew the man, how on earth was she heading into this kind of conversation about fending off advances?

Frank's ready laugh reached her once more. 'You might guess this is a relief for me. Being away from the other lads at the base, free to talk honestly to someone because our paths are unlikely to cross again.'

Rachel could understand, there must be no situation more uncomfortable than living among a group of people while not being in tune with their feelings. So often today this wartime life was thrusting together lots of folk who, for one reason or another, did not subscribe to common sentiments.

What would it be like when peace finally came? she wondered. Could enforced contact with people who had different motivations perhaps result in greater tolerance all round?

Her thoughts were interrupted by Frank's warning of storm-force winds ahead. 'Don't go into immediate panic, there's no need, just try to hang on in there – and to hang on to your last meal!'

Rachel had tried to comply with the latter ever since taking off, and was thankful that, thus far, the pills she'd taken were working. The turbulence was unpleasant but didn't last too long. And she was either growing accustomed to the cold or had been numbed into paying it less heed. The drone of the engine seemed to throb through her head, but the sickness antidote was soporific. With little or nothing visible beyond the window she was being lulled, this abnormal sense of suspension inducing the urge to sleep.

When, what seemed like hours later, Frank announced they were almost there, Rachel was jolted into full consciousness. If she hadn't actually been asleep, she'd somehow slipped into an unreal state where unaccustomed inactivity released her from awareness of her surroundings. Rachel was reminded of hospital nights on call when only one ear remained alert for an urgent summons.

They flew on and on, disproving her sudden assumption that they would arrive within minutes. Dawn was paling the sky over to their right. Ridiculously, having spent most of the flight untroubled by being airborne, she was beginning to feel apprehensive. But perhaps that feeling was generated by the, to her, unfamiliar prospect of landing.

Daylight had strengthened before they left behind what Rachel took to be the misty outline of the Scottish coast. Glancing beneath them, she spotted a group of islands – were they the Orkneys?

'There's Sumburgh Head,' said Frank, and she realised that they were already over the Shetland Islands.

Rachel supposed she should have expected Shetland to look barren, hadn't quite been prepared for such dismal-looking hills, dull-brown more than green, and with far less snow than she'd thought to see there.

The airstrip where they landed was unsophisticated by anyone's standards, and Rachel's instant sympathy went out to the aircrews who regularly operated out of there. She could be thankful that her normal bit of the war effort was concentrated on the more congenial hospital at Keld House.

When Frank had completed his routine drill in the cockpit he called to her and emerged to assist her as she was striving to bring her cramped limbs back to life.

'Don't forget to take all your gear, will you?' he reminded her as she removed helmet, parachute and the flying suit. 'I'll show you where to go, they know you're expected. One of the lads from the base will have transport to connect you with the officers in charge of the Bus.'

Rachel had been cold right through to her marrow during the flight; here on the ground she felt no better, and was shivering violently as she strode beside Frank to the edge of the airfield.

He left her in an outer office to wait for the RAF officer

who was engaged on the telephone. After acknowledging her thanks with a grin and saying goodbye, Frank departed so suddenly that Rachel felt bereft. Alone, acutely conscious that his kindness had generated an unrealistic optimism, she now admitted privately how scared she was becoming. So much for her claim of knowing boats!

'You must be Dr Skelton,' said the officer coming through at last to greet her. 'One of our recruits will drive you over to somewhere near the inlet where their vessels are moored. Don't expect comfort from our Land Rover—'

'Maybe discomfort will prepare me for the voyage ahead,' Rachel interrupted to suggest.

He smiled, shrugged. 'Maybe. Anyway, our chap is getting to know his way around the island, so he *shouldn't* get you too lost.'

The young airman looked extremely immature, Rachel doubted that he could be old enough to drive anything. And then she recollected: assuming these chaps were *too* young was becoming a habit. One she must curb, or she'd be obliged to admit she was guilty of a prejudice she hadn't thought she possessed.

Cheerful, and evidently glad to be of use, the lad helped carry her belongings into the vehicle, then gave a hand as she clambered after them.

'Your first time here as well?' he enquired.

'Oh, yes. When did you arrive?'

'Seems like a year already, but actually just a couple of weeks. The place might go down better with me when I'm allowed to do some real work.'

'Perhaps that won't be too long, all the forces need lots of personnel.'

'Are you army yourself?' he enquired.

'No, a doctor, helping run a military hospital.'

'Couldn't do that, seeing all them folk with bits missing, legs an' stuff.'

Rachel was noticing his accent, north-country, but not Yorkshire unless she was greatly mistaken. 'And where's your home town?'

'Oldham. I wasn't so far from there when I joined up at first. That was all right, could get home now and again, see my pals.'

'I expect you'll make new pals when you've been here for a while.'

'When I've completed my training, I might. These days I seem to be the only one as knows nowt.'

'I suppose it's like that in most careers.'

'And yours would be a longer training than lots, must have taken a deal of determination.'

'I don't know about that. But medicine's something I wanted to do long before this war appeared on the horizon, that made the decision for me. I'm fortunate my line of work is as necessary today.'

'If not more so.'

They drove for miles over the unforgiving tracks across terrain that might, in summer, present a kind of wild beauty. Winter did nothing for the place, to Rachel's eyes, even when they finally reached a house, gaunt and dour as the hillside it surmounted. Her driver gestured towards its door.

'I'm told you're supposed to check in here. Think it's where the chaps in charge hang out. Their vehicle's outside, looks as though someone's around. If you'd like to go and try the door, I'll bring your stuff.'

'Thanks, and for the ride.'

'I'll wait until I'm sure there is somebody there.'

The door was opening already, and Rachel gazed up at the tall man who was emerging at a run. Thrusting on a thick coat, he didn't speak immediately.

'I'm Rachel Skelton,' she announced in a rush, and hoped with all her being that this person wasn't Norwegian. Tired as she was, and slightly bemused, she felt scarcely coherent in her accustomed tongue, much less any other.

'Ah, yes. I was expecting you. Terribly sorry, but I'm needed urgently.' The man was English enough, and sounded well educated, but he evidently had overlooked her arrival. Dashing off to deal with a crisis somewhere, he couldn't delay even to introduce himself.

'We'll catch up later,' Rachel reassured him, not wishing to be a nuisance.

'Go inside, will you? My apologies for leaving you to make yourself at home. A problem with one of the boats – got to rush down to the quay.'

Turning to take her things from the RAF driver, Rachel was glad someone had time for her. She thanked him again and wished him good luck. Her host indicated the general direction of the kitchen and told her to make a pot of tea.

'There's food in the cupboards,' he called over his shoulder as he sped towards his own vehicle.

Solitude was not something that Rachel had anticipated, nor was it a condition she'd experienced for several months. The last time she recalled being alone for anything other than sleeping had been when she was setting up Keld House while Hamish was away on that course.

I wish he was here now, she thought, and instantly rebuked her foolishness. He was a colleague who'd become a friend, a *valued* colleague, but she should not let his presence in her life assume any greater importance. Where was her independence? She was going to need that in full measure during this expedition. Those Norwegian crews would have their own tasks throughout the voyage, and no time to spare for ensuring her comfort.

The projected sailing trip which now seemed to have been so long in the planning suddenly became very real, perturbing, and all too unpredictable. She did not even know if this evening was scheduled for departure.

Making tea, Rachel wondered if she already ought to be limiting her intake of liquids. Facilities on board, she knew from her father's trawlers, would be basic. If in existence at all!

When she had drunk her tea and was still alone, Rachel decided that she ought to find herself some sort of a meal. If they were sailing soon, it shouldn't be on an empty stomach. Investigating the kitchen cupboards produced a large hunk of cheese, a dish of butter and some bread. Sandwiches would be better than nothing and could be consumed while she was waiting. If news came that they were setting out tonight, she wouldn't be causing much of a delay. Rachel was already afraid her arrival had caused the officer here a disturbance; she would have to bear in mind that her inclusion on the trip was being organized as a favour. She must not become a liability. The cheese was good, and the bread seemed freshly baked, rather more tasty than some of the stuff available through their hospital supplies.

Rachel had finished eating when she heard a Land Rover approaching. Instead of the officer who'd witnessed her arrival was a man who looked around fifty and was dressed in the kind of seagoing gear her father would wear.

'Major Mitchell has ask' me to explain how he had urgent work on the boat.'

'Problems?' she asked when he went to the sink to scrub his hands.

'Too true! But I must tell you who I am. Nils Brekke.' After drying his hands, he strode towards her and shook her hand. 'I believe you are Dr Skelton.'

'That's right – Rachel Skelton. I'm pleased to meet you.'

'I am to make sure that you eat something, and prepare for leaving today evening. The major has obtain' a new part for our boat. When it is fixed, then we go with the darkness.'

Rachel explained that she'd had bread and cheese, and a cup of tea.

'But nothing *varm*? I think you should eat some soup, yes? I find a can, and we make *varm*?'

While putting a pan of soup on the stove, Rachel enquired how long Nils had been on Shetland.

'Since the start of the winter. My friend he own our vessel, did anyone explain you that our boats here belong to Norwegian fishermen or merchant seamen? They are requisitioned for this purpose. When an engine packs up, or other crises arise, one of the English officers may have to organize to make them seaworthy.'

'I see.'

'Until this time we are not having an ideal base. You will see only dinghies can reach our pier, not deep enough you understand. Even so, our boat is soon ready for to sail. And you also?'

'The sooner the better,' said Rachel, finding a dish for the soup and offering some to her companion. Nils had eaten already, and shook his head before continuing.

'Bergen is one of our shorter voyages, we can make it there in around twenty-four hours. Depends, of course, on conditions at sea. Is right how I am told – your father is a trawlerman?'

'He's never been anything else.'

'So, you should know how it will be. Although not perhaps the degree of cold, or ferocity of storms this far north.'

'I think I've got the general idea.'

'Someone tell me you speak some *Norsk*. That is good. As you might guess, these vessels must to behave as if they are fishing out of local ports over there. There is a restricted zone, but our task is assisted by the hundreds of islands.'

'I remember those from pre-war sailings to Bergen.'

'How well do you know the region?'

Rachel wasn't certain what he was getting at. 'Depends how detailed the knowledge required of me . . .'

Nils smiled. 'Enough to find the way swiftly to your relative's home would be a . . . a *bonus*. But you need not worry if not possible to do it. You will be travelling with all of us who are out of Bergen, we are very good guides.'

'Once we were into the city, I could find Grandmother's home. But no doubt we should have to avoid some sort of German checkpoints?'

'There are those – initially, for vetting incoming vessels, and documents of those on board. Unfortunately, often they name specific sections of water "forbidden" areas – these they change to try trick people. But here your Englishmen take note of information that we bring across. And that aspect should not be your concern. Only any restrictions ashore.'

'I'm just scared that my being around could place your men in danger.'

'That is our life now, we accept. This we do for Norway, and for the peace. You will have your documents, and we learn the Nazi regulations always from our own people over there. They inform themselves.'

Nils was looking at his watch when Rachel finished eating the soup. 'We should depart from here at 17.00 hours. At the quay it take some time to transfer from the dinghy on to our boat.'

Rachel excused herself to hurry towards the bathroom. Nils' conversation had been good for her, preventing her from panicking, but it also had outlined the trip ahead of them, bestowing a vivid realism.

The ride down to the harbour in the Land Rover was bumpy enough to seem a fitting preparation for life aboard a ship. The surrounding darkness was so intense that she might have been anywhere – at sea or on land. How many years was it since her last trip on one of her father's vessels? Rachel couldn't remember, but knew it was unlikely to do much to make the motion any easier, riding these far northern seas which were reputed to be as rough as any in the world.

When they reached the quay and she blundered her way through the darkness from the Land Rover, Rachel began to wonder if her eyes would ever adapt to this lack of light. The smell and the restless sounds of the seawater told her of their position more than anything she could see.

A couple of people, identifiable only as darker forms, were heading towards them. Unable to distinguish anything more than paler smudges between their headgear and their enveloping clothing, she failed to recognize one as the British officer in charge until he spoke.

'Hope you've a successful trip, Dr Skelton,' he said as they drew level. 'Sorry not to meet you properly, see you when you get back.'

'Oh . . . right, thanks. And thank you for fixing this for me.'

'He still seems in a hurry,' she murmured to Nils, noticing that the major was again in earnest discussion with the man at his side.

Nils nodded. 'One of the other vessels needs repairing. I

think that they arrange that it goes to Lerwick. This part of Shetland does not have the big workshops.'

'Running this operation must be difficult.'

'Is more difficult at sea.'

Sensing some degree of friction, however slight, between the British in charge of the scheme and those who risked their lives to make it work, Rachel decided to say nothing. Her admiration was for the Norwegian crews, but without more knowledge of how the operation had originated, she had no idea of how it might have worked without British officers.

'They do well for us on land,' Nils admitted anyway. 'It is not their choice that English officers are not permitted to make the crossing with us.' Seconds later he stretched out a hand and grasped her arm. 'We have reach' the dinghy – can you not see?'

Glancing to one side, Rachel spotted a darker, duller patch amid glinting waves. 'How far down is it?' she asked, the toes of her rubber boots at the edge of the jetty.

'Do not be afraid, Dr Skelton, I step into the boat before you.'

Still apprehensive because of being able to see so little, Rachel waited. Nils released his hold on her arm while he grasped a low bollard roughly a yard from where she was standing.

'Be careful of the ropes,' he warned. He had lowered himself into the dinghy and was now extending a hand for her own. 'Step to this side of me and you will be in the centre, and so you will be safe.'

If it gets worse than this I'll never make this trip, thought Rachel, then hoped she hadn't voiced that thought aloud. Its being so dark still seemed far worse than anything she'd anticipated. She could only do as Nils was instructing her, and pray that his certainty of what he was doing compensated for her inadequacy.

Stepping down into the tiny craft, she steeled herself not to clutch at Nils, whose hold on her hand was the only thing steadying her. After a degree of rocking, the reaction to her weight subsided. Nils directed her towards the necessary seating, then checked that she had brought all her belongings aboard.

'There is no turning back now,' he added seriously, while unfastening the rope. Taking the oars, he set out with what felt to be remarkable speed. Leaving the quay, Rachel discovered that her eyes were at last growing accustomed to the darkness. She could distinguish the line of waves breaking as they lapped the jetty, and beyond that the rough path with the shaded headlights of the Land Rover as, she assumed, the major and his companion drove off.

I wonder when I'll next see an English person? she thought, and turned to Nils to ask if the rest of the crew only spoke Norwegian.

He laughed. 'If that is so, you will be proficient in our language by the end of our voyage, yes?'

'I hope so. At the moment I feel as though I've forgotten most of the words I ever knew.' Had there been more time before leaving Yorkshire, she might have brushed up her Norwegian with her mother. Only that would have entailed revealing her intention to Asta!

'You must be adept at subterfuge,' said Nils.

Rachel felt hot colour rushing to her icy cheeks. How did he know that she'd deceived both parents?

'Fresh documents await you on board. You must have for you a name, and your new Norwegian person.'

'My grandmother's family name is Larsen, perhaps—'

Nils interrupted sharply. '*Nei*! Not Larsen, I think. There is a Larsen who work' to resist the Germans. Is safer you have some different name.'

They had reached the boat, Rachel had sensed it towering above their tiny craft. Voices whispered through the night, voices she could not understand, but Nils was seizing a rope that dangled towards them, hauling on it until they were touching the vessel's side. While he was making fast, Rachel's head crashed into some sort of metal rail which she soon discovered was the ladder providing access to the boat. With both their dinghy and the larger vessel riding the waves, she dreaded clambering aloft.

But there was no alternative. This time Nils urged Rachel ahead of him in order to protect her from falling.

Rough seamen's hands clutched at her arms, hauling her aboard while she struggled to avoid toppling head first on to the deck. One to either side, the men steadied her, laughing.

'*Tusen takk*,' she said. Thank you very much.

Both smiled, nodded to each other, and winked. I think they might begin to like me, hoped Rachel.

Nils was beside her now, having quickly made the dinghy safe. 'You come with me now, and meet my friend Thor.'

Thor was in the wheelhouse, a tall, burly man well suited to his name. His voice, though, she soon found in no way evoked thunder. He was so softly spoken that Rachel struggled, and failed, to catch his first few words.

'I welcome you in my home,' he repeated, grey eyes smiling.

Thanking him, Rachel wondered if Thor slept aboard even when in port, if all his crew did. There were so many gaps in her knowledge of this set-up.

'A moment, and I will take you to a cabin,' he continued, then in their own language conferred with Nils, who appeared about to take over from him.

Leading the way aft, Thor explained that one of the men helping her aboard was their engineer. 'And myself also, but so many other tasks keep me from the maintaining. You understand?' he asked as they reached a small cabin and he thrust open the door for her while he continued to speak. 'Nils is the junior member of my crew, yet he is the oldest. Before this war he fish with me only in holidays. He is school teacher, but is Jewish and not a good idea to stay in Bergen now.'

'Yet he still makes these voyages.'

'But yes, to help people like him to come away. Also . . .' Thor paused to consider. 'I have to trust you – but first now I remember me of one important matter. You do not smoke the cigarettes?'

'No, during my medical training one of my tutors was extremely anti-smoking.'

'Good, good. I have to warn you, you see. No cigarettes must have British wrappings. More seriously than that – we carry armaments, you see. Not only for use if we are intercepted by the enemy.'

Rachel nodded that she understood. 'This little fleet of vessels does far more than I first believed.'

'We are proud to think that we do. And now for the matters which concern you personally. Your Norwegian documents are here. We think to make easy for you, you become *Dr* Gunhild Fana – do you know that on our west coast one may take as the last name the place of birth? You will see Fana on the map, is important you should know where it is, *ja*.'

'I think I remember Fana – there is a very old church there, isn't there?'

'A stave church? *Nei*.'

'Not a wooden one, no. This is stone.'

'Enough, you need only to know a little if you should be questioned. Were you told not to carry any English money?'

'No. Probably no one's fault, everything seemed to happen in a rush.'

'So – I regret that if you have any English banknotes they must be destroyed. We will burn them. Coinage must be thrown overboard here, before we put out.'

'Fortunately, I only have a one-pound-note and two of ten shillings. The coins aren't worth very much.'

'Had you known, they could have been left at the base.'

'It doesn't matter. Once we're back over here, I'll have to contact somebody if I need any cash. My colleague at the hospital has pals in the RAF.' The lack of currency could be a difficulty, though, if Grandmother Hedda proved to be unfit for travelling to Yorkshire immediately.

Thor was explaining more about the voyage, some of the information familiar already but reinforcing the serious nature of any German checks they might encounter in Norwegian waters. 'When questioned, you will be the doctor who came aboard to tend an injured crew member. Your story is that the man died from his injuries, and was buried at sea. I need not tell you that you would be suitably distressed.'

'I certainly would – no medic likes to lose a patient.' Rachel didn't even like the prospect of pretending to have lost one.

Thor smiled. 'We are hoping, naturally, that we do not suffer any questioning. As you know, the islands on our coast are numerous, and my men accustomed to evading those who would detain us.'

A few less detailed remarks followed, and then he told her that the cabin in which they were seated was to be hers. 'And for your relative also on the journey to Shetland. You may not be comfortable, but I hope you will not endure misery.'

Rachel was told to expect they would eat once they had put to sea, which would be within the following few minutes. Long before any food was offered, however, her appetite had disappeared. Emerging from the cabin when Thor was showing her the rest of the boat, Rachel could smell their evening meal being cooked. And then the engine started up, and diesel joined the odour of food.

To increase her discomfort, the engine created a vibration that seemed to generate an internal quivering quite beyond her control. Trying to ignore the wretchedness pulsating inside her, Rachel struggled to smile while Thor was explaining the layout of his vessel. All too soon she was compelled to excuse herself and rush to the side, where she was sick.

Rachel heard the crew laughing, was too ill to care that she must be the object of their ridicule. She could blame no one but herself. In all the haste to embark, Dr Rachel Skelton had made her first mistake – she'd forgotten to take her own medication.

'But we are not yet out into the sea,' Thor murmured.

No, thought Rachel miserably, and I'm the one who committed myself to at least twenty-four hours of this agony. God forgive me for being a blundering fool – and somehow help me recover. I was supposed to be of use on this trip, not a massive liability to the rest of the team, who are already fully occupied.

Five

The night was like a horrible dream. After remaining at the vessel's side until she had been so sick that she might safely assume she had nothing more to lose, Rachel tottered with someone's assistance as far as the cabin she'd been given.

Before lying on one of the bunks, fully clothed because now she was shivering, she belatedly swallowed one of the pills to counteract seasickness. It might not work as well as it should have earlier, but ought to do something to help her condition.

Enclosed like this, the vibration from the engine appeared totally inescapable, and that wretched diesel smell seemed to permeate everywhere. Willing herself to sleep, Rachel tried to concentrate on the medication she'd taken and her knowledge that it could generate drowsiness. It *would* make her sleep, it had got to . . .

Although she did eventually lose consciousness, it was only fitfully. Despite her earlier supposition, Rachel did still have something remaining inside her, and twice was obliged to stumble out on deck. Her only consolation was that members of the crew were either somewhere on watch, or resting ready for their spell on duty: no one witnessed these further bouts of nausea.

Her visits to the deck confirmed that they now were well out to sea, the strong swell providing, if nothing else, an excuse for her sickness. Rain mingling with sleet stung her face and turned her hair into a clinging mass, but it did at least ease her aching head. The power of the sea, though, roared alarmingly while the exhaust from their boat's motor sounded merely a stubborn protest against the onslaught. I might not survive this, thought Rachel, and felt too ill to care. But she did care that Grandmother Hedda might not be rescued, prayed someone would explain how she had tried to reach her.

After her second trudge out into the fresh air, Rachel began to feel fractionally better, believed she might sleep soundly. This time, when she returned to her narrow bunk, the motion of the boat seemed to be lulling her.

Jolting her awake, the dream she had as soon as she slept was so vivid that tears ran down Rachel's cheeks as she struggled to surface from its horror. Don't let it be true, she thought, and it was several moments before reality replaced nightmare.

She had been operating in a cabin fitted out as a makeshift theatre; Nils and Thor were her only assistants while the man under her knife was Hamish Wilson. In a macabre reconstruction of Thor's storyline to explain her presence on board, she was trying to save Hamish. And Hamish was bleeding severely, from what seemed to be every artery. No matter what she did, Rachel could not stop the blood flowing out of him.

'We'll bury him at sea,' the dream-Nils had told her.

'No, no – you mustn't!' Rachel was screaming as she awakened.

There was a knock on her cabin door and someone called: 'Dr Skelton, are you all right?'

It was Nils. When he opened the door and peered into the cabin to check, she laughed weakly. 'I am so sorry. It was a nightmare. Did I shout something?'

Amused, Nils nodded. 'We thought that perhaps you were very ill.'

'As you know, I was, only hours ago,' she admitted. 'I'll never convince you I'm a sailor, will I?'

'You leave the sailing to us. But you might try not to alarm us by shouting, *nei*?'

Rachel felt an utter fool, and even though seeing Nils had banished that dreadful dream, it was replaced by thoughts no less disturbing. She was ill-prepared for the voyage, more gravely unsuited to crossing the North Sea in a boat as small as this than she'd ever imagined. No trips up and down the Yorkshire coast in her father's trawlers came anywhere close to this experience. And if she'd believed that pre-war crossings to Norway in regular steamships bore any comparison to this, she had suffered under greater than normal delusions!

And I thought I would care for *her*, she reflected miserably, that I was the one person who could bring Grandmother Hedda home to us – how in the world will I even look after myself?

She lay restless on the bunk, would have turned from side to side had she not been afraid that a sudden lurch of the boat might toss her on to the wooden floor. The will to sleep had gone, evaporated by the struggling of her exhausted brain which was insisting that she must use this time productively. It was all she had, the only way to find some means by which to overcome this massive inhibition. Never in her life had she felt so afraid – *afraid that she would fail.*

Daylight brought a small amount of returning optimism. Their vessel appeared slightly more stable, its progress more positive as it continued on its course. After a hurried wash in cold water, Rachel went in search of the others. She could see Thor in the wheelhouse, one of the crewmen beside him.

Nils was at breakfast, relishing eggs and something else which Rachel didn't identify. Refusing even bread, she accepted a mug of what, in peacetime, would have been coffee. Here, it resembled the real stuff no more than anything she had recently tasted at home, but it was hot and began to fill the emptiness where soreness still warned her against incautious eating.

'I've remembered the pills this time,' she told him ruefully. 'Hope I'm not going to distinguish myself by being ill all the way to Bergen.' Or home again, she added silently. The homeward journey was the one that mattered.

As soon as Rachel saw Thor, she enquired if there was some task she might take on. Occupied, she ought to feel better, be less aware of the motion of the boat and its pulsating engine.

The skipper grinned. 'Even fishing boats cannot be allowed to smell,' he declared, grinning. 'My men will show you the cleaning. And, if you wish, the cooking – no one of them enjoy to do that.'

'Fine. I'll swab decks or anything. Then if somebody shows me what food we have on board, I'll see what I can manage.'

Alone in the tiny area designated the galley, Rachel risked eating a slice of dry bread. When that stayed down, she tried a second slice, this time with a scraping of butter – or was it margarine? No item in the entire stock cupboard bore an English label. Remembering what she'd been warned about packaging on cigarettes, she recognized how serious it might be for those on board if German eyes should find items sourced in Britain.

Strangely, the gravity of their situation created within her fresh strength, supplanting the fears and misgivings of that dreadful night with a resolution to be useful. So long as she was aboard this boat she had a job, if only to play her part by doing whatever simple task might be required of her.

Providing hot drinks for the men and keeping soup warming in a stockpot, Rachel soon discovered that an additional warmth was permeating her – from the regular crew members.

Several times, when she wasn't occupied at the stove, she would go out on deck, and was pleased that her small experience of her father's trawlers bestowed some appreciation of this vessel.

Thor told her the kind of cutter she was: a Norwegian type, of course, its name meant nothing to Rachel. But he proudly declared her the 'queen' of the boats utilised for the operation. 'She is so compact, *ja*? No others used for our Shetland Bus have so fine a wheelhouse.'

Rachel had judged her overall length to be around sixty feet – not great to endure such relentlessly harsh seas, but no doubt of a size commensurate with the need to appear normal when supposedly fishing her native waters.

How soon they might expect to see land was a matter that engaged Rachel whenever she was working alone, but it wasn't something she would bring herself to ask any of the others. Still sensitive to how soft she must have seemed when laid low by that wretched sickness, she would say nothing that hinted at the urgency with which she longed to reach the other side.

When busy in the galley that afternoon, tidying the lunch things away, Rachel noticed that between the galley and wheelhouse there was a tiny chartroom.

At last, when Nils emerged from there, she could resist enquiring no longer. 'How is the trip going?' she asked. 'Shall we arrive on schedule?'

He smiled. 'If all remains this quiet, yes. Before darkness falls we should arrive near the outermost islands. From there it will be much slow journey, watching, waiting, alert for the patrol boat that could stop us and examine documents.'

'Speaking of documents reminds me – I was wondering if false papers will have been prepared for my grandmother?'

'I would think that they have – if not on board, someone ashore will have organise the matter. You should remember that our people are making this voyage many times.'

Now reassured, Rachel felt better again. When she later returned to the galley to begin preparing an evening meal for everyone, she was feeling excited about reaching Bergen.

Thor was in the adjacent chartroom with one of the crew when Rachel heard a word that sent concern coursing through her once more. Talking urgently and looking perturbed, they already appeared anxious when, amid the usual mass of barely decipherable words, the name Larsen emerged to unsettle her.

Could it be that Olav's new work was in helping this outfit to function? If he *was* the man they knew, did his having a family connection in Britain increase the danger he faced in German-occupied Norway?

Electing to keep silent rather than risk repercussions for anyone by mentioning what she had heard was far from easy.

Rachel's recently acquired optimism immediately dwindled to nothing. All excitement over the prospect of reaching Bergen and her family withered with the thought that her presence might increase the hazards these men already faced.

Only common sense encouraged her to eat her share of the food that she had cooked for the evening. The crew were quiet as they moved about the vessel, completing tasks while they steamed in, negotiating narrow straits between the offshore islands.

The water here was noticeably calmer, the air surrounding them dreadfully cold, but dry. Rachel recalled the expression 'too cold to snow', and thought it far more applicable here than whenever it was used in Yorkshire.

She had expected to see lights, had looked forward to their approach to Bergen harbour being well lit. Realizing how foolish that expectation had been, she wondered how many more disappointments would mark her return to this city she loved so deeply.

All too soon she discovered that there would be no opportunity for her to watch while they sailed in through Byfjorden and towards their anchorage. Finding her on deck Thor frowned, and when he spoke his soft voice had taken on a sharp edge. 'You will go to your cabin, please, Dr Skelton. We may yet be stopped by a patrol boat. If they come aboard I wish to avoid unnecessary interrogations.'

His circumspection was only just in time. Concealed in the cabin, Rachel lurked behind the door ready to hide should someone try to enter. Her heart was pounding agitatedly when she heard another vessel come alongside, then German voices and Thor's steady response. Footsteps, sounding purposeful, echoed across the deck, entered the chartroom and voices thrust out further questions, which Thor answered. They tramped into the wheelhouse and out again, and then away towards the side of the boat. Following a further brief conversation, Rachel heard the unmistakable sound of the Germans returning to their own vessel. She was immensely thankful.

Nils rapped on her cabin door a few minutes later. 'Do

you have all of your possessions ready for disembarking?' he enquired. 'Please you are not to leave anything on board here. I give you now papers for your relative, and wish you safe.'

Rachel was thanking him, leaving the tiny cabin after a final check for any mislaid belongings, when Thor joined them.

'We are docked now, and no serious incident. We sail this time tomorrow, Dr Skelton, and wish that you will sail with us. You should remember the registration number of our vessel, to recognize in darkness. If you are prevented to come we will try to arrange for another boat, another day, to call here.'

'I'll do my very best to make it in time. I can't thank you enough for all that you have done to help me.' She shook his hand, and they said goodbye.

Nils was still beside her. 'Do you think that you will find your way to the home of your grandmother? One of us might be able to assist if . . .'

'Can you tell me where we've tied up? I can't see a thing.'

'At the heart of the Vagen – the Torget, naturally.'

Rachel smiled. 'Then I will be fine, thank you.' She knew the fish market well – even on a holiday visit, Andrew Skelton had always been too interested in the fishing industry to keep away from here.

Descending to the quayside in darkness was frightening. The lapping of water against the side of the now silent boat was a clear enough warning of the hazards of a missed footing. Stepping ashore at last, Rachel turned for a final wave to the men who had brought her to Bergen.

No one remained at the vessel's side. She realized afresh the importance of doing nothing to attract attention. Turning to face away from the water's edge, she lurched suddenly on legs weak beneath her. Ruefully, Rachel sighed. She must make allowance for the effect of the voyage, take her time until she felt steadier. Not an easy matter, she feared, while all she longed to do was run and run, until finally she could trudge up the hill to Grandmother Hedda's home.

Hoisting on to her shoulder the canvas bag containing spare clothing, Hedda's new papers and her own, Rachel turned to her left, hurrying as swiftly as she was able towards the Bryggen.

Glancing nervously about her, expecting to be challenged at any moment, she crossed towards the familiar wooden buildings. Distant voices reached her on the icy night air, but few pedestrians were in sight. Darting into one of the wooden alleyways between the businesses of the Bryggen, Rachel found the cover she was looking for, and hastened onwards and upwards. At the next intersection with a narrow street she turned right, hurried on and, remembering, turned left once more.

Her eyes were growing accustomed to the darkness, even in so ill lit an area she could distinguish the bulk of the Floibanen station, the funicular railway. Although she didn't require a ride to the summit of Mount Floyen, Rachel was relieved that it proved she was on course. She was young and fit enough to climb the rest of the way towards the house that she remembered so well for its position overlooking the city.

With proof that she was on the right route, her unease focused ahead to her moment of arrival. Was she expected? Would Olav have received the message that she'd attempted to relay via the RAF and the Shetland Bus system?

Through residential streets and along elegant roads Rachel walked, at times rendered breathless by the gradient, until at last she stood, staring towards the white-painted wooden house of so many pleasant visits.

Perhaps reluctant to risk disappointment, Rachel remained motionless, just looking. A section of moon, which had seemed long-absent, hung above Mount Floyen, casting just sufficient light to reveal the old house unaltered. None of the windows was showing a light – was Grandmother Hedda at home? Asleep maybe, but this early . . . ? Unwell, and in bed, unable to be moved? Only by knocking at the door would she learn the truth. No matter the power of the dread generated, she must act immediately.

The sound of her own knuckles striking the door startled Rachel, making her feel foolish. But bolts were being withdrawn at the other side of its staunch timber, and a key was turning. The door was opened a few inches. The old familiar voice was asking who was there, Norwegian words which Rachel could not have forgotten any more than she'd forget their speaker, ever.

'Grandmother, don't you know me?'

'Rachel Hedda! Little Rachel Hedda, come in, come in. Olav told me to expect you. I could not believe it, would not allow myself to think that possible.'

She was drawn into the narrow entrance hall, and the outer door closed swiftly behind her. For a moment they gazed at each other, but Rachel could not wait to hug her grandmother. Tall, yet never more than slightly built, Hedda felt as fragile as some elegant bird when she held her.

'How are you?' Rachel asked at last as they drew apart.

Both women were weeping. 'I am well. Yes, really well,' the elderly lady told her. 'But what of you, my little love, you have travelled so many gruelling miles, for the sake of this old one who does not deserve you.'

'We want you with us,' said Rachel simply. 'I hope Olav has explained.'

'I did not dare to believe,' said Hedda, drying her eyes while fresh tears sprang from between silver-fair lashes. 'But I have packed a few clothes. Olav told me – and those people bringing the message – how I must not carry much with me.'

'I'm afraid that is so. But you have a friend, a neighbour perhaps who may look after your home until . . . er, while you are absent?'

'It is all arranged. They are good people, always have been kind. But they are older even than I, ought not to bear the burden of caring, if I were to remain here and should become ill.'

'So, you are not as healthy as you claim?'

Hedda smiled as she took Rachel's outdoor clothes, showing her into the warm living room. 'Most of the time, I am well enough,' she said, indicating the chair beside the hearth, and going to the sofa when her granddaughter was seated.

'You don't neglect your medication?'

'You speak like the doctor you have become, Rachel Hedda. And oblige me to admit that I do not always control this wretched diabetes. I suspect Olav has told everyone that I am not very good about the tests that I should do.'

'Don't worry, that's why I'm here. To watch that you do not become ill during the journey. And afterwards – we shall see. I believe my mother will love taking care of you.'

'*Believe*? You have not arrange' with Asta that I go to her? Is she not well perhaps?' Hedda Davidson had relished her independence, did not wish to rely upon anyone, especially if she was unsure of her welcome.

Rachel smiled. 'I had to keep this journey a secret. You remember how Mum worries, but she is quite well. It is only because, with my father out on the North Sea, she doesn't need to know that anyone else faces its hazards.'

Hedda shrugged, shook her head. 'This world at war often seems beyond my comprehension. So many half-truths, so many lies, subterfuge all around us. It should have been so simple, I felt so sure that it would . . .'

Rachel looked questioningly at her.

Again, the thin shoulders were shrugged. 'The only certainty to me was neutrality, the refusal to fight. And look where we are! Overrun, no longer able to live the lives we wish, afraid in our own homes, glancing nervously about each time we visit the market. Afraid for family . . .'

'For Olav? Is that what you mean?'

Gravely, the old lady nodded. 'He has some secret work, refuses to confide its nature.'

Rachel frowned, recalling the name Larsen being mentioned while she was aboard. *Was* Olav's task connected with the Shetland Bus?

Hedda suddenly sprang to her feet. 'Of what could I be

thinking? You must have something hot to drink – coffee, little one?'

'Coffee would be lovely, *takk*.'

She followed when Hedda went out of the room and along to the kitchen. After years of separation Rachel couldn't bear to have her out of sight.

'You see – I have *reinsdyrstek* cooking for our meal tonight.'

'Reindeer? That is a treat!'

'And for us here, also, now. Olav bring to me. I do not ask from where, he would not tell me.'

'Do you see him very often?'

'Now, alas, no. He has his work, out beyond the city somewhere. All I know is that he no longer is a manager with the public transport system, he refused to run services for the enemy.'

'So, he had a responsible job?'

Hedda laughed. 'I hope you do not believe you yourself the only one of the family who chose a useful career!'

Rachel laughed with her. 'It's just that I didn't know . . . what Olav did, how he's . . . well, turned out.'

'And between the two of you always existed a rivalry.'

Really? thought Rachel, somewhat surprised. She would have said that it was apathy, rather than anything livelier, between that plump schoolboy and herself.

Hedda poured coffee and offered a plate of *wienerbrod*, the pastries they both loved. She had gone short earlier in order to provide this small welcome. Sitting in the kitchen – the warmest, and to Rachel most familiar, room in the house – they began reminiscing about her past visits to Bergen.

'It's so sad that I can't stay here long this time,' she was saying when they heard rapping on the door behind them. When Hedda went to open the door, she gave a tiny cry of delight and was immediately swept into the arms of the man who came into the room. When they had hugged, she hurried to close the door and smiled towards Rachel.

The man, much taller than Rachel's own five feet nine inches, wore ski clothing that emphasised his athletic figure.

His eyes were blue, gleaming with the smile that enhanced a high-cheekboned face.

'Aren't you going to introduce us, Grandmother?' Rachel asked.

Hedda and the young man laughed. 'You do not remember Olav, the fat schoolboy?' he teased.

In a couple of strides he reached her. Catching Rachel off guard, he hugged her now, and kissed both cheeks before releasing her to gaze into astonished eyes. When he finally moved away, Olav ran a hand through his blond hair and grinned. 'You have not changed very much, Rachel. I would have recognize' you anywhere in the world.'

'Sorry, I didn't know you . . .' she began.

'But that is a compliment, I think. Today I am very fit. I ski a great deal, and play football in season.'

'To good effect!'

Olav laughed delightedly. 'So, the good doctor approves of me. That is excellent, proof that I am becoming the man I wish to be. And you, Rachel – are you well?'

'Normally, yes. I'm afraid I was foolish and didn't take the anti-sickness pills soon enough; that crossing could have been better.'

'And you are here for – how long?' He was sipping from the mug of coffee that Hedda had given him.

'Until tomorrow evening. We're due to board at around six p.m.'

Olav glanced from Rachel to her grandmother. 'So you both must sleep tonight in readiness. I shall see you before you leave.'

'You're not staying the night then, or even to eat with us?' Hedda asked him.

'Alas, no. There is something that I must do.'

Rachel watched her grandmother's grey eyes clouding with anxiety. *Could* it be that Olav was connected with the operation to ship people in and out of Norway? Much as she would like to understand, she didn't feel she knew this new Olav well enough to ask him.

The house felt strangely subdued after Olav had departed.

Rachel exerted quite an effort to try and distract her grandmother, bringing her up to date with family news from Yorkshire, while insisting on helping to prepare vegetables for their evening meal.

'And our family over here?' she enquired at last as so much about her people in Norway felt strange to her. 'Are Olav's parents still alive?'

'You do not recall?' Hedda asked and sighed. 'The two of them were killed in a terrible fire at their house. So many of the old houses here are wooden, and flare up all too readily.'

'I do remember something about that, now you remind me. Mum told me, would it have been while I was studying?'

'I feel sure it was then. Olav was at university, thankfully, and was not harmed. Except by the shock, naturally. When he returned to Bergen, the old house was demolished, too badly damaged. I am fortunate he considers me his family now.'

'Who has he married, someone you already knew?'

Hedda shook her head. 'No one. Olav tells me nothing of his personal life. I believe that there has to be a young lady somewhere, but I do not meet her yet. He always work so hard, and now for the war . . .' The old lady sighed again. 'I do not like to think that he risks his life, but who can know? These young people must do whatever their conscience dictates.'

'Well, I'm glad he got the message I sent through about taking you to England.'

'As I must be thankful also, despite regrets concerning leaving my home. And worries too – about what your grandfather will think of my arrival.'

'He will be all right about that, I'm sure. Bernard Davidson's still the genial doctor he always was.'

'Towards me? I doubt that can be so. I deserted him, did I not? An unforgivable disloyalty, I fear.'

Rachel shook her head. 'I don't think so, but we shall see. This war is altering perspectives, you know, for many people.'

'Does Bernard . . . does he still visit all those old abbeys and churches the way he used to?' Hedda longed to know that he wasn't changed too utterly.

'Not very often now. He is extremely busy, you know. Lots of civilian doctors are covering for those with the forces.'

'And for doctors like yourself who are founding military hospitals.'

'Who told you about that?'

The old lady raised thin shoulders. 'I cannot say, only that I had the news from someone.'

'Did I mention it perhaps in the message I managed to get through to you?'

Throughout their meal Rachel remained puzzled that news of her current work had reached Grandmother Hedda, but their conversation turned to the old days, and the joys they had shared when Rachel and her parents had visited Bergen in happier times.

After they had eaten, cleared away and washed the dishes, Rachel suggesed that they ought to sleep. 'Tomorrow will be stressful while we wait for darkness to come so we can depart. And if the night aboard is anything like last night we need to get what rest we can before sailing.'

In the small room she barely remembered from girlhood visits, Rachel felt exhaustion overcoming her and was thankful. She yearned for sleep more than anything in the world, and would need to be in prime condition to cope with what the following day might bring.

That difficult and dangerous voyage across the North Sea was far enough into the future to seem an unreal prospect. The one matter which was now disturbing her was something that would happen before their departure.

Returning to this house in the city she loved had resurrected all her affection for Bergen, for Norway. And today she was discovering her emotions had found a new focus – in Olav Larsen. Rachel couldn't imagine how she had failed to know him instantly. Despite his changed physical appearance, he should have been the man whom she recognized immediately as perfectly complementing herself. Olav, she felt certain today, was the only one she'd ever met who might erase the dreadful feeling that some part of her was missing. The half of her once personified in her twin.

And within hours they must say goodbye. Rachel was afraid she would never bring herself to leave him here. Nothing she might say or do could make that parting any easier. The whole point of her visit was to enable her grandmother to escape, there was no alternative to departing. Yet she knew in her heart that the situation in occupied Norway was so uncertain that she could not be sure of seeing Olav again.

Six

Rachel was awake early and bathed slowly, relishing the comfortable surroundings while preparing her mind for a day which offered little comfort of any kind.

Making coffee in the kitchen which was beginning to feel so familiar again, she wondered if her grandmother was still sleeping or would appreciate a hot drink. Hearing a sound, she turned and there Hedda was; in her dressing gown, appearing older and thinner than the previous evening, and extremely tired.

'Have you found all you need, little Rachel Hedda? I am a poor hostess, I fear. I did not sleep at all, I seem altogether too excited.'

'Then you should go back to bed. But only after eating something. And first, have you done your test?'

Hedda smiled. 'Yes, Doctor – and everything is registering that I am well!'

She did agree to eat some bread and an egg, however, and was then persuaded to return to her bed, if only until time for lunch.

Alone, and partially reassured about the elderly lady's well-being, Rachel took her time over another cup of coffee. She still could not guess what the rest of the day would be like, was trying to resist trying to visualise it. All she could do was prepare the two of them for the journey, and perhaps also check that Grandmother Hedda had thought of everything with regard to leaving her home unoccupied.

Beyond the house, the surrounding darkness continued, disappointing Rachel for she'd hoped to see something of

Bergen, if only from the windows. She ought to have remembered how little daylight there was here during these winter months, but her previous visits had been during the short Norwegian summers.

Hedda had shown her already the food set aside for their meals, and had explained that she would take everything else that was perishable to her neighbours. After washing the breakfast dishes, Rachel began to prepare vegetables and the fish they were to eat for their last meal there.

When the time came neither she nor her grandmother had much appetite for any food as both were too preoccupied with what lay ahead. Sensing that they were each eating because of the other, they struggled on, sighing, chewing, swallowing.

Eventually Hedda rose, unable to endure the pretence a moment longer. 'I have had enough of this.'

Rachel knew that she wasn't referring only to their meal. 'I'll clear away.'

'Then I must call on my friends.' Hedda walked briskly into the kitchen, and snatched up the provisions she'd set aside. It seemed like she was angry with those harmless items, rather than the circumstances necessitating this evacuation of her home.

As the door closed on her grandmother, Rachel wiped tears from her eyes. Was this really the right thing to do, right for the old lady?

She was washing dishes in front of the kitchen window when she saw him. Skiing rapidly from the top of Mount Floyen and, unaccountably, recognizable even from that distance. Several times, concealed by other dwellings or the many trees, Olav disappeared from view but then he came into sight once more, carrying his skis after he reached the lower slopes where the snow lay thinly scattered.

She opened the door at the first rap of his knuckles. 'Very stylish! I hadn't realized how much snow there was beyond the city, but I'm glad it's there. I wouldn't have missed the sight of that for anything.'

'*God dag*, Rachel,' Olav said, leaning his skis against the wall beside the door. All the while he was holding her gaze with eyes that seemed even more intense than they had on the previous day. He came towards her then, held her by both upper arms, and kissed each cheek in turn. Rachel felt a pulse awakening deep inside her.

'Did you sleep?' Olav asked, concern darkening his blue eyes.

'Surprisingly, yes.'

'And your grandmother?'

'I sent her back to bed this morning. She's finding all this traumatic, isn't she? The poor dear has gone next door to say goodbye.'

He nodded.

'What about you?' Rachel asked. 'Did you sleep, Olav?'

'Me – I am an owl. My work is in the night.'

'I was going to ask you about that. Someone on board mentioned a person called Larsen who's one of the other seamen. Is that person you?'

Olav threw his head back and laughed. 'I wish! *Nei*, I am not connected with the Shetland Bus. The Larsen working with them is far more brave than I could hope. He is no relation of ours, either.'

'I see.'

Olav went to one of the bedrooms, and emerged wearing a sweater and slacks which he evidently kept in Hedda's home.

'There seems to be a great deal more going on here than I can comprehend,' said Rachel, replacing cups and plates in the cupboards. 'For instance, Hedda knows I'm working in a military hospital, yet I'm sure none of us ever told her.'

Olav's smile appeared well pleased. 'Our country may be occupied but *isolated* we are not, my dear cousin.'

'What do you mean by that?'

'Do not forget the message that I got through to your father's trawlers. News travels in more than one direction – was it unnatural that I should wish to know what kind of work engages you?'

'I see,' she said again. Only, Rachel didn't really understand, and all she could think of was how delighted she felt because Olav had needed news of her.

'Even if Andrew Skelton did not speak personally to my contact, the men sailing his vessels are aware that his only daughter is a clever doctor – one who now devotes her life to men injured in the fighting!'

It was Rachel's turn to laugh, deprecatingly. She might, one day, be pleased by the opinions held by her father's men, but Olav's interest *thrilled* her.

'It's been such a long time, I thought you'd have forgotten me.' She hoped this would excuse her embarrassing ineptitude with words, which was caused by him.

He was gazing at her left hand and she saw he smiled to find it ringless.

'My elegant cousin, who always looked so lovely? I would not forget her.'

Olav was calling her 'cousin', yet she was sure that if they were indeed cousins, then that relationship was a distant one. And that mattered not at all, for in claiming this kinship he was filling her with a new warmth – *filling the part of her that for so long had felt so empty.*

'We must talk, and talk,' he insisted, smiling into her eyes once more.

Rachel smiled back. 'There is so much I don't know about you. Grandmother's told me hardly anything.'

He came round the kitchen table, took her hand and drew her to him, hugging her close. 'I was not anticipating boring you with my life history. Time today is sadly too short. Most of all, I just need to hold you. Where has this grown from, Rachel, this feeling that you mean so much?'

'I don't know, I'm only glad we seem special to each other. Special, because of getting to know somebody who . . .' Her voice faltered, and she sighed. Rachel couldn't explain that she felt Olav was a part of her. She realized this was so new, and she'd only once been really sure of belonging, with her twin.

'Someone who makes a difference to life, to oneself?' Olav suggested.

'That's it, yes.' And far, far more, thought Rachel. This was indeed the difference that made her complete, more complete than she had ever felt since the loss of the one person who had physically been a part of her.

'There are things I must say,' Olav went on. 'Let us find somewhere to sit, very close, while we use this time that could never be long enough for what I have to tell you.' They hurried to the living room and to a sofa where he drew Rachel down beside him. His arm felt strong, holding her against his side. 'I had a kind of hope,' he began slowly. 'A hope that you might come here to take our dear Hedda to safety. Without any reason, I sensed it was the sort of thing that you would do. When word came confirming your plans I became more excited than ever I remembered. Until the fear overtook me . . .' Olav sighed, kissed her forehead. 'That I have initiated this journey which could place you in serious danger is a grave responsibility for me.'

'I offered to come, I didn't have to,' said Rachel lightly.

The arm holding her to him tightened. 'Except that you *did* have to – I know you, Rachel, I know you now. And you would not have shirked the task. I can only pray your voyage to Shetland may be safely concluded.'

Listening, feeling him close at her side, his breath on her face while she inhaled the scent of his soap, Rachel recognized the amazing truth. She now had every reason in the world to survive. *For Olav*.

'I will try, somehow, to let you know that we are safe,' she told him. 'So long as that won't place you in any danger.'

'You should use only the methods of sending word that served for us before. Your father's men are good, and the air force know that messages for despatch through the Shetland route are important. We must hope that they will reach me.'

'You *are* working with them, aren't you? With the men organizing escapes?'

'Not directly, no. But there exists a great network of . . . of partisans who are all the time learning fresh ways of assisting each other. It is better you should not know too much, although away from our coasts knowledge of our activities should not harm you.'

And what harm might befall you? wondered Rachel again, sickened by this prospect of months, if not years, of never being sure that he was safe.

'Now that we have met once more,' said Olav quietly, 'I shall hold my thoughts of you here inside of me, each day until this wretched war is ended.'

'And within me you have a special place,' Rachel assured him. 'A place like no one else's.'

He kissed her then; for the first time on her lips. Along with the bliss of affection was the force of passion, a passion that was no more than a promise of the way things might be, the way they ought to be between them. One day. Deep within her, yearning surged. Rachel kissed him back, her mouth lingering.

Olav was smiling when she moved her head. He stroked her hair tenderly.

'God keep you safe,' he murmured.

'And you.'

They heard footsteps on the pathway outside the door. Olav glanced towards the clock as he gently slid his arm away before standing up. 'I should leave in a few minutes, but I need to say goodbye to Grandmother Hedda.'

'And so you shall.' Hedda walked in through the doorway.

Olav strode across the room and wrapped both arms around her. He was speaking softly, in their own language. Rachel couldn't translate, but the sheer tenderness of his embrace made tears spring to her eyes. So much love flowed from him to the elderly lady.

'You must not worry about a thing,' he said finally in English. 'I shall return in the morning to make certain that all is secure here. You will deposit a second key with your friends?'

Hedda nodded. 'I did so as I went to tell them goodbye, and to give to them the remaining food from my cupboards.'

'I shall collect my skis and the rest of my things,' Olav told her.

Smiling, he extended a hand to Rachel. 'Would you walk with me to the door?'

He hugged her to him as they reached the kitchen. 'Be safe, sweet cousin,' he said, and kissed her.

Too distressed to watch Olav walk away, Rachel closed the door on him and sighed. No one could even guess at how many years would pass before they might meet again, how many dangers they each might encounter.

Hedda was seated on the sofa, staring dismally towards the front windows. 'This once was such a happy place, so *free*. And now life here is so furtive that my dearest people are obliged to slink in and out through the back kitchen.'

'Perhaps it is good then that you are going to stay in England?'

'You think that?' Hedda shook her head. 'I leave only because I am too wearied to resist. You should not fool yourself that my gratitude for what you are doing means that I shall be happy.'

When Rachel frowned, her grandmother rose and walked over to pat her arm. 'You must forgive me, Rachel. I do not wish to be soured. I will try to be better.'

'Once you arrive in Yorkshire and see my mother again, you'll feel differently.'

'Warmer, certainly. I look forward to your gentler climate. Even though it lies so many miles away, across that unforgiving sea of separation.'

During the afternoon Rachel grew increasingly concerned about her grandmother. She was so evidently restless, wandering from room to room of her home, touching first one beloved item then another. The few things she could take with her had, in the main, been packed in anticipation of Rachel's arrival. Together they had unpacked and repacked them all, and had added scarcely anything.

Being unable to carry very much to her new home was making it all the more difficult for her to leave the old. While understanding how her grandmother must be feeling, Rachel was deeply disturbed about what she was doing. From the moment she received Olav's message, Rachel had been sure of his judgement. Until coming here. Now, filled with so many doubts, she seemed unable to rationalize that her grandmother had made the final choice herself.

Hedda had returned with eyes reddened from crying after leaving her friends in the next house, and that had made Rachel feel worse than ever. But just as doubts threatened to overwhelm her, Hedda surprised her, sounding quite exhilarated as she demanded to be told more details of their journey.

'It will be a shorter crossing, will it not? Shorter than the steamer route we took to Newcastle.'

'Much shorter, and I'm afraid you'll be thankful for that. Have you ever ventured out to sea in the winter?'

'No, no. Why would I?'

Rachel's smile was rueful. 'Quite.'

Hedda shrugged. 'And so – between the two of us, we should remember to swallow the pills against the sickness, even if *you* could not, alone! You have checked on this silly diabetes of mine so many times already that I could not be in better condition. And if you think me senile enough to overlook my medication, I know that you with your hawk-eyes will watch over me.' Despite her misgivings, Rachel laughed. Perhaps between them they would muster sufficient spirit to endure until they reached Shetland.

Waiting, even after darkness had covered the city, was the greatest drain on their spirits. Not until it was time to set out for the fish quay did Rachel experience any degree of relief.

Walking quietly down towards the city centre, Rachel noticed few signs that Bergen was under enemy occupation. Olav had warned of local onshore observation posts and those equipped with artillery. Planning a route to avoid them, she had wondered what life there had really been like. There would be time enough for Hedda to tell her about it during their perturbing voyage.

Despite the absence of any overt indications of the German occupation, Rachel remained cautious. She led Hedda through narrow streets to emerge near the Bryggen, which left them with only one road to cross in order to reach Torget and the quay where the boat should be moored. Both wearing trousers and with knitted hats and scarves concealing their hair, they had laughed before leaving the house. They were thankful now that neither's appearance should look out of place striding along the quayside.

Here there were German troops, armed and alert, yet paying little heed to the few fisherfolk engaged in tasks around their vessels. Rachel supposed that these soldiers would be more interested in whoever might be coming into, rather than leaving, the harbour. Praying that her assumption meant that they might continue to be ignored, she hurried with Hedda across the road.

Finding their boat was less simple than Rachel expected, even though she had memorized its registration number. In the darkness, distinguishing one vessel from another was difficult, and the one Thor owned was not where she had last seen it. Panic sent her heart racing while she struggled to conceal her alarm from Hedda. 'Not quite sure where we're tied up,' she whispered. 'Try to look as if we know where we're going while we trudge on, searching.'

Nils was on board, doing something with one of the nets which were being used to disguise the boat's purpose, otherwise Rachel could have left the vessel unrecognized.

'Thank God for that,' she murmured. 'We're here, Grandmother.'

Wary of attracting enemy attention, Rachel called 'Nils' very softly. He did not hear her. She glanced around, checking that none of the Germans were within earshot, then called again, slightly louder.

Nils looked up from his nets, nodded, and came to the side of the boat. He was gesturing further along to where they should come aboard. The engine was running already, its busy pulsing indicating the urge to be moving. 'Do be careful where you place your feet,' Rachel hissed to Hedda. 'I'll hold you steady as long as I can.'

Her grandmother giggled quietly. Surely she can't be enjoying this? thought Rachel.

Despite Rachel's anxiety, Hedda clambered unfalteringly on to the boat. When she joined them Rachel found her grandmother introducing herself to Nils and shaking his hand.

'We have a third passenger tonight,' he told them. 'An important man who is on his way to London. I cannot tell you more, except you will address him as Edvard Fasmer.'

'When we have been introduced,' said Hedda. She possessed a keen sense of the courtesies.

Rachel smiled. 'I don't suppose that's his real name,' she told Hedda. The elderly lady shrugged.

Nils was taking them to their cabin when Thor emerged from the wheelhouse with a distinguished-looking stranger. Seeing Rachel and her grandmother, Thor smiled and was introduced to Hedda before they both met Edvard Fasmer.

Thor became businesslike. 'We are prepared now, I think. As we sail, is wiser you ladies occupy your cabin. The patrol boat has inspected us one time, but we cannot be certain they will not still be curious about us.'

And there are lookout posts also, thought Rachel, we must not alert anyone to our presence on board.

'Quite a compact little place,' Hedda observed as she entered the cabin.

Rachel grinned. 'You know now why we couldn't carry much with us.'

'Also earlier, for the time when we were arriving at the boat. I do not believe the fishermen will set out with suitcases!' Her evident good spirits delighted her granddaughter who had been afraid that leaving Bergen would prove terribly upsetting.

Hedda was watching Rachel's expression, guessed what she was thinking. 'I have said goodbye already, little Rachel Hedda, to my home and to my country. The friends I have and people like Olav that I love *are* my home. If I am granted life long enough to return, I pray I might see them once again.'

But how can you not feel sad to be deserting Bergen? thought Rachel. She herself had always loved the city, and had found that love renewed on this trip. Or had her deepening affection for the place owed far, far more to Olav Larsen's presence?

She pictured the crew moving about the boat, their tasks well learned, their eyes schooled in navigating through darkened waters. Since the occupation began any lighthouses facing seaward had been extinguished or masked. Only their years experiencing these coasts enabled the men to negotiate their outward course, where so much involved navigating narrow channels between the many islands.

Once or twice the women heard planes fly low overhead. Even Hedda's determined spirit faltered and alarm narrowed her eyes.

'They patrol the fishing areas, I understand,' said Rachel. 'I'm sure that Thor will have made certain there's nothing to reveal us as anything but an innocent trawler.'

They were out on the open sea when Thor came to speak with them. 'We should be safe from the Germans, for the night,' he assured them. 'Word has it from Bergen that they are on the lookout elsewhere, for vessels crossing to the north of here, towards the Lofoten Islands. If, as I believe, those vessels are ours, they are well primed on what to expect.'

Rachel shuddered, disturbed to think that any boats like their own might have German forces awaiting them. But Hedda had taken Thor's assurance as it was meant, and accepted the slight comfort of knowing that, for the present at least, they were not being shadowed.

'May we go on deck?' she asked him.

Thor laughed. 'If that is your wish. It is snowing hard, the wind increases.'

Hedda's smile was rueful. 'Some other time perhaps . . .'

She is so *calm*, Rachel marvelled. Whatever she'd expected of her grandmother, it had not been this quiet acceptance of what they were tackling.

Thor was speaking again, turning now to Rachel. 'My men and I were hoping – well, that you might please us with your cooking again.'

'Of course.'

'Then I must help,' Hedda insisted. Smiling at Thor, she spoke in their own language. 'I think your crew might prefer good Norwegian food, yes?'

He laughed. 'Even if many ingredients were purchased earlier in Scotland!'

In the galley the two women divided the chores between them, and allocated the restricted working space to avoid potential clashes – of personalities as well as utensils. Rachel had rarely cooked since her student days, but the cramped situation in her digs had conditioned her to being tidy.

Hedda was the one who felt the limitations keenly, but she was determined that no one should detect her misgivings concerning any aspect of this journey.

As the men came off duty and one by one showed their appreciation of the food, Rachel began to feel this voyage would prove far better than the outward trip. Her grandmother had needed no persuading to test some of her own cooking, and they were both taking the anti-sickness pills too regularly to allow illness to overtake them. Probably because she was eating well and not neglecting her insulin, Hedda's diabetes also appeared adequately controlled.

Being occupied in the galley had been good for Rachel as much as Hedda, they both seemed healthily tired by the time they went to their bunks. Lying down was what unsettled each of them in turn. As soon as Hedda's head settled on to the pillow, she groaned. 'Oh, no! I feel quite dizzy now, and rather nauseous. How can that be when we have swallowed all those pills?'

'Maybe they're not quite strong enough. The way this boat's tossing, the sea must be extremely rough. Try lying still for a while and see if you feel any better, Grandmother.'

But as soon as Rachel had taken to the other bunk she was obliged to admit that she felt almost as bad. 'We can't sit up all night, can we?' It seemed, however, that they *would* be obliged to spend most of the night sitting upright. When Hedda was afraid she would vomit and Rachel took her on deck to lean over the side, she too succumbed to sickness.

Fortunately their nausea soon abated, but the blizzard

and stormy seas did not. Lashing at them as though from every side, the wind-borne snow froze on their hair and faces. Retreating to the cabin, they rubbed themselves dry before putting on every sweater and all the outer garments that they had brought on board. Enveloped in covers, they sat on one of the bunks, leaning into each other for support.

'And we started out so well,' Hedda remarked wryly.

'One improvement on my last journey, I suppose.' Rachel wasn't comforted, she had felt so sure that, this time, she would be fine.

They had become reasonably comfortable when she remembered that Hedda ought to have replaced the food and liquid that she had lost. 'I'm going to get you something, promise you'll try and keep it down.'

'Or my diabetes will go out of control,' said her grandmother, well aware of the potential problems. 'Can you not let me sleep, Dr Skelton!'

Rachel heated soup remaining from their meal and found some of the crackers that were popular in Norway. If they each managed to take something they should be strengthened to cope with the rest of the night.

En route to the cabin she met Edvard Fasmer who was turning away from the side, wiping his lips, his face looking ashen despite the limited light. He tried to smile and failed, shrugged his shoulders and said something in Norwegian.

Rachel had reached her grandmother by the time she translated his words. 'Yes, even naval captains can suffer seasickness!'

Hedda was amused, and also sympathetic. 'Might we spare him some of our pills perhaps? So long as you explain that they are not guaranteed to work. Tell him you are a doctor, he will be impressed.'

'He might be happy to try them. Even when I say they are only a recent development.'

Edvard was grateful to be offered the medication. Going back to the cabin again, Rachel realized that she would be very pleased to return to her profession. Looking after Hedda was not the same at all, much more like caring for a family member as any relative would.

The women talked intermittently through the night, each drowsing from time to time without really sleeping deeply. Whenever Hedda dozed, Rachel found her thoughts turning to Olav, her heart aching with anxiety as she wondered what his work really entailed. Intuition told her danger was involved, and she could not bear to even think that he might be injured. They had found one another after such a prolonged absence, an absence created only by their original failure to recognize in each other a vital half that had long been missing.

Tired, she and Hedda eventually struggled out of the tangles of bed covers and heavy garments, washed to freshen up, and headed towards the galley.

Nils was there before them, cooking eggs at the stove and ready to tease Rachel. 'I know how it was with you when we sailed from Shetland. I did not expect that you would come anywhere near food today!'

'I wasn't sick this time. Well – only the once. But I would hate to usurp your position as chef.'

'Usurp – what is that? I do not comprehend such clever English.'

'I only mean I will be happy to have you cook everything.'

'*Nei, nei, nei*! Unless you think to have the old lady make the good Norwegian food.'

Rachel laughed. 'We shall see, I will ask if she is willing.'

But before either of them could take over from Nils, a crisis distracted everyone from anything so mundane as cooking. The blizzard had hardly abated at all, and was battering the vessel and driving snow across the deck, obliterating sight of anything further than a few metres away. Rachel heard the drone of a plane overhead and guessed it to be one of the German aircraft that patrolled the coastal strip around Norway. She hadn't reckoned with the distance they had covered overnight, and the fact that they now must be out in the middle of the North Sea.

The strafing came as a shock, striking the deck in several places and finding its target of the wheelhouse. When a yell from Thor alerted them that he was hit, Rachel ran with Nils and found the skipper slumped over the wheel.

'Take his weight, if you can,' said Nils. 'I must seize the wheel.'

The rest of the crew came running, with Hedda hurrying behind them. Thor remained conscious but clearly in great pain, and blood was emerging through the shoulder of his sweater.

'I will keep watch.' Edvard had appeared to the side of Nils and was training binoculars towards the skies. 'From the sound of his engine, the plane is departing. If he returns, be ready to take cover. And man our guns, someone.'

'Guns?' Hedda echoed softly. She had not suspected the little boat was armed. And Rachel had avoided mentioning anything that would indicate to her the level of potential danger.

Rachel was kneeling beside Thor, already wondering how she might treat him when she wasn't even carrying elementary first aid equipment, much less her doctor's bag. There had been no room for that. One of the crewmen assisted as Rachel struggled to move Thor away from the wheel.

'That is far enough, I can steer now,' Nils told them.

The skipper was still conscious, but moaning with pain. Rachel eased him into a corner of the wheelhouse and called for a knife to cut through his garments and locate the wound. Thinking rapidly, Hedda rushed to bring a clean knife from the galley.

One man ran to the machine gun concealed in a converted oil drum, another sped to uncover a second weapon set up in the bows.

'Any sign of that aircraft returning?' gasped Thor.

Edvard lowered his binoculars. 'Not yet. Let us hope he believes he has done enough to finish us.'

Thor tried to move and groaned. Rachel eased him back on to the floor. 'I've got to attend to that wound before you even think of doing anything. I'm afraid I'll have to slit your sweater and whatever's underneath.'

Turning his head towards them, Nils enquired what equipment she carried.

'Very little. Painkillers and anti-sickness stuff, there wasn't space for more.'

'I will bring your bag,' said her grandmother.

'We have a first aid box in the galley,' Nils told her. 'If someone can take the wheel I shall go and fetch.'

Edvard Fasmer crossed to take over steering. 'Rather different from a battleship,' he said wryly. 'But I believe I might be entrusted with handling her.'

Nils gave him a look. He hadn't known this passenger was a naval man.

'Please, Nils, just do as he suggests,' Thor insisted.

The skipper was wincing, even after Rachel had given him painkillers, and despite disturbing him as little as possible while gaining access to his shoulder.

'I'm afraid the bullet's in deep,' she told him. 'But the wound is moderately clean. If I can dress it to help stop the bleeding . . .'

Nils came running back to them with the first aid kit. Rachel found several large dressings which could form a pad, and there were big rolls of bandage plus a couple of triangular slings. Working steadily, she anchored the dressing in place with bandages, then finally utilized a sling to immobilize his shoulder.

'Do you think you could stand?' she enquired. She needed to get him to somewhere more comfortable.

'But of course. I shall take over now, I am fine.'

'Not quite,' Rachel argued. Thor seemed unaware that he was shaking as a result of the shock. 'You need to rest. We must get you to a cabin.'

Assisted by Nils, Rachel supported their skipper as they hauled him to his feet and began heading out of the wheelhouse and along the deck. The wind had strengthened, beating heavy snow against their faces, and making every step difficult. Even before they reached one of the cabins Thor was faltering, his breathing troubled, feet slurring across the boards. By the time they reached a bunk he was losing consciousness.

'It might be simply the shock,' said Rachel, wishing with

all her heart that she had some of her hospital equipment there – and most of all, Hamish Wilson! 'I'll keep an eye on him, hope he comes round again soon.'

If Thor didn't regain consciousness pretty quickly she would need to disturb him further to try and discover if he had other injuries that she hadn't yet noticed.

'I will send to you the older lady, yes?' Nils asked, hovering worriedly. He did not like to leave a stranger alone to sail Thor's boat, no matter how experienced a sailor the man might claim to be.

'Yes, you do that,' Rachel agreed. With Hedda beside her she could send word to a member of the crew if Thor's condition should worsen.

What any of them might do to help him while they were out at sea like this, Rachel could not imagine. She was such a fool of a doctor to set out on a wartime voyage carrying nothing suitable for coping with a major crisis.

'God help us,' she prayed. 'But we lack just about all the resources needed to keep us going until we reach Shetland.' She was so afraid, not only for everyone aboard – she herself was terrified of dying. She had got to stay alive, or she would never see Olav again.

Seven

Thor was growing impatient. Rachel was greatly relieved that his spell of unconsciousness had lasted no longer than fifteen minutes after they manoeuvred him on to the bunk. Now that he was difficult to restrain from hurrying out to take command of his wheelhouse, that seemed evidence enough that the shoulder wound was the only injury troubling him.

His pain was succumbing to a double dose of the painkiller, plus a swig of some spirit that Nils had brought to them. And while their analgesic effect was good reason to prevent him from taking the wheel, it was also slowing his reactions enough to facilitate keeping him on the bed.

Hedda appeared to regret that her granddaughter was the one whose skills were more useful, and was trying to find herself some role in tending Thor. 'I am sure a cool cloth on his head will help him to feel better,' she began, and headed towards the door. It was such an age since she'd had anyone to look after.

Rachel detained her gently. 'I think resting quietly is what he needs most of all, Grandmother. Perhaps later, eh? In the meantime – well, now that I must watch our patient, I can't return to the galley. I believe the men would benefit from hot drinks on such a foul night, don't you?'

In their concern for the skipper they had paid less attention to the lone aircraft which had attacked them, and only now were they beginning to appreciate that they had heard nothing to suggest that it was returning to fire further rounds at them.

'Thank God he didn't come back,' Rachel murmured.

'I feared that he would do so, until everyone aboard was

killed,' said Thor. 'And I am the one person responsible for safety aboard.'

'But there was nothing you could have done, surely? Through a blizzard like that, any plane could approach without being spotted.'

Thor shrugged, winced with pain, and sighed.

Despite the tossing of the boat and the ceaseless roaring of the wind around them, Rachel felt strangely reassured to be occupied with concern for a patient in a way similar to her work in the military hospital. She began telling Thor about some of the men she had treated there, and found that distracting him was a means of easing both his pain and his anxiety regarding their safety.

Nils came into the cabin once or twice, to check on his friend's condition and provide assurance that everyone was coping. Edvard was handling the vessel with great expertise while Nils and the rest of the crew were tackling all other tasks satisfactorily.

'They do not need me,' said Thor regretfully after Nils had left them. 'I trust they do not forget who owns this boat.'

Rachel smiled. 'You will remind them, I feel certain, just as soon as you have been ashore long enough to be patched up.'

'I can tell you that it will be so,' he said firmly. 'But can you tell me how quickly that may be? How long before someone take the bullet away?'

'That depends how swiftly we get you to a hospital. Is there one on Shetland?'

'It is no use to ask that of me – I am a fit man, and my crew also. We do not need medicines or hospitals.'

'No doubt if there isn't one near your base, the RAF will fly you off to one.'

She wished that the destination could be her own Keld House, yet she knew that having Thor treated somewhere in Scotland made greater sense. The bullet ought to be removed with all possible haste to avoid complications.

Rachel was forced to smile when her grandmother was again providing meals, and reminding everyone that they must eat and drink in order to remain fit to endure the rest of the voyage. Hadn't she once presumed Hedda needed *her* to ensure that she didn't destabilize her condition by neglecting her diet! During the rest of the voyage Hedda occasionally interrupted Rachel's care of Thor to report when she had taken her medication or checked her sugar levels.

'You are quite a naughty old lady, aren't you, Grandmother Hedda?' Rachel teased, delighted the woman was in control of her condition to the degree that they could joke about it.

'On the contrary, Dr Rachel Skelton – I am being exceedingly good.'

And you enjoy being so necessary aboard this little vessel, her granddaughter realized, beginning to wonder how they would occupy Hedda Davidson once they arrived in Yorkshire.

The storm continued to thrash their boat while daylight lasted, and Hedda insisted she must dry off clothing for the men. Nothing they wore was sufficiently waterproof to withstand the wind-driven snow that found its way through to their skins. She was using heat from the galley stove to dry things, and had an answer for one of the crewman who tried to caution against risk of fire.

'You are from Bergen also, aren't you?' said Hedda. 'You should know then that our tradition of wooden houses has educated us in taking every precaution against such a catastrophe. I was reared to respect every little flame, and to be watchful. I do not leave such things to chance, nor leave drying clothes untended.'

When Rachel heard this, she smiled to herself. Grandmother Hedda possessed far more self-assurance than she had credited her with – a fact which no doubt owed a great deal to years of living on her own.

When darkness again fell during their exhausting crossing, Nils reported from the chartroom that he estimated they were only a few miles from shore. But time now seemed to move more slowly, and the rest of the voyage felt interminable.

Thor had dozed a little due to the sedation, but was becoming restive and insisted on leaving the bunk. Struggling to keep his feet on the reeling vessel while unbalanced by having one arm clamped in a sling, he nevertheless prowled, mostly between the chartroom and his wheelhouse.

Edvard was tired from concentrating for endless hours after insisting that, as senior officer aboard, he ought to remain at the helm. His hands and feet felt as solidly encased in ice as much of the boat's superstructure, and his features had long since ceased to respond when he attempted to smile.

For him, though, there was quite a lot to smile about. He was on his way to join his fellows in London and he was rehearsing here, if in miniature scale. The Norwegian navy was reforming in Britain, readying itself to join the Allied fight. Never since their own king and government had been obliged to quit had Edvard Fasmer held so realistic a belief that he would indeed once more engage in major conflict.

As they sailed closer in towards Shetland he was glad of Thor's presence at his side, offering advice as they negotiated inlets and narrow channels between the islands that reminded him of parts of Norway. Only with experience of these waters could any skipper reach harbour through this black night without risk to those aboard his vessel.

Edvard's look was wry when Thor explained that they must anchor short of the quayside and be carried ashore by dinghy. 'But I was hoping to take her in proudly, and be acknowledged by your colleagues onshore.'

Thor laughed, then grimaced as his shoulder pained him. 'They will acknowledge you, yes, but more for your naval rank, I believe, than for your handling of my tiny boat.'

It was Edvard's turn to laugh with him. 'Will it surprise you that I confess it is some many years since I did anything more practical than issuing commands from a bridge? The benefits of senior grading do not include the joy of putting your own two hands to steering.'

With Thor back on his feet, Rachel had packed her own belongings and tidied the cabin and was helping Hedda to collect her possessions together. Nils had looked into the galley and approved the way that Hedda had put everything in order there.

'Thor takes pride in his boat, and will be happy that you have left everywhere so clean for him.' Nils was interrupted by a toot of their siren. He laughed when they jumped, then explained that they were announcing their arrival to their colleagues ashore.

Edvard had been surprised that none of the vessels engaged in this enterprise yet possessed radio equipment capable of contact with those ashore. When it came to clambering down into the dinghy, however, he relished the few minutes of simplicity that reminded him of days long past when leisure sailing had sown in him the desire for a career at sea.

With the relentless wind still hurling snow at them Rachel could not share his enthusiasm for taking to the tiny dinghy, but tonight she was more concerned for Hedda Davidson's safety than her own. For once, her grandmother was behaving according to her age, visibly scared, and clinging to the strong arms of a crewman.

When they gained the quayside, climbing out of the dinghy was no easier than their descent from the fishing boat, but Rachel tried hard to encourage Hedda.

'This really is the worst experience you'll have to face before we're home, Grandmother. Just think – in a few seconds you will be on dry land.'

Rachel couldn't believe she'd forgotten the effect of many hours spent on a storm-tossed boat. With legs wobbling so badly that they hardly supported her, she was steadying herself against a bollard when she turned to see Hedda stumble.

'Gran—' she began, and tottered towards her.

The seaman bringing them ashore reacted more swiftly, catching the elderly lady by her arm and holding on while he took a few steps with her.

'I shall take you to the Land Rover,' he promised her in their own language. 'I do not leave you until you are safe with the Englishman.'

The Englishman proved to be the same major whom Rachel had barely met when she first arrived on Shetland. As he urged them into the vehicle to escape the blizzard, Rachel began by ensuring that he was introduced to Hedda. He smiled and nodded in their direction, but he evidently had instructions to give special attention to the Norwegian naval officer. When Edvard clambered aboard, Rachel soon gathered that it was for his benefit that the trip to Bergen had been arranged.

Together the two men were laughing as Thor was assisted into the vehicle by his crewman. Thor grinned despite his pain when they ribbed him about being obliged to surrender command of his boat.

'Ah – so,' he retorted. 'But never again shall I permit others to handle her. Edvard acquitted himself capably enough, but no one knows that boat like her own master. You will see – this wretched bullet will be removed, and I shall be back at sea tomorrow.'

Rachel knew that, even if the operation should prove straightforward, Thor would need some while to recover. She knew also, however, that the skipper needed to compensate for what he considered to be loss of face.

The major was joking with him, evidence of the sound relationship that existed between them. 'A bullet, you say? But I understood that you had fallen over after drinking too much of your aquavit.'

Thor muttered to himself, but good-naturedly slapped the major on the back when settled into the seat behind him. After they all waved off the seaman who had brought them from the fishing boat, Thor continued speaking as their vehicle drove away.

'*Ja* – it was from a German plane that I was shot. He fired several times but fortunately no one else was hit. And I was fortunate in two further ways: our young doctor here checked the bleeding for me with this impressive array of bandages. Also we had on board our fine Norwegian naval officer. I make the joke, I know, but I was thankful to have him there. You know how it is with my men – they are a very good crew, but only with an experienced skipper in charge.'

While he was speaking Rachel recalled how well the crew had coped during the voyage in such dreadful conditions. She realized that in what had seemed a suddenly hurried departure, she hadn't said goodbye to Nils. He had been especially helpful, and she wondered if she could leave a message of thanks for him. Disembarking from the boat might have been somewhat hasty and, for her, confusing, but Rachel was soon to learn that their departure from Shetland was likely to be even more rushed. When the major didn't drive towards the house but continued along a rough road scarcely visible through the snow, he began explaining, initially to Edvard.

'Our people in London have arranged to fly you to one of our RAF bases, then from there direct to your colleagues assembling in the south of England. I'm hoping they may also take the two women.'

'If they have room for us,' said Rachel to Hedda. She didn't want her grandmother to be too disappointed if they were later delayed.

The major heard her and smiled. 'The RAF were flying in three people for transfer out by our team, there's a good chance they could take you. The only problem is the weather, forecast to worsen, which is the reason I'm driving you straight to the base.'

Edvard asked what provision was made for Thor's transfer to hospital, and was assured arrangements were in hand for the skipper to be treated in Scotland.

Rachel remembered little about the air force station where she had first touched down, although that was only a few days previously. With snow still blowing all about them, she was thankful to be driven to one of the buildings so she didn't have to find her way around the site.

Her legs still felt to be sailing while the rest of her was more or less static, but she somehow managed to assist Hedda as they left the vehicle. When it became evident that the major was going to drive off again, Rachel turned to thank him.

'I'll always be grateful for everything that you and your people have done. I wish there was some way I could repay you, but nothing could do that.'

He smiled. 'I'm pleased we were able to help.'

Thor grasped her shoulder. 'If you pray, just remember us.'

'Oh, I will, I will,' she said, and thanked him for all he had done. 'I hope your wound heals quickly.'

There was no time for more. Their pilot was waiting, already kitted out. Rachel saw he looked familiar from her visit with Hamish to the base in Yorkshire. How long ago that seemed – it might have been a different lifetime!

Again, she noticed that Edvard was treated with extreme courtesy. Whether or not that was his real name, and whatever his position within the Norwegian navy, he certainly was a man of considerable importance. They left while Thor was being welcomed by the officer in charge of the base. Rachel wished she could have seen him safely to hospital, but had to be content that there would be room in the plane for her and for Hedda.

'I have not flown before,' her grandmother whispered. 'I hope that I shall not make a fool of myself.'

'There's no need to be scared, love. And we'll take another dose of anti-sickness pills – we're due some, and it could be a bit turbulent.'

Turbulent was something of an underestimate on her part. Rachel was quite frightened as the aircraft, which felt very small for coping with the elements, seemed to lurch continually. Hedda was plainly terrified, and Rachel put her arm around her, while she steeled herself not to cry out in alarm each time the plane was buffeted. Gradually, as they flew southwards and Rachel guessed they were over the Scottish mainland, their progress steadied.

'It's not so bad now, we're going to be all right,' she said.

Hedda's wan face failed to convince that she was reassured. At least, as yet, neither of them had been sick, which was fortunate as it seemed like hours since they had eaten and her grandmother's blood sugar level could already be deteriorating.

'Did you do your tests before we left the boat?' Rachel asked. Too little was known about diabetes to continue considering it lightly.

Hedda surprised her by laughing, however weakly. 'Here am I, dying a thousand deaths of sheer terror, and all you can fuss about is my medication!'

'It is the reason I came to fetch you in the first place.'

'Very well, very well – fine. And I am fit – or was fit when I last did a check.'

'It's just . . . we've done all right so far, I don't want you to end up in hospital.'

'From where I am seated, Rachel, hospital would be welcome. And seems to me a likely destination – I cannot imagine that his horrible aeroplane will avoid falling out of the sky.'

'You needn't think that. These RAF pilots are very experienced.'

'But have you not looked around you . . .?'

Rachel smiled ruefully. Their plane was indeed extremely basic, and clearly intended for military personnel engaged in wartime action.

'There are seats for us passengers,' she observed.

'That is so,' Hedda concurred, smiling. 'I only wish that I possessed more cushioning, for these seats do not!'

Her mood appeared to lighten after her own introduction of a little humour, and even when further turbulence made the aircraft lurch she clung less fiercely to her granddaughter while they exchanged wry smiles.

The landing in Yorkshire was no less bumpy than the rest of the flight. Snow had been cleared from the runway to the best of someone's ability, but had since compacted in some patches, in others had thawed only to refreeze.

'Take care,' their pilot cautioned as they prepared to leave the aircraft.

Hedda giggled, making Rachel give her a look.

'But think how it would be!' her grandmother exclaimed. 'If I were to break a few bones now, your dear mother would never believe that I had survived two such horrific journeys quite safely.'

'Yes – well, just do as the man says, and watch your step.'

Edvard was listening, and came between the two of them to offer an arm to each. 'May I prove myself a . . . a *stabilizer* as we trudge towards the offices over there?'

'I shall miss your company,' Rachel told him as they approached buildings recalled from her outward trip. 'I do hope you don't have long to wait for your onward flight to London. And all the best for . . . well, for the rest of the war.'

Hedda was adding her own good wishes, in Norwegian, and looked surprised at his reply to one of her questions. They said goodbye to him, and thanked their pilot.

'My car's somewhere out there,' Rachel told Hedda when they were ready to leave. 'Can't say I'll be sorry to set off in a mode of transport that I'm more used to.'

Some thoughtful person had cleared the snow off the car's windscreen and windows, she noticed as she opened the passenger door for her grandmother and stowed their baggage in the boot. From the window of the building behind them Edvard was waving. Rachel waved back to him.

'I'm taking you to the hospital where I work first of all,' she told Hedda. 'It's nearer than home.' What she didn't explain was that she needed to phone through to Asta Skelton in order to warn her. Arriving suddenly with her grandmother would be rather more of a surprise than would generate a good beginning.

When the car didn't start as soon as Rachel switched on the ignition, she sighed and tried again. At her third attempt there was still no sign of life from the engine. 'It's no good, I'll have to resort to the starting handle. Just settle yourself comfortably while I sort this out.'

Rachel had crunched back and forth through the snow to the front of the car, and was bending to slot the starting handle into place when a hand closed over her own. Startled, she looked up into the smiling eyes of Edvard Fasmer.

'Permit me,' he suggested.

'But you . . . you . . .' Rachel began, and faltered. She couldn't refer to his very senior rank, could she?

'I am really quite capable. And certainly would bring more weight to this.'

Whether because of his weight or not, Edvard had the engine running seconds later. Thanking him warmly, Rachel couldn't resist giving him a hug. As Edvard left them he was laughing delightedly.

'He is such a lovely man,' said Rachel, taking the driving seat again.

Leaving the airfield, her mind gave a tiny jolt. She was now driving towards another lovely man, Hamish Wilson, wasn't she? And unfortunately that prospect reminded her that *his* generous gestures were not without motivation. She knew him to be capable of being completely altruistic, but towards herself he was behaving like any young man who wanted a girl, and would do anything to make her fall for him.

'What are you thinking, Rachel?' her grandmother asked. 'I expected you to be greatly relieved to have brought this old person safely to England. Instead of that you appear very serious, are you no longer happy?'

'Of course I'm happy, Grandmother Hedda. But I am tired – we both are after losing so much sleep.'

'Ah – so. And I must not forget that you younger persons require more hours in bed than people like myself.'

'I'm having to concentrate on this snow-covered road, an' all,' Rachel added, and hoped that might preclude further questioning.

'But naturally. I was not considering that. You handle this car so proficiently that I am impressed. In my day, you see, it was not thought that a young lady should even wish to drive.'

Nor in mine, if the truth were known, thought Rachel. Both parents had been reluctant for her to learn. They had even, at one time, kept from her the documents that enabled her to continue driving. She had *listened* when they explained that they acted only out of concern for her safety, but she had failed to understand actions that had seemed so uncharcteristic. Even though with time she had forgiven them both, she hadn't forgotten. Sadly, she never would.

Recollecting their actions, and the resultant sourness that had taken months to heal, did not help when Rachel looked ahead to reaching the family home later that day.

Arriving at the hospital, something that had potentially been another problem, went far more smoothly than Rachel had hoped. By chance, Hamish was in the first of the wards leading off the entrance hall, and he saw them as soon as they entered and set down their bags.

Excusing himself from a patient's bedside, he spoke briefly with Shirley Trent and came hurrying towards them.

'Grandmother, this is our surgeon in charge, Hamish Wilson,' Rachel began, and then she smiled at Hamish. 'My grandmother, Hedda Davidson.'

'A fine Norwegian name plus a British one,' he exclaimed with a grin, shaking her hand.

'While this hospital of yours possesses links with Scandinavia, did you know that?' Hedda remarked quickly. 'Is there a stream near at hand, perhaps? Or a water spring? *Kelda* has those meanings for us.'

'There is a burn,' said Hamish and grinned, recollecting. 'Sorry – that's Scottish, I meant a stream.'

'Ah, from Scotland,' said Hedda. 'We saw Scotland – well, almost. I confess the blizzard did rather obscure its visibility.'

'Not much better here, I'm afraid.' He turned to Rachel. 'You'll be heading for your home now.'

'When I've made a phone call, yes. And had a snack, we've not eaten for ages. How are things here? I'll be back on duty as soon as—'

'This is your leave, don't forget. You've not been away that long.'

'Feels like I have.'

It was the wrong thing to say. She read in his eyes the meaning Hamish took from her careless words.

He smiled. 'We'll soon make up for that,' he promised, confirming Rachel's misgivings.

'I'll look after your grandmother, Rachel. You go and make that call.'

Asta was at home, and became anxious immediately she heard Rachel's uneasy voice. 'Whatever's wrong, love? You've not had an accident or anything, have you? This snow's that dangerous.'

'No, nothing like that, stop worrying, Mum. The news I've got is good, very good. You know how Olav suggested we should try to bring Grandmother Hedda over here to us?'

'You're going to be able to arrange that? Oh, that will be a good thing.'

'It's better than that, she's here now.'

'But how? Did she come all that way on her own?'

As briefly as she could, with numerous interruptions, Rachel related the experience of travelling to Norway and back. Editing out most of the hazards, she evidently made the expedition sound exciting, even enjoyable.

'That must have been lovely for you both. Is she staying with you at the hospital now?'

'Not exactly, no. We don't have that kind of accommodation. You've rooms to spare, haven't you, and I know you'll have heaps to talk about. Getting to know each other all over again.' If her mother could make assumptions, so could Rachel, and she was compelled to do so. Her life at Keld House didn't allow for including family.

Although taken aback by the suddenness of her mother's arrival, Asta rallied and even sounded quite pleased. 'Well, naturally, she must come here. I'd better get busy airing a bed. She can have your room for a start, it's nearer to being ready than any of the others.'

Rachel smiled ruefully to herself. Relieved though she was that her mother was welcoming Hedda, she'd expected to spend at least one night in her own room to recover from the trip. However, she must act immediately before Asta Skelton unearthed more than a few misgivings. 'We're on our way over soon, Mum. When we've had something to eat. Expect us when you see us, depends what the roads over the moors are like.'

'All right then, love. Mind how you drive. Eh, this is all so sudden . . . I wonder whatever your grandfather will make of it!'

Given time in which to think so far ahead, Rachel too would have wondered about that. As things stood, she would be thankful just to deliver Hedda and leave the rest of the family to sort any difficulties. Suddenly, returning to the wards appeared quite attractive.

Hedda was very evidently nervous when they set out,

unsurprisingly, but Rachel didn't need this additonal problem when she herself was so exhausted that driving as far as Scarborough was as much as she could tackle.

'Mum's expecting you to stay there, naturally,' she assured her, sympathizing with the elderly lady's feeling lost after leaving her own home. 'She's always been a good home-maker, takes after you. In no time at all you'll be settling in so well that you'll feel you've never been away.'

'Oh, really? Rachel my dear, you don't have to exaggerate so entirely. You know as I do that but for this wretched war I'd still be in the home that I love. Most of all, you are well aware that I'm unlikely to feel very comfortable in such close proximity to the man I deserted.'

'Perhaps, but—'

'I have always tried to face the truth, even concerning my own actions. I do not propose now to begin lying to myself about the way others will react. The comfort you anticipate me finding in Asta's house may exist, but I shall be surprised if its boundaries extend to making me feel easier about past traumas.'

There seemed nothing Rachel could say. Concentrating on the road became a welcome alternative to rustling up the reassurances that Hedda seemed disinclined to accept. Asta had not said if Andrew Skelton was home from the sea. Rachel hoped that he was. Her father was so gentle a man, normally given to smoothing over any difficulties. The quiet life that he loved was maintained largely by his understanding of his wife, and a certain knack of finding the right words to offset her outbursts.

They all knew that anxiety was often the mainspring of Asta's sudden bouts of agitation which could set them all on edge. Humouring her, Andrew allowed his quiet strength to endow a much needed calm.

'Here we are then, Grandmother,' said Rachel enthusiastically, and unnecessarily, she feared. Hedda might have been absent for years but the Skelton home had not altered enough to become unrecognizable.

Hedda was getting out of the car slowly, and not only on

account of her bones being wearied by travelling. Even when Rachel came to her side, she hesitated. But she was taking something from her bag, an envelope which she gave to her granddaughter.

'We want you to have this.'

Before Rachel could unseal the envelope, the door was opening. Instead of her mother, a man came out on to the step. And the man was not her father.

'Good God, Hedda!' said Bernard Davidson. But then his genial doctor's manner took over. 'How are you? You're looking well. Do come in, come in.'

Asta appeared at his elbow. 'Hello, Mother. I didn't know Dad was calling round today. And I didn't know what to tell him.'

Evidently! thought Rachel. Her grandmother *seemed* quite composed, although she herself had no idea from where Hedda was finding words.

'Thanks to Rachel's attention, I have been well throughout our journey. She has inherited your expertise, Bernard. But how is everyone here?'

In the general confusion and kissing, Rachel stood a little apart. She was too exhausted to be more than concerned for the others, too shattered to be able to sort anything out for anyone.

Remembering the envelope in her hand, she hoped Hedda hadn't done something stupid like trying to pay for their journey. She would have to put her right on that.

The photograph was of Olav, on skis – somewhere at the top of Mount Floyen, she could tell from the backdrop of hills, fjords and Bergen itself. His lovely golden hair looked to be stirring in a breeze, and he was smiling. What have we done, Olav? thought Rachel. What have we stirred up by bringing her here? And then Rachel smiled too. With Olav Larsen somewhere in her world, it could not be all bad. It might even become better.

Eight

Rachel placed the photo carefully in its envelope and then into her bag. 'Thank you for the picture, Grandmother,' she said, and kissed her.

Hedda nodded, but she was preoccupied already. Asta was hustling her towards the stairs after promising to make tea shortly.

'You'll want to see your room, Mother, and to freshen up. Was it a long journey then? What was the weather like?'

Rachel concealed a smile. Her mother wasn't panicking because of Hedda's sudden arrival after so many years. Perhaps sounding as though she thought the voyage had been a relaxing summer cruise was her way of coping.

'Been quite busy, haven't you?' Bernard Davidson was looking serious.

'I didn't mean any of this to upset you,' Rachel began.

Her grandfather had seen worse things in his long life than the reappearance of the wife who had deserted him. 'I should have guessed you might try to go over there to bring her back, just the sort of thing you would do. Once young Olav sowed the idea in your head.'

'But you didn't think it'd be this soon?'

He shook his head. 'I didn't think you'd manage to make the trip. Your father doesn't conceal from me how bad things are out in that North Sea.'

'I was lucky. Hamish knew something about the Shetland Bus – the people who operate these crossings in and out of Norway. He also introduced me at one of the RAF bases from where they fly up to Shetland. Coming back we were lucky again, they were picking up a fellow passenger, a Norwegian naval officer on his way to London.'

'And the crossing itself, or don't I ask?'

'Not without incident, we were strafed by the Luftwaffe, they hit our skipper.'

'Not fatally, I hope?'

Rachel shook her head. 'A shoulder wound.'

'Which you patched up?'

'I'd have done more, with my medical bag. There hadn't been room to take it along.'

'Quite, but you were glad you're a doctor.' They looked at each other and smiled.

'What will you do, Grandfather?'

'About Hedda?' He shook his head and shrugged. 'Don't ask me today. Haven't the slightest notion. Initially, avoidance tempts me, but that's no long-term solution. Adopt my professional smile, I suppose, and the complimentary tolerance useful with difficult patients!'

'Only you don't have to see *patients* all that often.'

'I don't have to see Hedda. I have my own place, haven't I?'

'But you'd regret losing your frequent visits here?'

Bernard grinned. 'Everyone else might regret the atmosphere if such visits sparked contention!'

'I am sorry this makes it awkward for you.'

'When life's too smooth we can forget that we are alive. Any road, I'm glad Hedda's looking well. As for the future, we shall see how the land lies.'

Asta came rushing down the stairs to make the pot of tea. 'Mother's ever so glad she can have your room, Rachel love. Says it's really lovely. She'll be down in a minute, just having a bit of a wash. Are you two stopping for tea, or what?'

Bernard shook his head. 'Think I'll be on my way. Got a surgery at seven.'

'Did you come in your car?' Rachel hadn't noticed it, or she'd have known he was at the house.

'Walked, economising on petrol.'

'I'll drop you off, if you like.'

'Thanks, love, that'd be nice.'

'I'll just wait and say goodbye to Grandmother.'

When Hedda joined them she looked less tired already, and she responded warmly when Rachel hugged her and advised her to take things easy.

'Thank you so much, Rachel, for bringing me here to your mother. I know I'll be fine now. If you manage to get word through to Olav, thank him for me. And give him my love.' Hedda paused, sighed. 'Pray God keep him safe.'

Rachel echoed that, fervently if silently.

Stopping her car outside the old York stone house that was surgery as well as home to him, she turned to her grandfather. 'You're not going to spend the night worrying, I hope, about how things will be now that Hedda's around?'

His silver-grey eyes were rueful. 'You know me too well. Of course, you could see me through this initial shock – spend the night here. I gather you've lost your old room.'

'I was going back to Keld House.'

'You're surely not on duty yet?'

'No. I did call in, and Hamish insists I'm still taking leave. Are you sure about my staying?'

'I'd love it. I'm told there's stew and dumplings in the oven, and that housekeeper of mine always caters for an army. There'll be a few veg out of the garden, I'm a firm believer in "Dig for Victory". There might not be a pudding, but you and I know they're not always best for your health anyway!'

It seemed years since she and her grandfather had had much time on their own. Rachel loved pottering with him in the old-fashioned kitchen, then sitting at its scrubbed table to enjoy their meal.

'Don't use the dining room, these days,' he told her. 'Too much trouble really, though I tell myself it's only to save on fuel for heating.'

'You seem to have an agreeable life here, despite wartime restrictions,' she suggested.

'I do – *did*. You're making me reflect on too many "might-have-beens", you know.'

'By bringing Hedda home?'

'Call it home and you do have me worried!' he paused, sighed. 'Do I have to admit to you that I was pleased to see her? Severely shaken, but pleased.'

'Oh.'

'Life deals out the odd cruel trick, Rachel. Being fond of someone, and discovering they don't want you to love them.'

He *wasn't* meaning Hamish and herself, yet the evening was ruined for her. If she'd known how to find an excuse that wouldn't be hurtful, Rachel would have left. But where could she go? The hospital was the last place . . .

Bernard was preoccupied with his own torment. 'Your mother doesn't know, never has, Hedda certainly hasn't. I did try to harden myself, to hate her. 'Twould have been so much easier.'

Rachel said nothing, she didn't know what to say. Even if she hadn't felt exhausted, being made to realize how Hamish must be feeling was enough to prevent her from trying to work out a solution to anyone else's emotional difficulties.

Her grandfather shrugged again. 'Who knows? Hedda's being around might disturb me sufficiently to finally get her out of my system.'

His words saddened Rachel, making her so uneasy that the mood remained with her, despite a good night's sleep. Setting out for Keld House next morning, she was oppressed by misgivings concerning her attitude towards Hamish.

It had been so good to work together on having the building converted, turning rooms into wards, ordering in all the equipment. She loved her work, and that had been enhanced by learning to assist Hamish in surgery, by sensing that her care in the wards was complementing his skills. Had she ruined all that by paying too much heed to sexual attraction when she couldn't reciprocate all his feelings for her?

Arriving at the hospital, however, Rachel immediately felt reassured. Hamish was coming down the stairs, still dressed for theatre. Similarly attired, Shirley was beside him. His arm was around his fellow surgeon's waist.

Shirley was smiling up at him, nodding her understanding while Hamish made some suggestion about speaking with a patient's relative.

They are attracted to each other! thought Rachel, and relief flooded through her.

Seeing her, they both paused to ask if she'd recovered from the journey. 'You did look ghastly yesterday,' added Hamish. Rachel couldn't have been more delighted with any compliment.

Shirley smiled. 'I gather your trip was successful. You'll have to tell me about it. Don't know when, though. We're pretty busy.' She gazed up at Hamish again.

He turned back to Rachel as Shirley left them to go to an elderly couple waiting near the door. 'What time did you think of coming on? Shirley's been keeping flexible hours, filling in when needed rather than sticking strictly to shifts.'

'When do you plan to go off duty, Hamish?' She should be able to arrange that their hours didn't coincide, at least for a day or so.

'Ah – that's a tricky one. We're due another influx of wounded, yet we're not sure when. Just heard it's unlikely for today. I'm sticking around, other than a few hours off tonight – taking Shirley for a bite to eat, thanks for her co-operation, and so on.'

'Well, I'll start this evening then, give you both the night off.'

'I need a word with you first of course, catch up, that sort of thing.'

Hamish's brown eyes began seeking her gaze. Rachel blinked, turned her head slightly.

'Now, in the office?' she suggested.

Hamish didn't agree. 'Give me an hour first. See you in the sitting room.'

Eager to reacquaint herself with their patients, Rachel took off her coat and went into the nearest ward. Most of the men had been admitted before her journey to Norway, and she was interested to learn who had progressed and if any needed special attention to ensure they might improve. The men were, in the main, glad to see her without her white coat. Some called to her that they thought they'd got a glamorous new visitor. Although still tired by the trauma of her voyage, Rachel smiled back. She had nothing to fear from the odd flirtation by any of these men – *they* weren't likely to grow too fond of her.

Nearing the second ward, she sensed Shirley approaching from behind. Evidently the young surgeon had finished speaking with her patient's relatives.

'Any chance of a favour from you?' Shirley enquired.

'Try me.'

'Instead of coming on duty now, could you sort of . . . defer that a bit? I've got the chance of a night off with Hamish, you see, and that means we both need cover.'

Rachel smiled. 'Fine with me.' She didn't tell Shirley about her brief discussion arranging that with Hamish. Suddenly the mood here augured very well indeed for eliminating her problems.

Her own room still looked rather bare, typically institutionalized, with function superceding aesthetics. But it was an improvement on that cabin she'd experienced aboard – best of all, it was completely motionless! Earlier that morning the unsteady feeling of still being at sea had waned, but only after a night of clinging to the edges of her grandfather's spare bed, afraid that her own restless limbs might toss her to the floor.

Unpacking the few belongings she had taken with her, Rachel decided all the clothes she'd worn must be washed immediately. The medicines remaining from the stock she had carried must be returned, and she set them aside to take with her when seeing Hamish.

She took out the photograph of Olav, smiled as she already had on several occasions, then returned it to the envelope. Finding a frame for that must be a priority, she would walk as far as the nearest shops that afternoon.

Olav's smiling face reminded her that she should try to send word of their safe arrival in Britain. If she asked Hamish he would surely co-operate.

Rachel was so intent on getting a message to Olav that it was the first thing she mentioned when she joined Hamish in the sitting room. Brown eyes clouding immediately, he refused to assist.

'Sorry, no can do. And you'd be well advised to stop sending messages over there. You might endanger this Olav. Worse, you could jeopardize the entire Shetland Bus scheme.'

'But he says he's not involved with running that.'

'Can you be certain? Nevertheless, you could generate trouble for people who surely don't deserve it.'

'I definitely wouldn't want that.'

'Well then. Best just be thankful you pulled off the trip, let it go at that.' He paused, thinking. 'Now – one or two things I want to put you right on. About tonight, it truly *is* just to say thanks that I'm taking Shirley out for a meal.'

'It doesn't matter to me either way,' Rachel began.

She was interrupted. 'To me it does. I tried before you left to make plain my feelings for you. While you were away on that dreadful mission, I couldn't stop thinking about you.'

'Hamish, don't. Please don't say any more. I like you, I like you a lot but—'

'*Like*?' This time his interruption was furious. 'Everything we did together convinced me that you loved me, that you feel like me that we're meant to have a future.'

'I'm sorry.'

'I'm surprised at you, if that's the way you behave with every man you have a necking session with.'

'I don't, it's . . .' Feeling particularly inept, Rachel let her voice trail off. Even to herself, she could not really explain why she'd permitted their relationship to promise quite so much passion.

Hamish shrugged, then astonished her by smiling. He didn't believe that she had suddenly become so cold. 'Don't worry. You're obviously still exhausted by that trip. Tiredness always ruins the libido. We'll leave this until you've caught up on some sleep.'

Although thankful to have any discussion postponed, Rachel wished she could find some kind means of convincing him that their relationship would progress no further. When Hamish's next words were only to seek agreement to the hours he wished her to work during the rest of the week, she gladly gave her consent.

Leaving the sitting room, she reminded herself how keen Shirley had seemed to spend the evening with Hamish. There was hope that this new doctor would soon be keeping him interested. In the meantime, Shirley would often be around anyway, preventing too many occasions when Hamish and Rachel were alone.

She wondered how on earth this problem had assumed so massive a proportion. It seemed quite ridiculous when compared to her recent experiences in the attempt to rescue Hedda Davidson, and with the possible dangers that Olav Larsen might be facing. She wished with all her heart that she could know what had happened to him since she had left Norway.

From his hideout on the hillside he had watched them go safely aboard. Lowering his binoculars, Olav trudged uphill to Hedda's house. Changing his plans, he'd opted to collect his skis and other belongings that night. Word had reached him of the early arrival of another boat from Shetland, one bringing the agent he'd promised to escort.

They were to travel on foot far into the mountains, halting only to rest with families known to be trusted, moving on by night until they reached their rendezvous at Stalheim. There, in the spot where years ago the Royal Mail coaches changed horses, Olav's charge would be handed on to their contacts.

He knew no more than that this British agent would be training more men like himself as they prepared to outwit the occupying Germans. Olav had been glad of his experience within Norway's transport systems, which bestowed an understanding of their terrain. Coupled with his ability on skis, he was making himself useful, and that was sufficient.

Every agent that was brought into the country, and each

concealed radio transmitter they had, widened the range of their activities, covering enemy actions and reactions until fewer opportunities for surprise existed. Contact was being maintained between the many partisans risking life to further their struggle towards freedom.

Rumours of German intentions were many, and reached the ears of men engaged in resistance – preparedness was their watchword. And if knowledge of future planning by fellow partisans was not always widespread, it was withheld for good reason. Knowledge might be extracted under duress, certainly under torture.

Olav could respect the threat of possible torture without letting it deter him. He acknowledged the sense in having his love of adventure curbed by remaining watchful. No one else need know how he felt thrilled and challenged by danger.

The boat he was meeting was due in by the time he had collected his skis and sticks and stashed them, near the snowline, in the garden of a friend he could trust. Striding towards the Torget in his fisherman's gear, he ran his keen gaze along the ranks of vessels at anchor.

The one he sought had not yet arrived. Stamping his feet to warm them, he drew back into the shadow of a quayside building and waited. In the distance, almost out of sight from where he was standing, a German patrol boat was moored alongside one of the trawlers. Olav visualized the tension aboard while documents were examined and the vessel searched. He hoped that this enemy reception was not destined for the boat he expected.

When his vessel finally put in he had crossed back over the road to wait in the lee of a building in the Bryggen. The arrangement was that one of their crew would bring the agent to him, rather than risk attracting attention as the men disembarked. The glint of binoculars from a German observation post revealed that their watch of the quayside was unrelenting.

The two fishermen coming ashore looked innocuous enough, warmly wrapped against the freezing night, both carrying – if ostentatiously – samples of the catch. Olav recognized the smaller man, an old schoolmate who'd followed his father as a trawlerman. Despite this familiarity, when they approached he hesitated until the chosen password was spoken. Olav beckoned and they followed silently along the narrow alleyway between two wooden buildings.

Heading on towards Ovregaten, Olav introduced himself to the strange Englishman, was told his name was Paul Drake. Olav smiled, grasped the man's hand, then turned to thank his companion. The Norwegian nodded, handed the fish he carried to Olav, and walked away into the distance.

Paul Drake – if that was his true name, no one queried identities – was smiling. 'Will you take this fish also?'

Olav grinned. 'You do not look very comfortable with it! In fact, there is a place – I have left my skis. You will see where in a moment.'

'Forgive me for seeming amused. I really am terribly impressed by the success of every part of this journey. But bringing ashore evidence of a catch . . .' He shrugged strong shoulders, smiled again.

The skis that Olav had left behind had gained a similar pair. He nodded approval of matters going to plan, took the second fish and walked around the house to a rear door. He rapped three times on its panels, laid both fish on the icy doorstep and rejoined his companion.

'Settlement for the skis?' enquired Paul.

'I do not believe so. The additional skis should be returned – eventually. The fish . . . A token, that is all, of appreciation.'

Paul was fixing on his skis efficiently, assuring Olav that information as to his prowess had been correct. His own skis in place, Olav offered a pair of sticks across and nodded towards the road. After a dozen paces they turned sharply to their left and Olav pointed a ski stick towards the steep mountain ahead.

'I hope that you are fit!'

'So do I, but they put me through commando training. And I played rugby for my university.'

'Sounds fine to me. My game is football. Less now, of course. I rely on the skiing mainly for fitness.'

'And you do a lot of journeys like this?'

Olav smiled. 'Let us say this is not my first time.'

'Always to the same place?' Paul asked him.

'No. Wherever necessary. Quite often towards one or other of the fjords. Your people, and ours also, keep an eye on activity by the German navy. Though some of the time *in*activity is the description of what their vessels are about.'

His companion nodded. 'I had heard that they often anchor there for an age.'

'How was the crossing this time?'

'Bad. Exceedingly so, snowing like the devil with a wind to match. Yet not severe enough to deter the Luftwaffe. Only good thing was the poor visibility, it meant they didn't strike their target – us.'

'Was that when you reached Norwegian waters?' Surely those boats relied on their supposed purpose of fishing for disguise?

'No, far out to sea. Midway, perhaps, in the crossing.'

Olav sighed. He had known, of course, that any boat taking to the North Sea was at risk, but he'd heard so many good reports of their making it across unchallenged. He'd been foolish enough to believe the worst prospect Hedda faced was illness. And now he'd allowed Rachel to face danger alongside her.

Paul Drake was breathing heavily, but maintaining a good pace as they trudged uphill between the trees. 'I understand it's a fair distance to our first stop.'

'You might say that. Idea is we get people away from the coast soon as possible, in the hope there is less enemy interest inland. I do not suppose that applies near to the Swedish border, but we are not heading that far over.'

'For which many thanks!' said Paul fervently.

'You will say that, I am sure, by the time we arrive in Stalheim.'

If Paul was to reflect on those words during the following few days, Olav's worst difficulties were with the times when they should have been sleeping. Travelling by night, the daylight hours were scheduled for resting, chiefly in barns belonging to other resistance workers. The food they were brought was good, and in the main their makeshift beds were surprisingly comfortable.

Olav's trouble was the inability to sleep, and that was caused by the news Paul had brought, of Germans firing from the skies on to the boats gallantly attempting to cross a sea known already as among the stormiest in the world. He hadn't really thought that such vessels would be immune to attack, but having all but disregarded such a hazard made him feel even worse. Would God ever forgive him for exposing the woman he was beginning to love to what seemed like near-certain danger? Could he ever forgive himself?

Hamish did appear to have been right in assuming that tiredness had increased Rachel's concern about their relationship. Although it soon became evident that he wasn't greatly attracted to Shirley, Rachel found herself relaxing once more. Their work was absorbing, and even when patients arrived horrifically maimed, whatever she could do to aid their recovery was greatly satisfying.

Any men admitted with gunshot wounds reminded her of Thor's injury and her efforts to treat him which had been hampered by her lack of equipment. Inevitably, memories of that voyage sent her thoughts rushing to Olav, reawakening the yearning to know how he was. Rachel hadn't been able to find a way to get a message across to him, a fact that disturbed her, if not so gravely as her constant anxiety about his safety. Not knowing what work he was engaged in allowed too much room for conjecture concerning potential hazards. She hadn't found a frame for his photograph either, a disappointment somehow adding to her unease.

The good news was that whenever she telephoned the house her mother reported happily that Hedda was recovering well from the voyage, and settling into life in the family home. Asta suggested after a few weeks that Rachel should join them for Sunday lunch, but her hours on duty didn't allow that.

'I could make it on Monday. What time shall we say, Mum?'

Asta's hesitation came down the line. 'Oh, all right. But it is my wash day.'

'I'll sit with Grandmother if you're too busy. Do you still cook bubble and squeak to have with the leftover meat?'

Arriving at the house around midday, Rachel found her mother in the wash house and Grandmother Hedda looking quite disturbed as she sat in the adjoining kitchen. Without being asked, Hedda began explaining in a whisper after Rachel had greeted them both.

'She refuses to permit me to help, yet persists in wearing a frown that complains to the entire world of her martyrdom! And I, meanwhile, am extremely bored, driven to flip the pages of magazines which are an effort for me to understand, while I try to accept the trouble I am creating since I arrived.'

'Trouble?' asked Rachel, pausing as she was removing her coat. 'But Mum said only the other day how well you've settled . . .'

'As I have, here. Except for days when Asta is so busy and irritable. No, Rachel, it is the changes that my presence is forcing upon other people that distress me.'

'Not Dad – he's away most of the time, surely?'

'And the dearest, kindest son-in-law imaginable. No, it's poor old Bernard's routine that I am destroying.'

'What's he been saying?'

'Nothing. Not one word. Or none to me. I wish that he would speak of his . . . his concern. Rather than that, he stays away from here, and Asta always tells me of the way that Bernard was accustomed to joining them for meals, or of an evening. He is growing old, like me, and should not be deprived of the few small comforts still left to us in wartime.'

'He has a good home of his own, his housekeeper is active enough and goes in daily. When I was there last the place seemed very comfortable.'

'If *he* is not. Or not comfortable with my being in Yorkshire, as I say. It was selfish of me to fail to consider what this would do to him.'

'I think you're worrying unnecessarily, you know. He told me how pleased he was that you had come here safely, that you were looking quite well.'

'If only Bernard would talk. I need for us to clear this matter between us. He must hate me for what I did, but . . .'

Shaking her head, Rachel interrupted. 'I don't believe that he does, he sounds to be fond of you still.'

'That cannot be, I would not expect it. All I would hope is that we might agree to establish a kind of truce. While he absents himself as though I would contaminate the air he breathes here, there can be no such agreement.'

Before Rachel could contradict or suggest how she supposed Bernard Davidson might be feeling, Asta came through to begin preparing their meal. The instant silence that befell Hedda made Rachel realize that none of this had been confided to anyone before. Not until she was leaving later that day was she alone with her grandmother for long enough to attempt to make her feel better about her former husband.

'I do think that Granddad is still remarkably attached to you, considering what an age it is since you got divorced.'

'But we did not divorce, Bernard always claimed that he did not believe in it. And I – well, I was not sorry to avoid the disparagement which, in those days, divorce brought on those involved.'

'I certainly didn't know you weren't.' Rachel was astonished, would have liked to have been able to discuss this with Hedda, but she should be on duty shortly and had left herself barely enough time to drive back to the hospital.

Hamish was still on one of the wards when she had donned her white coat and picked up her stethoscope. He smiled at first, then noticed that her silver-grey eyes were shadowed.

'Not your grandmother, I hope? You're looking so worried . . .'

Rachel shook her head. 'Physically she's fine, thanks. It's just – well, a long story. Anyway – briefly, she's upset because her ex has stopped visiting the house now she's staying there. Only he's not strictly her ex, in any case. I didn't know they were never divorced. Not sure if that makes it better or worse. *She* doesn't seem to have closed that chapter, even though it was years ago.'

She glanced up at the clock. 'Shouldn't be keeping you, going on about family problems. I've got to get on. Is there anyone needing particular attention?'

Hamish brought her up to date on a few worrying cases. As he turned to leave the ward he grasped her arm. 'You know where I am if you need to talk.'

Pensively, Rachel watched him walk away from her. Hamish could be such a good friend, she wished they could revert to the easy relationship they had enjoyed originally. Before she let sex create difficulties between them.

Shirley was working a split shift again, and appeared no less perturbed about a personal matter than Rachel herself was. When they took a few minutes off for a hurried cup of tea, Shirley began to confide. 'I've done something really stupid, Rachel. Made an utter fool of myself. The night Hamish took me out to dinner, I thought it was because he fancied me. We had quite a lot to drink and, well – when we came back here I suppose I left him in no doubt that I'm keen on him.'

'Give him time, and he might feel the same,' said Rachel in what she hoped was an encouraging voice. 'After all, you are stunning, he can't fail to notice that. And there is no other woman in his life.'

'Really?' Shirley's brown eyes brightened. 'Are you sure? He implied that there was someone.'

'If there is, I've never heard of her existence. There was somebody he was engaged to once, but she died at the beginning of the war.'

Rachel felt her own spirits rising. If only Hamish might begin to reciprocate Shirley's feelings, two people would become much happier. And she herself would gladly revert to her original good, *professional*, relationship with Hamish. She would settle for that to carry her through the rest of this wretched war.

Nine

Rachel couldn't refuse when Asta next invited her to have Sunday lunch at home, and she wouldn't have wanted to anyway. Having brought her grandmother back to England, she felt responsible for ensuring that somehow the elderly lady would become really happy there. Telephoning several weeks after they'd arrived in Yorkshire, Rachel had been pleased to hear her father's voice but less than delighted by what he said.

'Hedda's settling in better than I, for one, expected, but it's the effect that this is having on my dear old father-in-law that has me worried.'

Rachel had sighed, perturbed to discover the situation was no better than Hedda had claimed. 'What's wrong with Granddad, he's not making a fuss is he?'

'On the contrary. You know Bernard Davidson, he is simply keeping away from us. That isn't good, but I've heard he's cramming in additional work, helping organise the local Home Guard unit.'

'At his age? He ought to be retiring, never name working harder than ever.'

'Exactly. Unfortunately, there's no talking to him. Your mother's tried, so have I – to no good purpose. He claims he's right enough. Anybody with half an eye can see he's only keeping busy to avoid Hedda.'

'I'm sorry, Dad.'

'Nay, love, not your fault. What you did was great, none of us will forget it. And Hedda does need somebody to keep an eye on her. Your mum says she gets muddled sometimes about testing for the diabetes, and so on.'

'But she is all right?'

'Putting on weight, I'm told. And getting a bit of colour in her cheeks, even though it's not really even spring as yet.'

Her grandmother's well-being was certainly in evidence the day that Rachel arrived. Benefiting from regular meals eaten in company, she looked less haggard when Rachel found her in the kitchen. She also seemed in good spirits.

'Your mother and I share the chores now,' Hedda was quick to tell. 'This gives her more time for Red Cross work, while I have begun to knit socks which are sent to men in the Allied forces.'

'So you're not getting bored then,' Rachel remarked with a grin.

'Not at all. I have another task to begin also – Asta is to give me one of the spare bedrooms, and I shall sew for it a bed cover of patchwork. There are a great many pieces of material here, most of them too small for making anything else.'

'And how is your Red Cross work?' Rachel asked her mother who was bringing plates through to warm in the kitchen.

'Very interesting,' Asta told her, smiling. 'I'm quite proud actually, they say I've picked first aid up that fast they're going to give me a test. If I pass that, they'll have me teaching other women. I dare say you'd think it's all very basic stuff, but if it helps folk to cope with emergencies at home, that's got to be good.'

'I'll say,' Rachel agreed, hugging her mother. 'Now, anything I can do to help?'

'No thanks, love. Your grandmother and I have got it all organized to a fine art now. And I'm afraid there's only going to be the three of us for dinner today. Your dad's at sea yet again.'

During their meal it seemed to Rachel that her mother was also gaining a great deal from having Hedda around, to provide company when work kept Andrew Skelton absent from home.

They were finishing their rhubarb and custard when Rachel glanced away from the other two women and noticed the photograph of Olav on the kitchen dresser. It appeared to have been taken on the same occasion as the one she treasured, but he was sitting on a low wall instead of standing, and looked more serious.

'Is that a good snap of him?' Asta enquired. 'My mother says it is.'

'Very good.'

Asta nodded. 'He looks fair grand, just as I picture our Richard might have looked if he'd lived to that age.'

Rachel saw Hedda reach out and cover Asta's hand with her own. 'Olav could not have cared for me better had he been a closer relative – like my grandson. The worst part of leaving Bergen was deserting him. Yet I know that his work takes him far away from the city. I can only hope that when this war is won, he and I may be reunited in our favourite place.'

And that is exactly what I hope for myself, thought Rachel. She could not visualize Olav anywhere else, and the yearning for him was turning into an ache for his home town. She wished that there had been more time for seeing Bergen during her visit, especially in daylight. Those few recent memories were already becoming less clear.

On her way back to the hospital that day Rachel called to see her grandfather, only to find that he was not at home. His housekeeper, Mrs Hardaker, explained that he was off with the Home Guard. 'Why don't you stop and have a cup of tea with me,' the old lady suggested. 'I've been clearing up after high tea, but I'm not in any rush to be off to my own home.'

'No, thank you. It's a lovely thought, but I only wanted to see how Grandfather is. I'll come another time.'

'I can tell you how he is – doing far too much, if you ask me. But you know what he's like, won't be told. I blame *her*, of course. Coming back here, stirring up the past.'

'You'll tell him I called, won't you?' said Rachel. 'And that I'll be seeing him before long.'

In fact it was weeks before she managed to arrange time off when Bernard Davidson wasn't busy with either his practice or the Home Guard. In the meantime, many inhabitants of the Yorkshire coastal towns were alarmed when there was heavy bombing of Hull, which happened at the same time as the bombardment of Clydeside and the region around the river Mersey. There could be no believing any longer that the Luftwaffe were only interested in destroying London and the south of England.

Because of all this aerial activity, Rachel could understand why her acquaintances at the RAF station couldn't promise to ensure that her message to Olav Larsen would be delivered. After all, no one's life depended upon her getting news through to him. No one else would comprehend that she felt her own life was clouded by each day that she remained out of touch with him.

Together with Hamish and Shirley Trent, she was busier than ever as wounded men who'd been evacuated from the fighting in North Africa were admitted, along with some locally based airmen who had suffered injuries.

Rachel was badly shaken when Frank Smith, the pilot who had flown her to the Shetlands, was brought in with his face badly scarred and most of his hair burnt off following a plane crash. The only good thing was that his sight wasn't impaired, otherwise he seemed a wreck. Quite unlike his former self, Frank would not believe their assurances that he could and would receive treatment to help repair the damage to his features.

Being the first person she had known prior to his being injured, Frank's distress hit her really hard, and for several days after his arrival Rachel was nearly in tears whenever she saw him. Eventually, she felt compelled to admit to Hamish that she was doing more harm than good by being the person to treat him.

'I know I owe him a lot for flying me up to Shetland that time, but I'm only making things worse for him now. He can see how upset I am, and he's not stupid, he knows it's because he looks so terrible.'

'I'll speak to Shirley, she'll take over from you until he's transferred to East Grinstead.'

'It is arranged that he's to be seen by Archie McIndoe then? I wasn't sure.'

'Oh yes, spoke with them the day Frank came to us. He knows it's on the cards, just wish we could make him believe how effectively they can treat that kind of injury.'

Rachel was thankful to see that as soon as Shirley took over as Frank's doctor he began to seem more hopeful. She nevertheless felt disappointed in her own ability, and admitted as much to the other doctors when they were having one of their regular meetings to discuss the progress of their patients.

Shirley merely shrugged. 'Doesn't matter so long as one of us is beginning to get through to him. And *I* didn't see how handsome he was before this happened.'

Hamish nodded agreement. 'We're not in this to prove how well equipped we are for dealing with patients' hang-ups. If we understood how to cope with every person's anxieties we'd develop massive egos.' Which I certainly shall not, thought Rachel dismally.

She was still feeling deflated about being unable to provide all that Frank Smith had needed by the time he was transferred south to Archibald McIndoe's unit. Having finally arranged a bit of free time to coincide with Bernard Davidson's, Rachel was driving over to see him, and trying to plan what she might say to help the situation between her grandparents.

Opening the door to her, Bernard whisked her into the house before light flowed out to disturb the blackout, and then he hugged her fiercely.

'I'm that glad to see you, Rachel love. Your dad's called once or twice lately, but I've seen nothing of your mother for ages.'

'Oh, dear. I'm sorry.'

'Nothing you can help. I gather her loyalties are seriously divided now, and Hedda's the one she's got living with her, isn't she?'

'I want to talk to you about that, it's really what I've come for.'

'Aye, I expected it might be. Trying to get me to start going round there again, are you?'

'That would be nice.'

'Nice?' He laughed harshly. 'Happen so, for somebody. I don't quite know who. Can't say I'd find it very comfortable. And what Hedda would feel is anybody's guess. I wouldn't hazard an attempt at guessing. I dare say Asta would be the one to be pleased. But then, she's always liked a quiet life, while being one of the world's worst for coping with anxiety.'

'Couldn't you just try it, perhaps – drop in again, like you used to?'

'Tonight, maybe? Are you offering to come with me?'

'I will if you like, Granddad.'

Bernard laughed. 'Nay, Rachel lass, I'll not inflict that on you. I imagine you have problems enough to deal with at that hospital. Is that why you're looking so peaky these days?'

'Trust you to notice. I have been quite upset recently.' She told him about Frank Smith, and how perturbed she had been by his injuries. 'I could hardly function at all, Granddad, I felt so awful.'

'And still do, if that shadow behind your eyes is owt to go by. You seem to have forgotten, Rachel, the way it is for doctors and nurses. You can only do your best for folk if you leave emotions out of it. As soon as you begin to *feel* too deeply, you stop working at your optimum. Don't you know that's why doctors are never encouraged to treat their own families?'

'I do know that, naturally.'

'And the same goes for friends at times, especially when war's playing heck with our feelings any road. Often enough, we come to care more because of the situation we're in.'

'I do believe Frank became important because of the way he helped me get away on my journey to Bergen.'

'Well, there you are then.' He paused, thinking. 'And happen *I'll* bear in mind how much that journey meant to you. Maybe it wouldn't hurt me to go over yonder, see Asta and her mother.'

* * *

Rachel wasn't surprised that, following Bernard Davidson's very brief visit to her parents' home, she was invited for tea one Saturday when he was expected to join them. Andrew Skelton was home from sea, a bonus which promised to aid the smoothness of the occasion. Just seeing her father again made Rachel feel brighter – keeping in touch by phone was not the same. She might be adult and matured beyond her years through her work, but she still needed her strong relationship with her father.

Asta, naturally, was better for having him at home and Rachel noticed that Hedda still relished an easy friendship with her son-in-law. She hoped that when Bernard Davidson arrived the agreeable atmosphere would continue. But from the minute her grandfather walked into the house, Rachel wished that she had done nothing to encourage further contact between her grandparents. All colour seemed to drain from Hedda's cheeks when she saw the old doctor, while he was once again wearing his coolly professional smile.

After greeting Asta and Rachel in turn with a hug, Bernard looked rather at a loss when he gazed towards the woman who, legally, was still his wife.

'Hedda,' he said, and nodded.

'Hello, Bernard. Are you well?' Hedda enquired, her voice not quite steady.

'Thank you, yes. And you . . .?' Almost too hastily, he turned away to shake Andrew by the hand.

'With Asta's care of me, of course I am,' Hedda responded, and gave a tiny shrug towards Bernard's back.

If Asta was delighted to hear this confirmed, no one else was particularly at ease. But Hedda had insisted on preparing the family high tea, and she swiftly invited them all to come with her to the table. Rachel felt glad that her mother and grandmother still seemed to be getting on well together.

'Mother's adapting to our Yorkshire ways again,' Asta announced. 'Despite all the shortages, she's managed to get hold of some corned beef, and there's tinned salmon that I'd been saving for a special occasion. There's stewed fruit for after – apple was all we could get hold of, but Mother's cooked it the way she used to years ago, and that's condensed milk in the jug.'

'I'm sure everything will be lovely,' said Bernard, and smiled around the table. 'A rare treat for me, Mrs Hardaker's meals are very basic.'

'Mrs Hardaker?' asked Hedda, somewhat bewildered.

'Dad's housekeeper,' Asta told her. 'Been with him a long time now.'

'Since I left, I suppose,' said Hedda. And instantly regretted it. 'I should not have asked, should I?'

'Ask away,' Bernard said briskly. 'Anything else you wish to know?'

Had there been even one more thing, Hedda would have stifled the question. Her lips clamping tightly together, she began cutting the corned beef on her plate with a savagery more appropriate for the toughest of steaks.

Rachel quelled a sigh. 'We're very busy at the hospital,' she told them, to fill the descending silence. 'Some troops wounded in North Africa, and one or two airmen from bases not far from us are among the latest admissions.'

'I hope you're not too busy to stay the night with us,' her mother said. 'Your grandmother's in her own room now, you can have yours again.'

'Sorry, but I really ought to get back. Have an early start in the morning.'

'Did you ever hear how that lovely skipper of ours is? Has he recovered?' Hedda enquired.

'Was he taken poorly during the crossing?' asked Asta.

Rachel hadn't been sure if Asta had been told about Thor being shot, and wondered now how much she should say. But they had all survived the voyage, so no harm could be done by explaining.

'He was wounded, a bullet fired from a German plane. Fortunately it was his shoulder they caught, nothing fatal.' She turned to Hedda. 'I'm afraid I haven't heard anything further about his condition. He should be almost as good as new now, despite the makeshift nature of my initial treatment.'

'But you'd know far more about what should be done for him than those that only understand first aid,' her father said.

'Aye, that's right. Unfortunately, the only equipment I had there was first aid stuff.'

'But you did your best,' said Asta, her own recently acquired knowledge producing a welcome affinity with her daughter.

'From the sound of it, you could have done as much, Mum,' said Rachel ruefully.

Asta was pleased, making Rachel thankful that at least one person at their table was smiling. She was beginning to suspect the get-together was unlikely to improve, and couldn't help longing to escape. But as she had persuaded her grandfather to come, she felt obliged to remain there for as long as he did.

Her mother suggested that they listen to the BBC evening news. She'd long since ceased to be reluctant to hear recent events. When Bernard stated he must leave immediately afterwards, Rachel promised herself she might depart with him.

They all listened silently to the usual catalogue of battles lost and won, and the inevitable listing of casualties, of both Allied and enemy forces. The mention of Norway alerted them all instantly, and they listened intently to an account of the destruction by British forces of factories producing glycerine for German use in explosives. This raid on the Lofoten Islands had been followed by further bombing of a power station and oil storage tanks.

'Oh God, no!' Hedda cried.

Bernard rose swiftly from his seat and strode over to grasp her shoulder. 'Steady, love, steady. The Lofotens are nowhere near Bergen, are they? We must hope that the areas precious to you remain unscathed.'

Swallowing hard, Hedda nodded. Very briefly she put up a hand to cover Bernard's. When they drew apart her eyes were no longer dry. And nor were his.

Rachel had hoped for a private word with her grandfather, but although they left the house together they each went to their own cars. She sensed as he called goodnight to her that he was longing for the solitude of his own home where Mrs Hardaker would long since have departed for her cottage.

Although Rachel frequently wondered if Bernard Davidson had resumed his regular visits to her parents' house, it was months before she herself was present there at a time when all the family were together.

The Keld House hospital was busier than ever, with many RAF personnel being admitted after crashes or injuries due to enemy action. Amid this additional surge of patients, she and Hamish were faced with a further problem when Shirley Trent gave in her notice.

'I am sorry,' she told them, without looking particularly sorry. 'I've been offered a post I've been aching to get for some time – at East Grinstead.'

Recalling her mention of visiting the place, Hamish and Rachel exchanged a glance before he sighed. 'What can I say – McIndoe's gain will be our loss. We wish you well, of course.'

Replacing Shirley was far from easy. Few hospitals possessed a full complement of doctors, and available surgeons seemed especially difficult to find. Once Shirley had departed, Hamish was obliged to work all the hours he could, and consequently became exhausted.

Concerned for him, Rachel had ceased taking the days off that were due to her, but she'd started to feel that Keld House was like a prison. No matter how much she loved the work.

The only good thing was when they took on Jessica Thomas, a fully experienced theatre sister whose expertise often freed Rachel from attending operations. And if Rachel sometimes regretted missing out on theatre work, she was too busy treating her patients to worry about her personal feelings.

Several of the men were suffering burns, and quite a few had broken limbs which no longer required surgery once they had been set. She also tackled severe cuts and other open wounds, many where infection had set in while the patient was in transit to Britain. Gangrene was a threat if injuries had been neglected, and she constantly reminded their nurses to watch for signs of it developing.

Efficient though their nurses were, however, what they still needed most desperately was a second surgeon. As the weeks turned into months and spring warmed into summer, she and Hamish started to despair that they might ever succeed in finding someone. Ultimately, it was her grandfather who offered them a solution. Bernard telephoned Rachel one day to ask if they had filled the position.

'I only wish we had!' she exclaimed wearily. 'Hamish is constantly worn out, and I worry that he won't be able to continue like this for ever. No matter how willing.'

'Is there a top age limit?' Bernard enquired, making Rachel wonder if *he* was volunteering.

'I shouldn't think so,' she began cautiously.

'Don't worry, I'm not suggesting myself. There's a chap I trained with, while God was a nipper. He's a brilliant bloke, been a naval surgeon until they put him on submarines and discovered he suffered from claustrophobia. He was invalided out because of it, but otherwise he's fitter than most of us. Unless your surgery is performed underground!'

Rachel laughed. 'It certainly isn't. Sounds like he could be the solution. Let me have a word with Hamish and I'll come back to you. How do we contact this pal of yours?'

'Very easily, he's staying with me for a few days.'

Hamish snatched at the idea immediately and was pleased to interview Donald Barker when Bernard brought him along on the following evening. Rachel liked what she saw of the elderly surgeon, and left him with Hamish while she went off happily with her grandfather to show him around the wards. From the day that Keld House had opened Bernard Davidson had wanted to see the place, but his work and Rachel's had combined to prevent that happening. Being obliged to wait had made him all the more eager, and he strode at her side enthusiastically as she took him through the first wards.

'Takes me back to my own hospital days before I set up on my own,' he told her, then smiled. 'Except that all the equipment here, and the beds as well, look far more modern than any we had to work with. You and Hamish have done well to get this lot together while there's a war on.'

'It's all a bit crowded, though, we soon had to get additional beds in once patients started arriving.'

'I've seen worse than this,' Bernard said. 'And you only have to consider where a lot of these chaps will have come from – field hospitals, and worse – to know they'll be happy enough in these surroundings.'

'We don't get too many complaints,' Rachel confided. 'Except regarding the pain they're in, and that's understandable.'

'Quite. I dare say they can all see as well as I can that you're doing a grand job.'

They went through into the second ward where Rachel introduced her grandfather to the ward sister who had been with them since shortly after Keld House opened. She noticed how Bernard responded, smiling and with his silver-grey eyes lighting up when he spoke with the sister, who was fortyish, an attractive brunette.

I wonder how you're getting along with Hedda these days, she thought. It wouldn't hurt either of them to relish the stimulating company of the opposite sex. For the present, the attention he was giving this nurse proved illuminating.

The three of them were still talking shop when Rachel received a message to join Hamish and Donald Barker who had come down from theatre to continue their discussion in the surgeon's office.

Rachel soon found that Donald was just as pleasing on closer acquaintance, and Hamish was quick to emphasize that the man's experience couldn't have been more fitting to their needs. 'Donald can start on Monday, Rachel – I'm all in favour of going ahead. Do you agree?' he said, summing up.

'You're the one who knows best what's required in theatre. And since he's one of my grandfather's pals, I dare say he'll not disturb our harmonious set-up here.' She grinned at them both.

Introducing Donald Barker into their hospital worked very well. Having been the only doctor on board ship, he wasn't afraid of assuming responsibility. In theatre, he operated effectively with a minimum of fuss and the neatness of someone accustomed to severely limited space. The nurses soon loved him for his unassuming good humour, and the patients relished the presence of a man used to serving with the forces.

When Donald had been at Keld House for a couple of months he regularly insisted that both Hamish and Rachel take more time off. On the second occasion Hamish went home to Scotland. Rachel used her first time off to drive over to see her family. She was disappointed to hear that Bernard Davidson still only rarely called to see them.

'My only consolation is that your mother and your father do visit him when they can make time to do so,' Hedda confided. 'Otherwise my guilt over depriving him of so much would be compounded.'

Rachel tried to reassure her that she shouldn't be feeling guilty, but privately she acknowledged her own feeling that Hedda should never have left Yorkshire years ago. Loving her and Bernard equally, she would always have difficulty in accepting that their being apart was inevitable.

So fully occupied was she that the seasons had passed while she barely noticed, and Rachel was surprised when Hedda and Asta were both busy with preparations for Christmas. Andrew Skelton was determined that he would manage some time at home, and the two women began insisting that Rachel should join them for at least one day of festivities.

Before Christmas, however, Hedda and Asta had further plans. They both had good voices and were members of the local church choir. They offered to bring the choir to Keld House to provide a carol concert for their patients. Thankful to have arranged something for the men to look forward to, all the staff of the hospital were delighted to welcome the singers. The men, together with their nurses, sang along happily when required, and listened attentively whenever the choir sang unaided. The event took place on the Sunday afternoon prior to Christmas, and was voted an enormous success.

Elated by their good reception, both Asta and her mother were in ebullient spirits as their party got ready for leaving. 'What day are you coming to us, Rachel?' her mother asked. 'Can you make Christmas Day?'

'You must try to be with us, my special Christmas in England,' Hedda insisted.

Before Rachel could explain that she wasn't yet sure what duty she would be on, Hamish was telling her she must have Christmas Day off.

'But what about you?' Rachel asked him.

'No point in my attempting to make it home; my parents are going to my sister and there'll be no room for anyone else.'

'You must come to us again,' said Asta, while her mother smiled and nodded.

Donald Barker smiled. 'I can hold the fort here, if you'll permit me. My only alternative would be going to Bernard, and I may do that any time.'

Hamish's delight was so evident that Rachel hadn't the heart to try and alter the arrangement. After all, she reassured herself, there would be so many people around that no situation could arise where Hamish expected more than friendship.

Christmas Day was dry, but crisply cold as they drove over the moors to her parents' house. They talked most of the way there, mainly about hospital matters, but just occasionally relaxing sufficiently to discuss films that they'd each seen, and programmes they had heard on the wireless. These modest entertainments were the limit of their leisure activities now; even though Donald had joined them, work still demanded so much of their time. And of their energies.

Neither Rachel nor Hamish were slow to admit that they were losing weight, although she joked that she'd always wanted to be slimmer, even if she might have preferred some more congenial form of exercise.

'I suppose other hospitals are just as severely stretched,'

said Hamish. 'We don't have the opportunity to learn what their conditions are like, not that knowing would do us much good anyway.'

Arriving at the house, Andrew welcomed them, delighting Rachel that he was there, even though he admitted to being expected to go to sea that evening. Once again, Hedda and Asta were working amicably together in the kitchen, and Bernard was present, sitting beside the fire in the dining room.

'Your mother's insisting we use this room today, and I've got a blaze going. As you see, now I'm instructed to make sure it doesn't go out.'

If she had come here alone, Rachel would have used the opportunity to enquire if his relationship with Hedda was improving. With Hamish at her side she could not bring herself to ask. And she supposed her grandfather would refuse to give a straight answer in front of someone he hardly knew.

The day passed quite pleasantly, with wry comments about the food which was showing the effects of rationing despite efforts by Asta and Hedda to disguise the limitations. Fortunately, Andrew had been persuaded by his father-in-law to accept a few bottles of wine from his cellar, so they were not deprived of something good for toasting the season.

The wine certainly did make Rachel feel relaxed. Spending most of her life on duty, she'd scarcely drunk any alcohol in the past several months. By the time Hamish was driving her back to the hospital she was thankful that he was the one at the wheel. She herself had unwound until she was pleasantly drowsy.

When they arrived at Keld House and checked with Donald that all was well, Rachel headed upstairs to her room. Hamish would be going on duty at midnight, but she wasn't due to start until six a.m. Before she reached her own door, Hamish thanked her for a lovely day. 'It was great to spend time with your family again.'

'Glad you enjoyed it.'

'I'm going to allow myself just one small whisky, even

though I've got to work. Please don't make me resort to drinking on my own.'

Rachel hesitated, but it *was* Christmas Day after all, and from tonight they would be back into their routine of being fully occupied. The sitting room felt cool and she was glad that even though she'd discarded her coat, she was still wearing a thick cardigan over her sweater and skirt.

When Hamish poured whisky for her Rachel shook her head. 'You have that, I don't really want any more alcohol.'

'Oh, come on . . . Tell you what – I'll do another with masses of water.'

She still didn't really want the drink, but took a sip then placed the glass on the low table near the sofa as she sat down. Her head was anything but clear. Hamish came to sit beside her, and one arm went around her as he drew her close. When he kissed her, Rachel realized she'd been a fool not to anticipate that this would happen. Despite her tiredness and reluctance, she felt her body responding. He unfastened her cardigan and began to caress her breast through her sweater. Some latent fervour agitated deep inside her, willing her to urge him on, while her mouth developed its own will, encouraging his exploring tongue.

'I'm sorry, Hamish,' she said at last when the need to breathe superseded his urge to kiss her. 'I'm afraid I'm much too tired for this. Not really in the mood.'

The disbelief in his brown eyes challenged her to admit that she was concealing her desire, but Hamish had never been a man who would encourage a reluctant girl to make love.

After saying a hasty goodnight, Rachel walked out and along to her room. With every step she recognized more clearly that she was beginning to destroy her good relationship with Hamish. But there was no alternative. While he was arousing desire in her she had grown increasingly conscious of a powerful feeling that even just kissing Hamish was being unfaithful to Olav Larsen.

Ten

As 1942 began, Rachel was wondering how often she would have to remind Hamish that they were no more than friends. She was surprised that she hadn't already destroyed their good working relationship, which she still valued as much as she always had.

In no time at all, though, any personal emotions were submerged under concern for all the people who were engaged in fighting. Since the attack on Pearl Harbor, American forces were often in evidence, and news from the Far East became as disturbing as reports from Europe and North Africa.

For Rachel's family, hearing that Vidkun Quisling had become the prime minister of Norway was very upsetting. A man who had collaborated with the Germans since their occupation two years previously, there could be no doubting that Quisling was merely a figurehead placed there to facilitate German activities. Disturbed afresh on Olav's behalf, Rachel tried not to even think about the ways in which his life might now be worsened.

Closer to home, the war was inflicting its own problems on their part of north Yorkshire. During the early months of 1942, fencing posts and barbed wire were being erected just outside Malton amid rumours that a prisoner of war camp was under construction. From the local newspapers and their own excursions outside Keld House, the doctors and staff gathered that people in the area were giving anything but wholehearted support for the proposed camp. Hamish and Rachel were prepared to accept that such places were necessary, and had to be constructed somewhere. Donald Barker, having served with the Royal Navy, was less inclined to be so philosophical.

'We want none of them round here,' he declared, an opinion and that seemed to be echoed by several of their nurses.

Most of their patients were hospitalized as a result of enemy action and, predictably, were wishing extreme discomfort upon any such prisoners once the camp was completed. One or two of the more pugilistic men among them soon announced what they would do to any German or Italian soldiers they could lay their hands on.

In an effort to contain any contention, the three doctors got together with all nursing staff to discuss the feelings that had been aroused. Not surprisingly, Donald continued to resent the projected arrival of prisoners in the vicinity, and was backed by several nurses whose husbands or fathers were fighting somewhere abroad.

Hamish was trying to sound reasonable. 'There is the hope, of course, that any prisoners held over here may be influenced by the experience. As a result, they might come to believe that we have right on our side.'

Those totally opposed to the presence of prisoners of war remained unconvinced, while several others agreed with Donald when he moderated his own view, remarking that Hamish's notion was as clichéd as the words he'd used. Whilst taking that with a shrug, Hamish was perturbed that he had found no firmer means of encouraging a more tolerant outlook. Feeling she ought to speak up in favour of his more liberal view, Rachel tried to prevent the others walking away from the discussion.

'Can we at least agree that we must try to prevent our wards becoming a site of resentment? If we can guard our tongues a bit, just so that we don't incite any more bad feeling, that could be sufficient.'

Hamish was nodding. 'After all, this wretched camp is a good few miles from Keld House. We don't go into Malton, do we?'

'Only those of us who live there,' one of the nurses stated fiercely. 'This might not matter very much to you, but to us it could be vitally important.' Neither he nor Rachel had an answer to that, and the meeting broke up with the consensus that they would agree to disagree.

The unease generated by the projected prison camp did not go away, but it was overshadowed by the need to increase the capacity of their small hospital. With fighting in the air and on the ground extending to so many areas across the world, casualties were inevitable. All hospitals, especially those which specialized in treating servicemen, were under pressure to allocate more beds.

They cleared one of the upstairs rooms originally used for storage, ordered in everything necessary to furnish it, and immediately learned that more patients were already on their way.

A part of Rachel was content to be busier than ever. No matter how pressured, she still found the work satisfying, and it didn't allow time for dwelling on other matters. Although she had telephoned home to sympathize when Quisling's new position in Norway was announced, she hadn't seen her family since Christmas. Away from them, she was unable to even guess what the current situation between her grandparents might be, and Rachel suspected she might be better not knowing.

She had done all she could to help, and needed to conserve her energies for taking action where she knew that she might be of use. Several fresh patients had been brought back to Britain, not only badly injured but also suffering from what in the previous war would have been termed shell shock. The daily torture some of them still endured was no less dreadful for being nameless. Many cried out in their sleep, and several others cried because of *not* sleeping. Perhaps worst of all were the men who remained inert, and some even rendered speechless, by their experiences in battle.

There was never sufficient time for nursing staff or doctors to devote their attention to patients' needs beyond their physical injuries. Sometimes of an evening, or other times when off duty, Rachel would wander the wards, pausing to speak with this person or the other. She was always hoping to arouse a response, or at least to ease the isolation of some poor soul's torment.

One man in particular, an RAF pilot among the initial batch admitted to their new ward, seemed physically intact but was clearly deeply troubled. He spoke hardly at all, but just occasionally yelled out his despair at being isolated. 'There's only me,' he would protest, reliving some anguish. 'It's all down to me, the rest are gone. All gone . . .'

Rachel felt with him his dread of being alone, of being held responsible, of being obliged to cope while no one could assist. Something about him, not entirely his appearance, brought Olav to mind. Once there, she could not rid herself of the dread that Olav might suffer similar isolation. No matter how she tried she could not stop worrying about him. Would this war never end, would she never cease yearning to know what he was doing, where on earth he was?

He had skied for miles alone and, from all he knew, unobserved. Leaving the Hardangervidda plateau where he used to hike in summer, he had followed a trail southwards and to the east. Another day's trek and he would be overlooking the site. Over and around familiar mountains, alongside lakes, through remote terrain where snow would linger even into June, he had sped during these icy March days.

Olav found a certain delight in travelling while it was light, so much of his work was, of necessity, confined to the long winter nights. There was a degree of relief also in travelling alone, as all too frequently now he was responsible for others – and many of those were men and women whose lives would be more valuable than Olav Larsen's, should they reach German hands. Whilst not afraid of responsibilities, he could relish this freedom of risking no one's life except his own.

Today he was acting on orders based on rumour: from what he was told, nothing more substantial than Allied curiosity regarding the known German interest in the Norsk Hydro plant at Vemork. In common with many partisans, he was accustomed to following orders or requests without being fully aware of the significance of the work he was engaged in.

But Olav had his own theories regarding activity at Vemork, and would be interested when the truth emerged, as it inevitably would. For the present, his instructions were enough, and provided good reason to put his expertise on skis into practise.

His old life pre-war had made him acquaintances all over the countryside as he had investigated potential routes. Some of those friends now offered a night's hospitality or a meal, and some also gave further information which was helping him to form a composite picture of the purpose behind this exercise.

Today the summit of Gaustatoppen had been visible for miles, drawing him on. Olav's current regret was that he wouldn't savour the splendour of the view it provided, and nor must he risk travelling on to see friends in nearby Tuddal.

He was instructed to keep well away from the Norsk Hydro site while gathering the required information, and concentrate instead on fixing in his mind all possible details of the terrain for subsequent use by others. Even if he chanced on further useful information he must resist the urge to act, but pass on whatever he learned – again, to be used by others.

His value to the Resistance was in his knowledge of routes and potential routes, plus weather conditions and hazards local to this region that he loved. And if, once, Olav would have hated having his explorations curbed and resented the people destined to take action, for a year now he'd recognized the importance of staying alive. Not for even a day had he ceased to think about the dear, gallant woman who so often filled his dreams. No matter how preoccupied with a task, his mind and his heart remained full of Rachel Skelton. While hope remained that they would meet again, he would work only as directed, and quell the old Olav Larsen who would yearn to be Norway's bravest.

Hardships for British families increased during those early months of 1942, as rationing and taxes became more severe and the only lists that grew were of items in short supply. On the day their Keld House nurses arrived with word that the first Italian prisoners were being received at the camp near Malton, Rachel and the other doctors began to wonder who would be brought to Britain. But they were too busy to pay the news much attention. Both of their operating theatres were in constant use, which created more patients needing demanding post-operative care.

Hamish received a telephone call one day from a man who explained he was in charge of Eden Camp, but Hamish didn't immediately make the connection with the POW camp.

'I understand yours is a military hospital. What's the security like?' the man enquired.

'Security? Against bombing, is that what you mean?' asked Hamish, puzzled.

'Actually, I meant to prevent people escaping.'

'We don't need that sort of security. Our chaps are here for treatment, not as a punishment.'

'Of course, of course. So you only take Allied forces. The position is, I've an Italian seaman here. This initial intake is of men living under canvas while they assist in the construction of a more permanent camp.'

'I see. And . . . ?' Hamish prompted.

'This Italian fellow is a builder back home. We'd got him working on the roof of one of the huts when he fell. Knocked himself clean out, our first-aider is afraid there might be brain damage. He's also broken his right foot.'

'So he definitely needs hospitalizing. Trouble is, some of our patients here won't take kindly to his being around. Have you tried anywhere else?'

'A couple of the nearer ones. They're not keen either, we'd have to find guards for the ward, and we don't have that degree of manpower here.'

Hamish sighed. 'Nor do we. Although I suppose the heavy service presence amongst our patients might compensate. What have you done with this guy so far?'

'Not much we could do. We've set up a makeshift first aid room and fixed his stretcher between a couple of supports.

He was starting to come round when I left to use the phone.'

'Very well, you can bring him in. I'll warn all our staff and try to ensure that after we've treated him a responsible person will keep an eye on him. Can't promise on that, mind, we're pretty stretched already.'

The Italian seaman arrived just as Rachel was supervising arrangements for his reception. They had allocated him an upstairs room, a hastily prepared box of a place which led off from the recently adapted ward.

'We'll be popping folk into cupboards next,' she observed ruefully to the porter who was trying to manoeuvre a bed into the tiny space.

The Italian was fully conscious now, able to tell them that his name was Benito Cerrato. He was in severe pain from his foot as well as the gravely injured head. Hamish asked Rachel to take a look at an open wound on Benito's head while he continued in theatre with a tricky operation to remove shrapnel from another patient's side.

'We'll give Benito's skull a thorough examination then for signs of compression and so on, though I gather they've done that before bringing him to us. Once we're more certain of the state of his head, we'll fix the foot injury. It's waited this long, it can wait a while longer, and from their report on his foot the bones aren't too seriously displaced.'

Rachel soon began to like the Italian. A few years younger than herself, he spoke English which seemed to improve as he recovered from shock and regained some composure. She took that as a promising sign that his brain had not suffered too much damage, and he seemed very appreciative of their efforts to help him.

'Your foot will be X-rayed shortly and then given a plaster cast, do you understand?'

'Plaster, yes.' He smiled wryly, indicating with both hands the process involved. 'I break one other time, when . . . when child.'

'The same foot?' she asked him.

'No, the other one.'

Rachel mentioned this to Hamish when he joined her to put Benito's head through all the tests for more serious damage. Both agreed that he appeared to have suffered no more than the inevitable bruising and a nasty wound. Damage to the foot, however, was actually quite complex, with several bones broken, including the important tarsus forming the lower section of the ankle joint.

'Did you fall on to something?' Hamish asked him. 'You've smashed this very thoroughly.'

'I do not know, but there were tools around on the floor.'

'Sounds like you landed on one of them,' said Rachel. 'Could explain why this looks like an injury caused by an object being dropped on your foot.'

By the time the plaster had been applied, Benito was clearly exhausted. Rachel instructed one of the nurses to ensure that he rested, and added that he must be made to keep to his own quarters. He wouldn't be attempting to wander about at first, but would have to become accustomed to remaining in the one room even when he regained mobility.

Donald Barker was the duty doctor that night, and very evidently relished the prospect of keeping the Italian incarcerated. 'If I had my way, we'd have a guard on that door. Since we haven't risen to that, I'll have to content myself with making certain the ward nurses know he's stopping where he is.'

The situation soon proved far from ideal. As Benito swiftly improved, Rachel began to feel quite sorry for the young man. His head seemed to be producing nothing more than the unavoidable ache, and with his foot and ankle encased in plaster he was eager to be moving around.

'I would harm no one here, you understand,' he told her. 'You have been so very kind to me, and your treatment will make me to walk again.'

'Even so, that is the way things must be,' she told him. Had the prisoner of war camp been nearer completion and providing better accommodation, he might have been discharged to it. Conditions there being as they were, expecting him to cope with life under canvas really wasn't viable.

Despite the discretion with which his presence was handled among their staff, it soon became evident that the men on the neighbouring ward were fully aware that an Italian was occupying that small room. Going about the ward, Rachel could hear the men muttering among themselves, and quite often suspending whatever they were saying whenever she was within earshot. She would catch odd words, mainly to the effect that he was being given better treatment than they were – he had a private room, hadn't he? They also suspected that he was being given nicer meals.

Tired, as she invariably was towards the end of a long shift, on the crucial night Rachel wasn't paying much heed to what the ward sister was doing. The nurses working with them at Keld House were all so thoroughly trained by now that they were left to get on with the necessary tasks. They had had several new admissions that day and Rachel herself was checking the condition of an airman who had needed surgery for a chest wound dangerously close to the heart. Sleeping now, the man was breathing with difficulty, still clearly in pain, and she rang through to Hamish's room after he'd gone off duty.

'I'd be happier if you could take another look at him,' she added after explaining. 'He's probably all right, but a quick once-over from you might save trouble later on.'

'I'll be right there,' he promised.

Turning from the desk where the telephone stood, Rachel was alerted by a commotion down the far end of the ward. Several men were out of bed and making such a disturbance that they had drawn the nurses running towards them. At virtually the same minute a couple of patients close to where she had been standing sped towards the door of the Italian's room. Charging at the wood with a force that belied his own injuries, the older man burst through into the room.

'Come out of there, you mustn't . . .' yelled Rachel, and tore after them.

Both men were in the room already and, in what seemed a preconceived plan, tilted the bed to toss Benito out of it.

He was struggling to overcome the encumbering plaster cast and stand up when Rachel reached his side.

'It's all right,' she reassured him. 'They won't hurt you.'

Half turning away from the other two patients, she helped haul the Italian to his feet. 'Get out,' she shouted at the others. 'Get back into your own ward.'

'Not yet. We haven't finished with him!' one man snapped.

'Oh, but you have!' Rachel contradicted, and turned to face them fully.

Appalled, she saw the younger man was holding a knife.

'Don't be stupid,' she began, as she sensed that Benito, just behind her, was trembling.

'Let us have him,' the other man said. 'We're only going to give him a bit of a fright, just to be going on with, like.'

'No, no – think what you're doing,' Rachel protested.

But the men had thought already, had been planning this action for so long that they were too keyed up to turn back. The one with the knife lunged forward in the tiny room. Rachel couldn't let this happen in her hospital. Instinctively, she reached sideways in front of the Italian. The knife struck the starched collar of her white coat and slid upwards. She felt its point pierce her neck.

'You stupid woman, you shouldn't have got in the way,' her assailant cried.

Rachel raised a hand to her neck as blood pumped from it. 'It's all right,' she told the Italian, who had screeched in alarm. 'Only a scratch.' Blood was spurting between her fingers, spattering her white coat, and splashing on to the upturned bed. This wasn't trivial. 'No,' she said despairingly.

Hamish pushed past everyone to reach her. He clamped the fingers of one hand over the wound, desperate to seal it. With his other he steadied Rachel, eased her towards a chair. 'Sister,' he yelled, and saw she was with one of the nurses detaining the man with the knife. 'You'll have to let him go, this is urgent. Get hold of a trolley.' Glancing about, he snatched a clean pillowcase from a nurse who'd held it when she came running. Folding the cloth into a pad, he thrust it hard against Rachel's wound.

She could sense she was losing consciousness, but Hamish was there, he knew what to do. She was vaguely aware of being hoisted up and on to a trolley while Hamish struggled to check the blood flowing from her neck. Then they were running with her. Rachel closed her eyes against increasing dizziness. The glare of theatre lighting made her open her eyes again. When the room reeled giddily about her, she shut them tightly.

'Don't worry, love, you're in theatre now.' Hamish's voice sounded strange, from somewhere far distant. 'Donald's here too, sister's giving you the pre-med while we scrub up. You'll soon come out the right side of all this, Rachel.' Please God, he added silently.

She was glad to feel the anaesthetic removing the final scrap of consciousness. There was nothing she had to do now, nothing she *could do . . .*

They told her afterwards that the operation had taken some time – how much time, Hamish didn't reveal. Rachel suspected he didn't want to alarm her, but she knew that after the scare with the knife nothing else would match that terror.

'Don't try to speak,' Hamish insisted when she attempted to thank him as she came round. 'You are going to be all right, but you've got to take it very easy. I'll let your family know.'

He anticipated that Rachel would try to shake her head, and she felt his hands steadying it. The hands that had saved her.

'Sleep now,' Hamish suggested firmly. 'There'll be someone with you all the time, just relax.'

Resisting would have been impossible; if all her blood had been drained away and not replaced, she couldn't feel weaker. Slipping into sleep was a welcome relief.

Hamish telephoned her parents' home himself. He felt heavily responsible for Rachel's injury. No one else had agreed to admitting that Italian, he didn't recall even discussing alternatives with either Rachel or Donald. Yet he had known there could be trouble from their own patients.

Hedda answered, sounding pleased to hear from him, but Hamish cut her short. 'Is your daughter there, Mrs Davidson – or Mr Skelton?'

'I am sorry, no. Asta is away on a two-day Red Cross course. Andrew's at sea. Is something wrong?'

'I'm afraid so, but the worst is over, we believe. There's been a . . . an incident here, Rachel was hurt, but we've done all we could to put that right . . .' He needed to give Hedda the truth, but was desperate not to panic her. Somewhere between the two, he found a few more words. 'We had to operate, but she's come through that very well.'

Hamish heard a gasp from the other end of the line and the scrape of a chair as the elderly lady sat down. When she swallowed, that sound also came through to him.

'I think you must tell me everything,' said Hedda slowly.

'One of our patients had a knife, he lunged at somebody else and Rachel somehow came between them.'

'Poor little Rachel! Where was she stabbed?'

'In the neck, but fortunately we acted swiftly.'

'I shall come to her at once. If only I could drive, I never learned . . .' Very briefly, Hedda considered. 'I shall tell Bernard, we shall come there together. Does he know?'

'Not yet. I'll speak to him immediately.'

'No. Please do not. I must tell him. He will be dreadfully upset, he is always so very, very fond of Rachel.'

Hedda couldn't bear to wait before going to see Rachel. She made a swift visit to the bathroom, checked that she had money and keys in her handbag, and walked briskly out of the house, locking the door behind her.

Striding out on the way to Bernard's home, Hedda realized that she hadn't left a note for either Asta or Andrew. Bernard would know what to do, though, and telling them in a note was hardly the gentlest means of imparting bad news. She couldn't recall what Bernard's surgery hours might be, but hoped that he would be able to set out at once for Keld House hospital.

A woman she took to be Mrs Hardaker opened the door

to her. Distressed though she was, Hedda noticed the housekeeper's smile and was glad she seemed the sort who would take good care of Bernard.

'I am Hedda Davidson,' she explained. 'Is he at home please?'

'I do believe you might have caught him at the right time. He just finished surgery a few minutes since. Would you step inside, while I find him for you?'

Thankful to have a moment alone to recover her composure, Hedda drew in several deep breaths then straightened her shoulders. Hurrying here had done her heart no good at all, but it had precluded time in which to contemplate Bernard's potential reaction to her appearance on his doorstep.

More than a few minutes passed, enough to cause Hedda to wonder if he too needed to compose himself for this encounter. She hoped he would not feel too perturbed; the shocking news she brought would do more harm to the old soul.

Looking around her, Hedda was surprised to find much that she recognized from her occupation of this house years ago. Certain items had changed, naturally. The carpet was new – or perhaps not all that new, as carpet manufacturing had been suspended for the war. The walls were oak panelled to dado height, and above that against a pale blue wallpaper were arranged her beloved antique plates. Had they all survived? she wondered, and was pleased that Bernard kept them in place still.

'Hedda, this is a surprise . . .'

Weary though he appeared at the end of a busy surgery, Bernard nevertheless looked to her just as striking as he had on the day they had married.

'Not a pleasant surprise, I fear,' she began. 'There is no easy way of telling you,' she began.

This time Bernard inserted a sentence when she hesitated. 'Andrew? It's his boat, isn't it?'

Hedda crossed the few paces to grasp his arm. 'Not Andrew. I am sorry to have to tell you that Rachel has been hurt. But Hamish says she will recover.'

'Hurt? At the hospital? How on earth?' Bernard was too shaken to form coherent questions.

'I did not hesitate long enough to demand full details. According to Hamish, some patient got hold of a knife.'

'God, she was stabbed!'

'Evidently, yes. I believe Hamish had to operate, someone certainly did. But, my dear, he assures me that Rachel has come safely through that.'

'We must get to her at once. But where's our Asta? Why isn't she with you?'

'Didn't you know? She went on a course, quite an important one with the Red Cross.'

'This is up to us then. At least we know what's expected of us. And you walked all the way here?'

Hedda smiled slightly. 'I never did learn to drive, you know. I don't believe you would have thought I was capable.'

Bernard patted her hand where it still lay on his sleeve. 'Today, there has been nothing lacking in your reaction to crisis. You have coped splendidly, Hedda.' From some men, that remark might have seemed patronising. She could not take it as such, as she knew Bernard spoke what was on his mind and never assumed to condescend.

He paused only to inform Mrs Hardaker that he was going out, and suggest that she should not prepare a meal for him immediately.

'I really do not know how long we might remain at the hospital,' he said to Hedda as they went out to his car. 'I can telephone and make arrangements regarding my surgery if we shall not be back by morning.'

He realizes how serious this could be, thought Hedda as he opened the car door for her. She was thankful that she wasn't the only one whose heart had felt leaden with anxiety from the first second of being told. Her own reluctance to deliver too massive a shock might so easily have left Bernard with a false impression of what might await them at the hospital.

'You haven't lost your old knack of tempering bad news with concern for the recipient,' he approved as he started up the car. 'Even when we see our Rachel fit and well again, there'll be things to remember about this day.'

Do not be too generous, thought Hedda, or I shall make myself a fool and weep. I am too old to suffer bad news like today's and emerge with emotions intact.

'Have you visited Keld House before?' Bernard enquired. He needed to introduce some conversation that did not involve the harrowing suppositions he was entertaining about his beloved granddaughter's condition.

'Oh, yes. We first went there before driving to Asta's house when Rachel brought me out of Norway. I liked Hamish then, as much as I liked him today for his consideration.'

'A grand chap indeed. Must admit to hoping he and Rachel make a go of it. After the war, naturally.'

'From what he said, she will owe him a great deal.'

'Perhaps. Yet doctors, you know, don't help folk and expect them to be indebted.'

'I did not suppose they would. I have known you well enough, Bernard, to understand that *giving* is its own reward, as is a satisfactory result.'

Despite his anxiety over Rachel, Bernard chuckled. 'Have you become a diplomat with the years, Hedda? Or are you trying to convince me that I did make some kind of impression, once upon time?'

'Once upon a time belongs in fairy tales, does it not? I try to see life's happenings as they really are, and behaviour for its true worth. And that, perhaps, is how I have altered. Expecting less of people might not be the fault which once I believed it.' Fantasies are an indulgence for the young, she reflected silently.

'But today we must expect the best,' said Bernard. 'And pray that fine young surgeon has indeed *given* everything required of him to preserve our little Rachel.'

Hedda swallowed hard, she already was trying to pray. But trying was as far as her desperate mind would go. In a way altogether too familiar, her ageing brain was struggling with the effort to marshal words. She hoped to God that her *intending* to pray might be sufficient.

Eleven

Keld House appeared so peaceful amid the wooded slopes and distant Yorkshire moorland. Hedda could scarcely believe that such a terrible drama had taken place there.

'You'd think it was all you wanted in a healing place, wouldn't you?' said Bernard, echoing her thoughts as he parked the car near the front entrance.

The massive front doors were locked and they wondered aloud if that was normal or a result of the earlier attack. The strident ringing of the bell brought a nurse to admit them; a pretty girl who looked too young to be qualified.

'We're Dr Skelton's grandparents,' Bernard announced. 'I suppose you know all about what's happened.'

'Oh, yes. I'm to take you up immediately; Mr Wilson's instructions.' The nurse escorted them to the lift which she entered with them, then pressed one of the buttons.

Hedda noticed her own agitated breathing and realized how anxious she was. Instinctively she reached towards Bernard's hand, then remembered, withdrew, and clamped her fingers to her side.

Bernard stifled a sigh. He grasped her hand, she felt his fingers caressing her own.

'Not long now,' he murmured.

He thanked the nurse after she'd conducted them to the room. Hedda's gratitude for having him there increased. *She* was too alarmed for courtesies.

Hamish rose and came to greet them. Hedda could have sworn he'd been kneeling by the bed.

'Rachel's sleeping, but quietly. There's nothing to indicate there'll be problems. Do make yourselves at home. This is her own room, actually. Simpler to bring all the monitoring equipment in here. We don't provide private rooms normally.'

'And are all your patients male?' Bernard enquired, his grey eyes already inspecting his granddaughter's face for indications of her condition.

'Yes, so far. Makes life easier, but as it is we've had to open up an additional ward. We'd have difficulty segregating if we were obliged to admit from the women's services.'

Bernard nodded. 'There's enough about being hospitalized to perturb people, without adding to their unease.' He paused, nodded towards the bed. 'So, this was a neck wound – where, exactly?'

'He caught the carotid artery, but only just. Luckily, this is the right place for receiving instant attention.'

'If also for being attacked in that way,' Hedda observed quite sharply, and sighed.

Bernard's arm slid around her shoulders. 'What went wrong?' he asked the surgeon. 'Someone suffering the after-effects of trauma induced in battle?'

'Perhaps. Look – I will explain as much as I know later, after you've spent some time with Rachel. I do have patients I must see, and one doctor short . . .'

'Sure. But first set my mind at rest on one thing. What's happened to the wretched soul who did this?' Bernard persisted.

'He's with the military police. At his own request, demanded that they be sent for. They took him away.'

Still with an arm around Hedda's shoulders, Bernard led her up to the bed as soon as they were alone with Rachel.

'She . . . she doesn't look too awful,' Hedda whispered, and dashed away her tears with fingers that shook.

'That's right,' Bernard agreed, willing his own emotions under control as he encouraged Hedda to sit at the bedside. A second chair stood across the bed from them. He walked around the foot and carried the chair to Hedda's side. She took hold of Rachel's arm as it lay on the covers; he grasped their granddaughter's fingers.

'Feels quite warm, doesn't she?' he remarked. 'But not overwarm, and not sweating.'

Hedda managed a slight smile. 'That is good, yes?'

'Encouraging. You do understand there's a long way to go?'

'I suppose I do. Damage to an artery is serious, is it not? And then there was the shock.' Strain was making her sound more foreign than usual.

Bernard nodded, sighed. 'What a world we live in, eh? When a doctor's injured in her work. And this is presumed to be a civilized country. I think perhaps you were not so misguided, all those years ago, in believing conflict should be avoided.'

Her wry laugh startled him. 'You think that, Bernard? While I have concluded that pacifism can have its flaws, observing what has happened to my homeland.'

'That hurts you greatly.' He nodded sympathetically, his free hand grasping her arm.

'I learn resilience. From that young lady there, for one, and she risked more than I over that voyage. Her projected life far exceeds my own.'

'You should not talk like that.' Bernard sounded dismayed. 'You must not devalue your own existence.'

Hedda gave him a curious look. Surely he had been indifferent to her for several decades? Eventually, she shrugged. 'It will be easy for you to speak that way, for yourself. You fulfil your life's work, and you have always your family to hand.'

'They are your family too.'

But only in this impermanence, thought Hedda. She had wondered so many times since returning if she might truly belong with them. One day.

When Rachel next opened her eyes she smiled, inwardly thrilled to find both grandparents, all but entwined, at her bedside. And then the pain kicked in as consciousness increased. She frowned, and felt their grasp on her tighten. She tried to tell them that she would be all right. No voice emerged.

'She will recover.' Hamish was speaking from the doorway.

'But she will need rest, sedation perhaps to ensure that. And the two of you – dare I say that you do not look much better?'

Hedda smiled at him. 'You young people will learn, one day, how it is to feel one no longer can quite tackle so many of life's difficulties!'

Bernard squeezed her arm. 'You do not age, love, you must not try to fool the man.'

Hamish turned towards the bed. 'You're in pain again, Rachel, aren't you? Let's give you something to ease that.' He glanced over his shoulder towards her grandparents. 'There's a sitting room two doors along; if you'd like to wait in there I'll be with you in a moment.'

Hamish had mentioned their evident tiredness, and his own was plain enough when he came to join them. 'I can offer tea, or coffee if you wish, though the latter is the ersatz variety now.' Initially, they accepted neither. He could tell them more about Rachel's condition and that was all they needed.

'How bad is she, really?' asked Hedda, unable to delay a moment longer.

'She's looking good. I do believe I've done a thorough bit of sewing.'

'So it was you who operated,' said Bernard, nodding in satisfaction.

'Couldn't bring myself to delegate this time. I think a lot of your Rachel. Plus I needed to ensure we hang on to the very fine doctor that she has become!'

Bernard smiled. 'Any idea how long recuperation might take?'

'Not the slightest, as yet. Much too soon to hazard guesses. How easily she takes these early days will contribute a great deal to the outcome. And I know Rachel – not given to taking things easy, is she?'

'She loves her work,' said Hedda and Bernard together.

'Even contending with me!' Hamish smiled at them. 'Anyway, we people here are going to need allies until Rachel's truly fit – glad I can count on you two. Did you say neither of her parents are at home?'

'I'm afraid that's so,' Bernard confirmed, and turned to Hedda. 'But can we contact Asta?'

'But yes. She gave to me her telephone number. I do not believe she trusted that I would look after myself, or her home!'

'Have you got it with you?' asked Bernard.

'Naturally. You know how we women always fill our handbags with every item of possible use!'

'Do you wish me to speak with her?' the young surgeon offered.

Bernard shook his head. 'I'm not at all sure anyone could prevent that daughter of ours from fretting, but I would like to attempt to reassure her.'

'That doctor's manner of yours, of course,' said Hedda. Hamish explained where to find a telephone they could use.

When Bernard returned, Hamish turned to him from speaking with Hedda. 'I've just been saying, regarding tonight, you may wish to remain at Keld House, although I do assure you that Rachel seems to have progressed well past danger point. I'm afraid we couldn't accommodate you in a room – *rooms*,' he corrected himself, remembering their situation. 'You might be reasonably comfortable in here, if you wish to stay. On the other hand, a night's sleep may not go amiss . . .'

'And for you, young man,' said Bernard.

Hamish shrugged. 'We have a long training, don't we, in sleeping with one eye, and keeping watch with the other? You may entrust her to me, you know. And we have good nurses as well.'

Bernard gave him his card, and didn't really need Hamish's assurances that he would contact him should any crisis arise. Their granddaughter would be well cared for here, and with loving attention.

'That is a massive relief,' Bernard exclaimed, getting into the driving seat after settling Hedda comfortably. 'Are you all right?'

'Exhausted, but yes. I shall recover.'

'And the insulin? Do you have it with you?'

'Well, yes – but I'm not due for any yet.'

'Good. But I suggest that you consider spending the night at my house. I don't want you going back alone to that empty place of Asta's.'

When imparting the news about Rachel's injury, he had succeeded in calming his daughter's natural alarm, but he had been reminded by Asta that Hedda would be alone unless Andrew Skelton returned unexpectedly from sea.

'Are you sure about this?' Hedda asked him.

They were nearing the house now, and she had refused to reply immediately to his invitation. She needed to think, and to contain her own longing to stay with this man she had once loved so completely. The companionship between them seemed as strong as ever today, and had seen her through that dreadful shock of seeing her dear Rachel Hedda injured. Letting go and having Bernard take care of everything would be so easy.

He was smiling at her as he drew up at his door. 'When I spoke with Asta that short while ago, I also rang Mrs Hardaker – she is now preparing food enough for two. And will have a spare room ready.'

'You assumed I would wish to stay the night?' Hedda felt at the same time pleased and perturbed, and still more confused about the wisdom of whichever decision she might make.

'If you do not wish to use it, the room will be ready for my next visitor.' Bernard suddenly sounded very dignified. And hurt. Hedda could not do that to him.

She smiled. 'I would be a fool to turn down your offer. In my own home, I quite enjoyed being alone – in someone else's there seems less to do. And today, I must admit to needing company that will prevent my thoughts from dwelling incessantly on that dreadful stabbing.'

'Quite.'

Bernard opened the car door for her, then took her arm when she got out. He is being kinder than I deserve, thought Hedda, while resisting the impulse to lean her head against him. She had always liked his being a big man, sensing that his bulk somehow epitomized Bernard's many strengths.

Mrs Hardaker had left a note, explaining that the casserole

was keeping hot in the oven, and vegetables were prepared and waiting in their pans.

'I'll just light the gas under these,' Bernard told Hedda. 'If you wish to freshen up, the main bathroom's still the first door along the landing.'

'Is there anything I can do?' she offered before hanging her coat in the hall.

'Not for the moment, thanks.' If he admitted the truth, he was needing a short time quite alone. Just being with Hedda again, and during such a shared trauma, was sending his emotions rocketing. Together they had expressed how dear Rachel was to them. What he could not, must not, express was this deep affection for Hedda herself.

She had spruced herself up when she found him in the kitchen. Bernard nodded approvingly. 'You look better now. More like the smart woman I once . . .' He let his voice trail off, sacrificing to caution his need to speak of love.

They ate in the kitchen while he told Hedda how Rachel had been his last visitor. 'Don't entertain much these days,' he confessed. 'Wartime shortages make a reasonable excuse, but it isn't really that. A snack at the pub with friends is more my style now.' It wasn't meant as a reproof, she could tell that from his tone, yet Hedda wished away the vision he'd conjured of a lonely man, driven to eating out by lack of a hostess.

'Do you have the same old friends?'

'The same . . . ?'

'People whom I knew.'

'One or two maybe.' He felt reluctant to name any, might have been afraid to add even one more stone to the bridge between them.

'Your housekeeper is a good cook.' And discussing the meal felt to be safer territory.

'You know me, couldn't have tolerated anyone who wasn't. But enough of my life, Hedda. Tell me how yours is.'

'*Was*, you mean. Before the invasion ruined everything. I created interests for myself. One woman with whom I went to school all those years ago teaches our local folk dances. She even encouraged me to try, although beside her I am anything but elegant. We do have fun. though. Or we *did*. Olav wanted me to improve my skiing, he is fanatical, but I have grown too old for that. My skiing limits itself, but serves to get me about when the worst of the snows come.'

'And now – are you missing everything about Bergen quite terribly?'

Hedda considered for a few minutes before replying. '*Now*, no. Because it is no longer the place that I love.'

'Is the German presence very obtrusive?'

'In some ways, but less so than we feared. One does adjust to regulations, to seeing their uniforms about the streets. The worst is this feeling that the city is no longer *ours*. No one knows when they are watching. On a mundane level, naturally their forces acquire the best of available food, just as they have commandeered many of our facilities.'

'A good thing that you had Olav to keep an eye on you.'

'He helped, of course, and helped some of my friends also – the ones who are Jewish, especially. I worry for them now, those who did not get away already.'

Bernard nodded gravely. 'Some of my patients are of Jewish stock, anxious for family members elsewhere in Europe. Lots of them came to Yorkshire years ago, you know, many in the clothing trade.'

'For which your county is famous – I do remember good Yorkshire cloth, you see, and the fine tailoring.'

Bernard was pleased, glad to have assurance that she hadn't chosen to forget everything about the life she had led with him.

'Do you see Asta and Andrew very frequently?' she enquired. 'Normally, I mean – when I am not there.'

He shrugged, his smile rueful.

Hedda frowned. 'Ah, so – that is how I supposed. You must not be this way, Bernard. Unless you hate to see me.'

'Hate? I couldn't.'

'Then we must make for us some changes. You may ignore me there, if you will, but you should not absent yourself from Asta's home on my account. Whatever has taken place in the past, I have found comfort always in knowing that you have your own people.'

Moved by learning that she had continued to care, Bernard found he was clattering the empty dishes as he cleared them from the table. Hedda joined him at the sink, and was surprised to discover how contented she felt while they worked there, side by side.

After showing her where the clean china and cutlery were kept, Bernard went to the telephone and rang through to enquire how Rachel seemed. The nurse who answered sounded like the youngster they had met earlier, and was happy to tell them that Hamish was pleased with Rachel's condition.

'And now we may be able to sleep,' he said to Hedda, relating the latest news.

'Presently,' she responded, leaning her head back against the chair where she was sitting.

Bernard went to his favourite seat, an old wing chair near to the hearth. He was happy enough to sit for a while, but rendered strangely restless by a massive conflict of feelings. Having Hedda so close was certainly a challenge – one by which he felt daunted. Beside the instinctive capacity for contentment that she induced in him was growing an intense longing that he'd once decided was dead rather than dormant. That he continued to love her was a fact he never could doubt. Discovering that desire could emerge from dormancy in such unpromising circumstances was a bit of a facer!

Her eyelids slightly lowered, Hedda gazed towards him. Bernard was a fine man still, the comfort of his touch while they were at Keld House had reminded her of the tenderness from which for so many years she had absented herself. But missing that reassurance was nothing to that other great abyss – the torment created by losing the intimacy of their lovemaking.

Both tired, and not yet entirely comfortable with each other, their conversation flagged. After chatting for a short while in desultory fashion on the few topics that felt safe, Bernard suggested that he should show Hedda to her room. She tried to check her instinctive frown, reminded herself that he had worked earlier that day and no doubt had a surgery scheduled for the morning. Why was she so selfishly eager to retain his company? Especially when, to Bernard, it must feel like a lifetime since she'd relinquished all right to expect anything of him.

'You will have no nightdress with you,' he said when they reached the landing. 'I've put out a set of clean pyjamas – hope they will do.'

'Thank you, Bernard, you're very thoughtful.'

'I'll say goodnight then.' He opened the door of her room, indicated that she should go in.

'Goodnight.'

Hedda turned abruptly, so sharply that she overbalanced slightly and banged her shoulder on the door frame. She had so longed for him to kiss her. Bernard steadied her, his grasp on Hedda's arm increasing her need for more. But she knew it was no use, must get herself out of this because he so evidently felt none of the emotions that were assailing her. Before he could turn away, she was through into the room, closing the door behind her.

Glancing around, Hedda saw that this was one part of Bernard's home that had hardly changed at all since her departure. The bed was a double; high, and old-fashioned even all those years ago. She remembered having difficulty in making its flock mattress comfortable for visitors who had come to stay.

The rest of the furniture was good, Victorian, constructed to last and evidently preserved by Mrs Hardaker's routine polishing. The walls were almost as Hedda remembered them, covered in a pale wallpaper, but now faded to render unobtrusive the pattern of roses which she'd once regretted selecting.

The bed was no more comfortable than she'd expected, and only made acceptable by the pyjamas Bernard had loaned. She smiled to herself, seeing that he still chose the classic blue and white stripes which, even in their younger days, she had designated an old man's! Wearing them, however, Hedda relished the warmth they generated, not by the quality of their cloth, but in association with their owner. Fresh from the wash though they undoubtedly were, they seemed so undeniably *his* that they held her secure, as though enveloped in a part of him.

Exhausted by shock and anxiety, Hedda had felt to be aching for sleep, and was sure that this was one night when that horrid mattress would not keep her awake. All too swiftly, she began to realize that the state of her own mind would be the culprit rather than any physical problem. Discomfort could be pushed to the back of her subconscious, but with her anxious thoughts she was experiencing greater difficulty. Even reassured, as they had been by phoning Keld House, she could not let Rachel's condition rest.

Troubled by concern for her granddaughter, she felt awareness of other things disturbing her. And then, as so often since developing the diabetes, lying in bed soon began to induce the urge to get up and visit the bathroom. For quite some time Hedda forced herself to wait, in case wandering about the house should disturb Bernard. He had been as distressed as she herself, and had more need to sleep in order to cope with his work.

Eventually Hedda was compelled to get out of bed and tiptoe along the corridor. Hating the condition that ensured these nightly visits to relieve herself, she wished some treatment could take her back to the days before being diagnosed, when she had been like everyone else. While tiredness overwhelmed her, Hedda wished with all her heart that she could turn back the clock.

In so many ways she was very different from the woman who had given up all the happiness she had known here in this house. Loathing the foolish person that she believed she had become, Hedda gave in to the misery that normally she wouldn't have permitted herself. She was emerging from the bathroom when the door of Bernard's room opened.

'Hedda, are you all right?' he asked. And then he saw the tears running down her face. 'You're not ill, I hope?'

She shook her head, tried to laugh off the state she was in, and hiccuped.

'Come here, love.'

His hands were outstretched towards her, she hurtled towards him and was wrapped in the arms she had so longed for. He took a handkerchief from his pocket and dried her face.

And then he kissed her. His mouth felt blessedly familiar, welcoming and at once exciting.

Hedda tested his lips with the tip of her tongue and recollected. She hastily withdrew. But Bernard pulled her closer against him, through their clothing she felt the hammer heartbeat in his chest, plus another insistent assurance of his need. He kissed her again, fervently, with all the passion for which she had yearned throughout that long, long absence. When he paused to breathe she gazed beyond him into the room they had shared so often.

Bernard sighed, shook his head. 'Not tonight, Hedda love. We must not surrender to impulse merely because we've experienced recent anxiety. Too much has happened. We need to think. I'm far too old to have sensuality overcome sense.' He did kiss her again, but on her forehead. 'Do try to sleep now.'

Away from him, she felt instantly chilled, and walked into her own room feeling dazed and distracted. Her own surging desire had surprised her less than evidence of his. This physical need had burdened her days, yet she'd never considered that Bernard might still desire her. And now he had sent her away, dispatching her to this spare bedroom as though to indicate that he could *spare* the life they once had known. Was his only need now simply to prove that he had mastered the attraction that had originally drawn them together? Put it behind him? While she made an even bigger fool out of herself, because of wanting him. Memory of that moment when she had teased his lips with her tongue refused to sink below the surface of consciousness, tormented her with the supposition that Bernard was shaken by her sexuality.

He might even be repulsed by what I have done, thought Hedda, and was appalled. Why couldn't she have thought before indulging her instincts?

Dread of the morning and the inevitable shared breakfast added to all her other worries, to ensure that she dozed rather than slept throughout the rest of the night.

Morning was easier than she had expected. Mrs Hardaker was

there when Hedda went downstairs, and Bernard looked as cheerful as he was composed while he sat at the table.

'You should not have waited for me,' she told him. 'You no doubt have an early start.'

'No more than you. Didn't I say I've arranged a locum for today? My first priority's our granddaughter. And, I'm thankful to say, the people at Keld House report that she's had a good night.'

'That is a relief. Was it Hamish you spoke to?'

'Actually, it was their theatre sister. She'd evidently just looked in on Rachel before going to scrub up. Sounds a nice woman, very genuine.'

'Our dear Rachel Hedda certainly seems well loved by everyone there.'

'As she should be. Setting up a military hospital wouldn't be to every new young doctor's taste.'

'I suspect she enjoys going the extra mile in caring. Much like yourself.'

Bernard gave her a quizzical look, then allowed himself to smile. Some aspects of Hedda's approach might perturb him, but he loved to discover these little indications that it might not have been dislike which took her away from him all those years ago.

They were finishing their meal when Asta arrived, breathless and a little dishevelled because of travelling since dawn.

'What's the latest on Rachel?' she asked immediately. 'I've not slept at all since your call, had to get away as soon as I could. Persuaded them to let me on to a troop train.'

'I've just spoken to the hospital. They're very pleased with her, so far. You'd better be warned to expect her to look poorly, though. It was quite a shock for Hedda and me yesterday.'

Asta nodded. 'And you're a doctor, used to folk that's ill.'

Bernard frowned. Did this daughter of his really not understand how different it felt when the injured person was family? He sensed Hedda's sympathetic gaze on him, looked up and realized that *she* knew him more thoroughly.

'I suppose our Rachel herself will be helped to recover by

knowing all the ins and outs of what's happened to her – the operation and that,' Asta continued.

Bernard sighed. Her words seemed to compound her lack of comprehension. In his experience, colleagues could find that knowledge of their condition and its inherent potential problems was a disadvantage. Each little symptom might present further cause for alarm, while the instinct to probe their significance generated an obsessive interest.

'I am sure that Rachel has inherited Bernard's informed optimism, and that will be a great aid towards her recovery,' said Hedda. She had sensed his tension and remembered how he'd always remained very fond of Asta, whilst admitting privately that this daughter of theirs was not overendowed with understanding.

Asta gave her a look. Her eyes revealed that she wondered if her mother was trying to sound clever. Hedda concealed a smile, and decided that Bernard wasn't the only one deserving of a little kindness.

'Do not look so perturbed, Asta. We go very soon to Keld House, and you will see for yourself how Rachel is today. In fact, if anyone believes that two persons only would be admitted, I shall remain here.'

'There's no need for that, love,' said Bernard. 'If there is one advantage of being a doctor, it's gaining admission that might be denied to other folk.'

When they arrived in Rachel's room at the hospital, neither Hedda nor Bernard could dismiss Asta's very evident distress on seeing her daughter. All questions regarding what might be of benefit were forgotten when they witnessed the depth of her concern for Rachel.

Hedda felt tears springing to her own eyes as they watched Asta struggle to find the words to tell her daughter how she was feeling.

'I'll never forgive myself for not being the first to come rushing here. I was away with the Red Cross, you know, Rachel love.'

'All right, Mum. These two came,' her daughter added, her voice barely audible.

'You seem as though you shouldn't be talking so much,' said Asta as she sat beside the bed and took Rachel's hand. 'So long as we can see you're going to be all right, you're better resting.'

Hamish came in at that moment, smiled towards the bed, greeted Asta, and turned to speak with Bernard and Hedda. 'Since yesterday Rachel has progressed greatly. We're pleased with the way she's come through the night. I suspect our next problem's going to be preventing her from trying too much too soon!'

Bernard smiled. 'I'm delighted to hear you're well satisfied with her. We can't thank you enough for everything you've done.'

'That is true,' Hedda agreed. 'How is it that in the really serious times one can never find words that seem adequate?'

Hamish smiled at her, laid a hand on her arm. 'You must not forget that it is for *our* sake also that we need to have Rachel well again.'

With only a brief word to Rachel and her mother, Hamish departed once more for the wards. But his reappearance had impressed Hedda as well as Bernard, relieving them from anxiety, which meant that by the time the three of them were leaving Rachel to rest they felt more contented.

When Bernard's car halted outside Asta's house, Hedda experienced a great rush of conflicting emotions. She was disturbed by the effect that being close to him for several hours had upon her, and might feel easier for a break from such intensity of feeling. On the other hand, she could not help resenting the fact that he was returning alone to the house that once had been theirs.

He got out of the car with them and said goodbye to Asta who was hurrying to unlock her front door. And then Bernard turned to Hedda. He took her hand and smiled as they said goodbye.

Perhaps this could be a fresh beginning, thought Hedda, and prayed that she would not make a fool of herself again and deter him by wanting too much.

Twelve

Rachel recovered remarkably well from the attack and her family began to let relief drive off their anxiety. Her father had been deeply affected by the stabbing, despite the fact that she was greatly improved by the time he was home from sea and able to visit her.

'I must admit I'm badly shaken,' he confessed to his father-in-law. 'I can't seem to get out of my mind what it would have been like if that knifing had proved fatal. I wouldn't have known – nobody can contact me when I'm on board. I'll never feel sure now while I'm out there that everybody is surviving all right.'

Although one of the inevitable consequences of war, Andrew's fear for his family during his own absences began to weigh down on his spirit. Right up until then he had done whatever was required of him, cheered by the belief that every contribution should be shortening the war. Now that was changing; where he'd once reckoned the possible cost might have been his own life, these days he was more fearful on behalf of the people he'd supposed safe at home.

Sensing this, Rachel tried to rid him of that dread whenever he visited while she was confined to bed, and to a greater degree when she went to stay with the family to recuperate. Despite her longing to get back to work, the lethargy she experienced for some time indicated that her recovery wasn't yet complete. She schooled herself to relax during the remainder of the summer.

There were disturbances, mainly private, which she had to conceal whenever Hamish Wilson visited her. She would have had to be blind not to see the tenderness in his brown eyes, and she had difficulty in avoiding the affection which he seemed eager to give. But Rachel was determined she wouldn't convey the wrong impression about her feelings towards him. None of her family helped. Without exception, each of them had liked Hamish on first meeting him. Since his skill in the operating theatre had saved her life, they would all do anything for him.

Rachel herself was grateful, of course, and understood better than anyone how vital his prompt action had been. She just wished she didn't feel this placed her under some obligation. Whenever her family disappeared in tactful efforts to leave them alone, she inevitably tensed as though preparing to ward Hamish off.

He didn't attempt anything more intense than a few chaste kisses, but Rachel's unease did not wane. She had read the emotions in his eyes and in his whole demeanour, and she was perturbed that he might simply be waiting for the right time to speak of his hopes for their future.

Rachel's personal misgivings were set aside after the attack on Dieppe during the August of 1942. It proved a disaster, with so many Allied forces killed or injured that every hospital was preparing to be inundated with casualties. She went back to work, and was provided with more than enough to occupy her.

Crowded before, the wards at Keld House had additional beds crammed into them while both operating theatres were kept open round the clock again. Hamish and Donald snatched sleep when they could, and most senior nurses did likewise. Rachel also put in longer than normal hours, and relished the tiredness that generally produced regular sleep. The other two doctors insisted at first that she must take care of her health until absolutely fit again, but that stipulation vanished during the increasing crisis.

Even when campaigns in Europe and North Africa brought success, there were still injuries among military personnel, and the great need was to patch them up and prepare them for returning to active service. The desire of most of the men to get back out there and fight was a sentiment that Rachel could now understand. And if she spared little time for wishing harm on the person who had injured her, she found satisfaction in trying to ensure that no one else harboured the urge to take revenge on enemy prisoners held in Britain.

The hospital had been told eventually that her attacker had been punished, and was now incarcerated with time to reflect on his hasty action. The Italian whose presence had provoked the incident had been returned to the prisoner of war camp near Malton. From what Hamish learned, he'd subsequently become one of the best workers constructing permanent facilities there. By this time there were so many German and Italian prisoners confined about the countryside that people were accustomed to seeing them being escorted on and off duty, most frequently as labourers on local farms.

Rachel's biggest surprise towards the end of 1942 was receiving a note from Olav. No more than one line which said simply: '*I am happy to know that you are well again*'. The message was written on parachute silk, with needle marks evidence of being stitched into someone's clothing. Thrilled to hear from him after such an age, Rachel listened carefully to what Hedda told her as she handed her the note.

'Your father's men naturally heard of your being attacked – he is so well respected among the trawlermen who patrol the North Sea that word somehow travelled from one crew to another and found its way eventually to Norway.'

'Using the Shetland Bus?'

'I do not know, but the man also named Larsen who is connected with them could have been involved.'

'I believe Olav knows of him, even if they've never met.'

'He could have known how to find Olav. However it was achieved, I was pleased to receive a similar note with this. It seems such a long time since having any word from family, from my homeland.'

'Do you miss Norway quite horribly?' Rachel and her parents were so used to having Hedda with them that they had ceased to question her feelings about living in Yorkshire.

Hedda smiled to herself, shook her head. 'Less and less with each day that passes. There are compensations, you know, if only one looks around.'

And Hedda did not need to look further than the York stone house quite close to where she was staying. Bernard made her so welcome there, and was increasing the occasions when he invited her to visit him. 'Asta is always busy with her war work, and Andrew off to sea, we mustn't all neglect you,' he had said. There was no way that Hedda could ever feel neglected in Bernard's company, and if she herself felt obliged to rein in her secret needs, that was a small price for seeing him so regularly.

Their hours together were simple enough by anyone's standards, generally begun by sharing a meal at his kitchen table, and then perhaps listening to the radio together. Once or twice, Bernard had brought out albums of photographs which led to hours of reminiscing. Hedda was not certain that was always a blessing. They both looked so much younger in those snapshots, causing her to wonder where the youthful Hedda had gone, and what had possessed her to waste so many intervening years. Bernard was such a dear man, admirable in the way he refused to retire so long as his patients needed him. And while tiredness might occasionally render him impatient with others, towards Hedda he was impeccably considerate.

Wanting him back was a feeling she'd recognized even before anxiety for Rachel reunited them. Wanting Bernard to love her, and love her completely, was her personal, very private, threat to the prospect of their having a future. Hedda knew her own body, had washed it and tended its shortcomings, had tried for years to disguise the ugliness which she felt age had created in her. How could he, how could *any man*, consider her desirable?

Through embarrassment, Hedda had blanked out memories of that night when she had let foolish impulse bring desire into her kisses. Blotting out such recollections had left her believing she must have been mistaken to think for a moment that he'd been aroused by her. But now nothing could stop her noticing how fit Bernard appeared, and how attractive, how out of reach to a silly, fanciful, old woman.

News of the stabbing had badly shaken Olav, despite third-hand assurance that Rachel was recovering well. Previously, when he'd heard of York being bombed, he had been concerned because of its proximity to where his loved ones lived, but nothing could have prepared him for hearing she had been knifed. He'd also been moved by the evident respect everyone felt for Rachel.

Thankful that there were still a few means of conveying messages across the North Sea, he had written to her and also to Hedda. Then he had tried to force himself to shelve his anxieties regarding Rachel's safety, as acute concentration was demanded of every Resistance member now that activity was increasing in several parts of Norway.

The state of emergency was extending, the occupying Germans were intensifying their campaign, retaliating forcefully against any Allied successes. In one Norwegian town they had shot nine patriots and arrested seventy others. There were tales of Allied attempts at sabotage and, from what Olav heard, not all of them successful. A daring effort to destroy the battleship *Tirpitz* while it lay in Trondheimsfjord failed, and he suspected revenge for the attack would be exacted in some form or another by the Germans. When news reached him of Jews from his beloved Bergen being deported to Auschwitz he wondered how many were friends of Hedda, people whose hospitality he might have enjoyed in the old days.

Olav's own work seemed unspectacular to him, although he relished, as any skier would, the increasing challenge when snow fell and the mountainsides turned to ice. Much of his time was spent helping to maintain communications between fellow partisans in remote areas, and acting as a guide for agents. And there was great satisfaction in learning that some of his earlier work was proving useful.

His exploration of the Hardangervidda and the region over towards Rjukan was now providing information for British commandos and their Norwegian colleagues. The plan was to sabotage the Norsk Hydro plant at Vemork where, as Olav and others had surmised, possible German interest in its production of heavy water was because it could be used to create an atomic bomb. Much as Olav might have loved to take part in such a raid, he was aware of the special skills which would be required, and could accept that his role was not to be in such an operation.

So far he had not been tempted to join the military organisation that had been set up under a high command in London. Admirable though their aims might be, Olav preferred to indulge in his own form of resistance. Most recently he was learning more about radio communications, and hoping this might become one of his more useful skills. The ability to keep abreast of Nazi intentions through the partisan network was fascinating. If obliged to endure a war that dragged on, he believed that radio waves might also facilitate his contact with those he loved in England. He was discovering that without reassurance that Rachel was safe, life could become unbearable.

The fact that Olav had got that note through to her cheered life for Rachel. The flimsy scrap of silk became a substantial link with the man who, after that very short time together, still seemed to be the one person she needed. She could not remember now how long it was since she'd last yearned for her dead twin. It felt almost as though life itself had been completed for her by being reacquainted with Olav Larsen. She did not need to have that feeling confirmed, but her early thoughts following surgery had certainly focused on surviving to see Olav again. Rachel preserved his note between pages of her Bible, to be read and reread, and smoothed beneath her fingers. Sentimental or not, she couldn't deny herself any fragile contact with his life.

The increase in admissions to their hospital had for some time warranted employing an additional doctor. The newcomer was himself an army man. Mike Preston had lost a leg while serving in a field hospital in North Africa. Now fitted with an artificial limb, he'd initially arrived at Keld

House as a patient. To his dismay, the site of his operation was causing problems that made adapting to the prosthetic limb very difficult. Mike would not be fit for returning to active service until healing really was complete.

Trained as a surgeon, he had experience of all manner of operations in the field and, naturally, grew interested in the work that Hamish and the team were doing. Sometimes Mike had more practical knowledge than they of particular kinds of wound, and he appreciated having his opinion sought. From there it was a matter of formalizing the arrangement to make him a temporary member of their outfit.

Rachel liked Mike from the start, and when his wife Jenny moved north with the land army to work on a nearby farm, the three of them became friends. Neither Jenny nor Rachel had had a close female friend during the war, and both loved the opportunity to compare notes on shortages in make-up and hair products, or the depressing effect of having clothing rationed. Matters that might seem trivial to the men around them.

With Mike's arrival on staff, the need for the other doctors to work such long hours dwindled. Determined to pull his full weight, he was soon suggesting that their duties should have a more regular shift basis. As Rachel might have anticipated, Hamish wasted no time in asking her to spend some time with him. Still acutely conscious of how greatly indebted she was to him, Rachel didn't quite know how to refuse without seeming churlish. Once or twice they went to the cinema – on one occasion to see *In Which We Serve*, which she found quite inspirational while Hamish criticized its overt propaganda. Many current films were pure escapism, welcome to Rachel in particular. She worried constantly about Olav, while at the same time treating some of the war's more cruel effects in the hospital.

One evening out with Hamish, early in 1943, was to another dance at the air force base. To her disappointment, none of the men she'd met previously were there any longer, but the two of them were made welcome nevertheless and enjoyed the exuberant atmosphere. Even well aware that the apparent light-heartedness was no more than an antidote to the tasks engaging the whole squadron, no one could remain introspective for too long there.

Rachel danced with Hamish a few times, and several times with RAF personnel, as well as chatting with a number of WAAFs newly arrived in Yorkshire. Towards the end and having drunk her share of light ale, Rachel found Hamish at her side once more.

They danced as they had before, but more slowly now as the evening was winding down and the music softening accordingly. Hamish was holding her very close, but the familiarity accrued over the years prevented her from feeling uneasy. After saying goodnight to their friends they went out to his car, and found stars glistening in the winter sky while a full moon gleamed down on to a light snow covering. Even parked beside the perimeter of an air base, it all looked quite ethereal.

'This suddenly appears so peaceful,' Hamish remarked, and wished he felt at peace regarding his personal life. For so long now Rachel had seemed to be blocking his every attempt to become closer to her.

'I can't help feeling enchanted by the night,' she agreed.

Surprised, Hamish resolved to use this opportunity – there might never be another chance. Over the moorland roads towards Keld House, he drove carefully, more slowly than his normal pace. When they encountered no other vehicle the experience felt like further proof that the night was special, theirs alone.

With Mike keeping an eye on the ground-floor wards and Donald on the rest, Hamish resisted his customary impulse to check that everything was in order, and was satisfied with signing in. He detained Rachel with a gentle hand at the door of her room. 'Don't desert me yet, please. I'd love another drink, had to watch it over there because of driving home.'

She felt too relaxed to be obstructive, and was well aware how frequently this war generated massive tension. She ought not to deny Hamish a few more minutes of her time.

'I don't want another beer, I'm afraid,' she said in the sitting room as he crossed over to pour.

'Fine, we've still got a drop of brandy.'

'I don't really feel like that either,' Rachel said, smiling. 'You go ahead with whatever you wish.'

Pouring a tot for himself, Hamish took a couple of sips, then went to the chair where she was seated. Placing his drink on a low table, he took Rachel's hand. Before she realized his intention, he had drawn her to her feet and pulled her down on to his lap. Hamish reached for his glass, took a further sip. When he kissed her, brandy moistened her lips. She relished its taste on his tongue but its potency threatened to make her gasp. His mouth moved on hers, and his tongue began exploring.

Rachel moaned. Hamish misinterpreted her protest as passion. Feverishly, he drank in more brandy, conveyed it into her mouth. Her inner being responded to the spirit, to his nearness: a pulsing here, a nerve end awakening there, and everywhere the need to belong. They had known each other so long . . .

Hamish *was* a part of her, and she a part of him because he had saved her. She would always owe him. He was stirring now, as were his fingers over one breast and at her spine, willing her to belong with him. His mouth again possessed her own, asserting a need impossible to ignore. Hamish ignited desire deep within her, driving Rachel against her will, compelling obedience to these electric sensations.

Her body seemed possessed of a power beyond conscious control, echoing each stirring of his, alive to his attraction. The force of their passion amazed Rachel. And suddenly repelled her.

'No, Hamish.'

'Not yet? Sure. Fine. We'll go to my room.'

'No, no.'

'Yours then.'

Where Olav's photograph was waiting? And the note she treasured, along with dreams of their post-war future. How could she, ever? Anywhere? 'I mean no, not at all. This is enough.'

'For you, maybe. Don't pretend you don't know what you're doing to me. We've been through this before. I thought you'd be more understanding.'

'I'm sorry.'

'It's not compassion I need from you, Rachel. I love you, feel that I've loved you forever. This isn't only sex.'

'For me it is. With you. I . . . I almost wish I felt more.' Her protest had slowed the rhythm of his stirring, but not its insistence. Rachel willed her own yearning to subside.

'You can't spend your whole life longing for the brother you lost, he wouldn't want you to deny yourself happiness.'

'This isn't because of him. It's just . . . *everything*. Nothing seems right.'

'That is this bloody war. Believe me, Rachel, when we've won through we'll all feel differently. And that's when I want you to marry me.'

'Marry?' Now she was totally appalled.

'I love you, and want you. For always, Rachel.' Hamish manoeuvred her off his lap and stood up, then drew her fiercely against him. Pressing at her, his hips moved once more, the message of his firm body forceful and unashamed.

But she was ashamed of permitting herself to need him. He cared too much. Gone was the time when they might sate mutual need by acknowledging the demands of attraction. Hamish wanted complete commitment.

'Marry me, Rachel. Marry me. Make me that promise.'

How easy life would be if she felt free to do so. But her love for Olav was the sacred bond, the feeling generating hope, belief in a better life. Her vision of the life she might have, all those miles away, which meant far more than anything.

Working together grew more difficult still. Rachel could have accepted daily frowns, a resentful attitude. Only Hamish wasn't like that. Hurt though he may be – that showed in the clouding of his brown eyes – he was neither angry nor affronted.

And she deserved that he might be both. Allowing him such intimate kisses and caresses had been entirely wrong, arousing him while she had known from the start that there would be no satisfactory conclusion for him. Certainly not marriage.

Worst of all was disapproving of herself, wondering what kind of a person she was turning into. Why had she become ready for loving, when she could not love Hamish?

The only solution was in escape, and that Rachel once more achieved by going home each time that she had a long period off duty. One of the best things about joining her family was discovering that the old awkwardness between her grandparents was easing considerably.

This ease between them became very evident on the spring day when Rachel and her grandfather decided to revisit Fountains Abbey. They were unsure how close they might get to the ruins in wartime, but even seeing the abbey from some distance would be good, and she had the following Sunday free.

'We'll take a picnic. I'll get Mrs Hardaker to pack something up for us,' Bernard Davidson suggested.

'Then we'll take my car,' Rachel insisted. 'I don't use all my petrol allowance, and I haven't driven anywhere to relax in ages.'

'Would you have room for another one?' Hedda enquired, listening. 'I have not visited Fountains Abbey since I first came to England years ago.'

'Of course you must come with us,' said Rachel.

Bernard was beaming across at Hedda, his silver-grey eyes bright with affection. 'You've got to come, that is a must! Do you remember how we explored its daughter abbey at Lysekloster?'

Hedda nodded, tears spilling from her eyes, and Rachel recollected hearing that visiting the Norwegian abbey had brought the pair together. It seemed to her that organizing this outing might be meant solely for the elderly couple. This feeling continued on the day when they set out, the easy good humour between them permeating her car to convince Rachel that the worst of the differences between Bernard and Hedda were over.

They reached Fountains Abbey in spring sunlight which

enhanced their mood. Rachel soon indulged in private smiles as Bernard was quick to take Hedda's arm or her hand to assist wherever the ground might prove tricky.

They ate their picnic lunch in a spot sheltered from the breeze, relishing the open air all the more because the reality of the work necessary during this long war so often deprived them of a chance to relax.

On the way back to the house Bernard took it for granted that he should sit with Hedda in the back of Rachel's car, and she smiled fondly when her rear-view mirror reflected their clasped hands. She couldn't have wished for a happier conclusion to their day out. Delighted for her grandparents, she herself felt more at ease than she had for a long time.

Finding her father at home pleased Rachel still more, and she smiled around the table while they all enjoyed high tea. Just for once she felt able to obliterate thoughts of the terrible war, and the suffering which depressed her so with each new intake of casualties.

Rachel didn't believe her own wound had played any part in this new depression. She'd always been horrified by the harm man could inflict on his fellow man. It seemed more likely to her that the increase in the number and severity of casualties was to blame. Whatever the cause, she was becoming sickened by dealing with all the traumas.

Naturally, her strained relations with Hamish did nothing to lighten the atmosphere at Keld House. She had become so wary of being alone with him that she caught herself devising elaborate means of avoiding him when off duty. After visiting Fountains Abbey she was staying in her old room and driving back to the hospital at dawn rather than risking a meeting when Hamish came off duty. Glad she could sit chatting with her parents and grandparents, Rachel was taken aback when Asta announced that she had to report for Red Cross duty.

'This war doesn't take account of Sunday evenings, does it?' Asta added, when her husband protested that he had only hours ago come ashore. Although she wouldn't dream of saying anything of the kind to him, Asta did rather resent the fact that Andrew could disapprove of her going off to work, while he was so frequently away from home for days on end. Away and in danger.

After Asta had gone out, Rachel noticed that her father moved to sit very close to the wireless set, and gave every appearance of being riveted by the programme which was turned down low so that none of the others could listen.

Bernard and Hedda seemed lost in their own world again, reliving old times from their courtship and early married life. Pleased for them though she was, Rachel was beginning to feel a little left out, and even contemplated returning to the hospital that night. She could surely manage to avoid Hamish if she was desperate to do so.

'There were good times,' Hedda was saying. Rachel saw her grandfather frown. 'I do know what you are thinking, Bernard,' said Hedda. 'But do you never consider that I might be regretting the way I left our home here?'

He shrugged. 'And how many years did it need before you reached that conclusion? The route back was open to you years before this war intervened.'

Hedda was frowning now, wondering how in the world she might encourage him to permit her another chance.

'We do enjoy some happy times together, even now,' she ventured. 'In quiet companionship, like today. That could work.'

'A pleasant interlude,' Bernard agreed, but sighed. 'But totally unrelated to real life. You have no idea of what I want.'

Rachel stood up, decided to leave them together to sort out what they both needed. 'Think I'll get back to the hospital.'

She turned to say goodbye to her father, and was conscious of Bernard getting to his feet behind her. So much for believing his relationship with Hedda had improved.

'Want a lift, Granddad?'

'Thank you, no, Rachel. Need a walk to clear my head.' Without a further word to anyone, Bernard strode from the house, shutting the door very sharply behnd him.

'Not like him,' murmured Andrew and returned to his wireless set.

Hedda was crying. Instead of leaving, Rachel went to put an arm round her. 'Want to talk, Grandmother?'

'You'll only think me a foolish old woman.'

'I'll risk it, if you will.'

'Were you really wishing to go back to Keld House tonight?'

'No. I just thought you and Granddad might need to be on your own.'

'Am I in the way now?' asked Andrew, still upset that his wife had gone out while he had a rare night at home.

Hedda smiled towards him. 'Not you. Not in the least, my dear. And I think that Rachel and I might speak quietly for a little while in my room.'

After climbing the stairs, Hedda seemed rather short of breath as she sat on the bed and indicated that Rachel should take the chair.

'Are you all right, Grandmother? You are up to par with your medication?'

Despite herself, Hedda smiled again. 'This reminds to me of the time when we were aboard that tiny boat. And yes, I have observed the dosage regularly and meticulously. It is only that I do not breathe so well when I am . . . well, *distressed.*'

'Maybe you're upsetting yourself unnecessarily. We did have a lovely day, and Granddad does think a lot of you.'

'If not enough!'

'Why do you say that?'

'It is the truth. Each time that I believe we might come somewhere near to recovering at least part of what we have lost, he walks away. Always walks away. How are we ever to find some solution when he refuses to discuss?'

'So, this isn't the first time?'

'More like the hundredth. And he tears from me my heart. I love him so much, Rachel. So very, very much.'

'And he loves you. He always has, even while you were in Bergen.'

'But not in the same way. You do not comprehend. Nor do you know how I made myself the fool with him.'

'You? I find that hard to believe.'

'I was so . . . so immodest. That night when you were injured, and we went to his house. He held me close, we both needed that, I think. He kissed me, just a little. And I . . . But no, I cannot tell it to you.'

'I shan't understand if you don't.'

'Bernard was to me so kind, so blessedly familiar. I did not stop myself when I tried to kiss him more fully, as a young woman would with her sweetheart.'

Rachel struggled to conceal a smile. No reaction of hers must seem inappropriate. 'If that was the way he made you feel, kissing him thoroughly might not have been a bad idea.'

'He turned away from me at once, in much the same manner that he left this house for his own today. It is plain to see that Bernard Davidson would not wish to share his life with me again.'

'Or would not wish the kind of life that you were outlining earlier this evening – one where you enjoyed companionship, but perhaps nothing more.'

'No, no – it is that he finds me repulsive now. I am old, Rachel, destined for a solitary life. I think perhaps it would be better for him if I returned to Bergen as soon as peace comes.'

'With your private yearnings unfulfilled? Have you ever considered the possibility that Granddad might experience similar yearnings, that he could be afraid that you only want that quiet life you mention, devoid of sex?'

'And *if* that were so, *if* – how on earth do you imagine he and I would ever overcome the lack of comprehension between us?'

'You have lots of spirit, Grandmother, enough to force you to endure that dreadful journey to come here. Are you really so terrified of appearing a little sexy for the man you love?'

Thirteen

Hedda remained distressed about her relationship with Bernard for weeks, yet without the least idea how she might improve their situation. He continued to see her with Asta and Andrew in their home, but less frequently invited Hedda to his own house. He remained genial with her, but seemed cold, as if he'd withdrawn the bit of affection shown during the outing to Fountains Abbey.

Hedda felt herself growing increasingly inhibited. Her head was an airing ground for all the early reminders from her mother, old codes stating it was unbecoming for a lady to reveal her emotions until prompted. *Emotions*, never mind desires, thought Hedda dismally.

Things finally changed with an event far beyond Yorkshire, miles to the north, in Arctic waters off Norway when the Royal Navy sank the *Scharnhorst*, the last major German ship. It was December and the entire family were delighted. As they looked forward to 1944, it did begin to seem that there might one day be an end to all the years of fighting. For Hedda, decision-making time began looming much nearer.

With Norway being near the site of the *Scharnhorst*'s destruction, Bernard increasingly wondered what Hedda might be feeling about her old country. Was it inevitable that she must be looking forward to going home? They had spoken of the good times spent together, had enjoyed each other's company again, but not one word had she said about wishing to stay in Yorkshire.

He had been left by her once, he wasn't about to expose his feelings to a repeat of that experience. Perhaps he would be wiser to start to curtail the time they spent together. He couldn't bear to think how terribly he would miss her.

Finding Hedda the one person left in his waiting room at the end of surgery a few evenings later, Bernard gazed at her. He hadn't any idea what he might say. 'Are you ill?' he asked eventually, falling back on his medical role because all others failed him. 'If you are, I'm afraid I am not the person to help. I'm not allowed to treat close family.'

'Not ill, no.' Hedda managed an awkward smile while she drew her thick coat tightly around her. 'I do have a problem, and not one that I am prepared to discuss in Asta's house.'

'She hasn't been upsetting you? Asta's not endowed with massive comprehension of other people's feelings. You must have seen that she can appear quite sharp – sometimes even where Andrew is concerned.'

'It is nothing remotely connected with Asta. And I do not know where to begin to tell you. However, you are a doctor, and I figured that I must be outspoken this one time, or live with regrets for the rest of my years.'

'This sounds very serious. You'd better come through.'

Bernard led the way into his consulting room, indicated a chair on to which Hedda sank very rapidly, then went to his own seat beyond his desk.

'Well . . . ?' he prompted. He stared down at her hands which were kneading at the gloves she'd removed.

Hedda sighed. 'You do not make this easy for me. Firstly, I need you to understand that if I am making even more of a fool of me than I fear, you must dismiss what I am telling to you. My trouble, you see, is embarrassing. And connected with you, Bernard.'

'With me? A problem of mine, perhaps?' Making a joke of it was a method he often used with troubled patients. 'I do try to maintain personal freshness, despite wartime shortages!'

Hedda laughed. 'You need not worry on such an account. On the contrary, the difficulty is . . . well, that you are too . . . too desirable.' Hot colour rushed up from her chest, over her neck, and flooded her face. She had meant to say *attractive*, had *rehearsed* attractive, but agitation had diminished her skill with the English language and created this eloquent substitution. When she dared to look at him again, Bernard's eyebrows were soaring. But he was smiling.

'How ridiculous,' he began, but his smile didn't falter.

'I know,' Hedda interrupted apologetically. 'I am probably much, much too old to be having any such thoughts. I do not know what on earth you must be thinking of me. You must not worry, though, I shall not expect anything of you.'

'Then I will be very sad.' He reached right across the desk and stilled her restive fingers with a firm hand. 'What a pair we are – thank goodness the family can't know! Don't you see, Hedda? I've been avoiding certain situations with you because I couldn't trust myself. I need you so desperately, my love.'

Hedda gasped, swallowed, drew in a long, slow breath. 'While I was speaking of companionship, because I dared not utter any hint of what I really wanted!'

He rose swiftly, impulsively, and strode around the desk to draw her to her feet. Hugging each other they kissed repeatedly, as fervently as ever in their lives before. Eventually, they went through from his surgery into the house. Surprised to find Mrs Hardaker still there, preparing Bernard's dinner, Hedda hesitated. He had no reservations. Standing with his arm about Hedda, he smiled at the old housekeeper.

'You shall be the first to know – Hedda and I are back together again. This is very recent, since ten minutes or so ago. We're not sure where we'll live or anything, but it will no longer be apart.'

'Eh, I am glad, Doctor! For you both, of course. I've seen how you've seemed happier with each other, even despite the war.'

Much later that night, Bernard asked his wife if her heart would be set on returning to Norway when the war ended. If that was what she really needed, he could be content to move there with her. They had spent hours in their old bedroom convincing each other that their love had endured all traumas. Hedda smiled serenely at his question.

'You should not need to ask that when we have just proved how well this home suits us.'

Bernard nodded, well pleased. 'It was only that I wished to do something to show I'm determined this marriage will succeed. There doesn't seem much scope for significant gestures when you wear my ring already.'

The months had passed and they were well into the summer of 1944 when Hedda suggested that they might ask the local vicar if he could arrange a ceremony in which to renew their wedding vows. 'I need something to show how committed I am to ensuring we shall remain together for always,' she added.

Delighted by her idea, Bernard agreed that her Lutheran background need create no problem. Asta and Andrew privately thought such a service rather unnecessary when the couple had lived together for several months now, but Asta nevertheless began thinking of how she might cater for a special party.

Rachel was very enthusiastic for both grandparents, sensing it was good for them to mark this renewal of married life. She made certain she could have time off in order to witness the ceremony, and was looking forward to celebrating with them on the last Sunday of August.

The shock came for Rachel a few days afterwards. Hamish greeted her, smiling widely as she came on duty. 'I'm delighted to receive an invitation from Hedda and Bernard, your grandparents are such lovely people.'

And they've done this believing they'll please me, she thought grimly. They could not have known of her everlasting struggle to avoid situations where she was alone with Hamish anywhere outside the hospital. There was nothing she could do, and no one she might tell, without seeming even more difficult than she was beginning to believe herself to be. No matter what reservations she held regarding him, Hamish still gave every appearance of remaining devoted to her.

On the day, Rachel insisted that she would use her own

car despite Hamish's suggestion that they save petrol by travelling in his. She was determined to surround herself with people and prevent any recurrence of situations where Hamish's attraction might arise. If she trusted him, she couldn't entirely trust her emotions.

Limiting their encounters to the hospital environment was serving her well: there they could co-operate on the job in hand, as they still did very successfully, and dismiss personal feelings.

At Keld House they were just as busy as ever before. The D-Day landings had produced inevitable casualties amid the success, and men brought back to English ports were being transferred further inland for treatment. Due to eventual progress in Normandy, however, there was a general air of optimism which made some wounded men less resentful of having to leave the battlefields. Military personnel and civilians alike were beginning to feel more hopeful that the war in Europe would reach a satisfactory conclusion.

On the eve of the Davidsons' church service, news came through that Paris had been liberated, a sure indication that the struggle to bring freedom throughout Europe was being won. On their way to the church Hedda spoke earnestly of her feelings. 'You know how I once loathed the whole concept of fighting, but I must admit now that some motives justify the actions taken. I only hope that you can forgive me for that time all those years ago, when I could not see a way to remain in a country that had chosen war?'

'Of course, my love. We would not be here otherwise.'

And much of the ceremony included words of forgiveness and understanding. Listening, Rachel wondered if a form of service already existed for such a renewal of vows, or if the selection had been made between the couple and the local vicar. However it had come about, the occasion moved her deeply, especially on account of being realistic, asking forgiveness for all that had been amiss, as much as sharing in the couple's joy.

Most of all, though, she was touched by the renewal of their wedding vows, ending with them saying together: 'Today, in the presence of our family and friends, we affirm our continuing commitment to this vow.'

Bernard then turned to face his wife. 'Hedda, I gave you this ring as a sign of my lifelong commitment to you.'

Hedda, with tears coursing down her cheeks, responded, 'Bernard, I received this ring as a sign of my lifelong commitment to you.'

They then said together, 'So may this ring continue to be a symbol of our giving and receiving, together in endless love.'

There were blessings of the couple, with a prayer that the pair may be granted wisdom and devotion in their life together, that each may continue to be to the other a strength in need, a comfort in sorrow, and a companion in joy.

Hearing those words, Rachel was overcome with the yearning for someone who could mean that much to her. The vicar's address, final hymn and blessing were lost to her. For all her joy for her grandparents' sake, she had never felt more terribly alone. Olav was so far away, their relationship so insubstantial.

Asta and Andrew were hosting a small reception which Rachel might have preferred to miss. She would not do anything of the kind, of course – she couldn't let her own longing to escape diminish her grandparents' happiness. In line beside her parents, the couple were welcoming everyone into the house where Rachel had grown up. She clamped a smile on to her lips and began passing around drinks and plates of food and felt her personal anguish easing.

As well as family, one or two of Bernard's oldest patients were present, plus friends from their early life in and around the area. Warm Yorkshire voices filled rooms open again after years when wartime economies had closed them. The local inflections made Rachel realize that at Keld House she'd grown accustomed to having most dialect diluted by the influx of people from other parts of Britain. But one voice that she recognized all too swiftly, and without turning, was Hamish's. 'A beautiful service, don't you think Rachel? Such a lovely renewal of promises does the soul good in these cynical times. Don't you long for the assurance of such devotion?'

'Naturally,' she responded quickly. 'Who wouldn't? With the right person.'

'Have you really never considered that one person ought to be given the opportunity to prove that they could be right?'

'Hamish, please don't. I'm making a real effort to keep contention of any kind out of this occasion. And I am still afraid that I'm not going to be more than a friend to you.'

Hamish hadn't even had time to speak or to turn away before the vicar began a short speech, preparing to toast Bernard and Hedda. 'There seems so much hope around on this day,' he began. 'I can't resist the urge to share with you my personal joy at having heard from my brother, a chaplain with the forces who've liberated Paris. Even those of us not permitted to engage in fighting may rejoice at its happy outcome. And so it is that this renewal of love between these two dear people here comes at a time when events allow us to look more optimistically towards the future. Their example in expressing a love that will sustain them throughout their lives is encouraging. And encouragement is quite often all that anyone needs in order to survive life's uncertainties. It is, therefore, my great pleasure to ask you to drink with me to the future of Hedda and Bernard.'

Hamish could have taken no more than one sip from his glass when he set it down and turned away. 'Do give them my apologies for leaving,' he murmured to Rachel while everyone was applauding.

Relieved to feel free to relax, Rachel continued to circulate among their guests and was pleased, if a little embarrassed, when her grandfather frequently reminded his friends or patients that she also was a doctor.

When Bernard and Hedda eventually left for their own home, Rachel stayed to help her parents clear up after the party. Asta seemed very tired, although Hedda had helped with early preparations for the celebration, and Andrew had been home from sea long enough to assist with moving furniture and organizing the setting up of trestle tables that he'd borrowed from someone.

'You've done wonders putting on a good spread, love,' he complimented Asta. 'Don't know how you've managed while so much stuff is rationed – or even unobtainable.'

'Well, I had to do my best, didn't I?' she said, grey eyes gleaming. 'It's not often we get a good excuse for a bit of a do nowadays. And they did look happy, didn't they, bless 'em?'

Her husband nodded, smiling. 'I know I wondered if they were daft to go to all this trouble, but the day proved me wrong. That ceremony suited their situation to a T. I'm sure it'll set them up for the future.'

Rachel couldn't have agreed more, and whenever she saw her grandparents afterwards she felt warmed by the very evident success of their marriage. They were planning together for the eventual end to the war, when they hoped renewed supplies of suitable materials would enable them to bring in a decorator to refurbish their home. Bernard was the first to admit that while living alone he had given little thought to improving the place, while Hedda was hoping to eventually bring some of her own furniture across from Bergen.

Their looking so far ahead was good, a reassuring reminder that peace would bring a very different way of life for everyone. Andrew Skelton was planning to rejuvenate his business when all his trawlers could be devoted to fishing again instead of participating in minesweeping and similar wartime duties.

Asta was yearning for the time when her husband's work would be less hazardous. To her, the North Sea had always seemed quite dangerous enough without threat from enemy planes, ships, or the dreaded mines. For any woman who was a worrier like herself, there would be no peace until everything to do with the Germans had been eliminated.

Rachel was inclined to be more optimistic about the remaining months of the war, despite the awful flying bombs that were now devastating several parts of England. Mainly these were in the south and in East Anglia, and upsetting though they were, they seemed no threat to her own family. She could feel thankful for that fact while sympathising with all who suffered these attacks.

Her optimism faltered on Christmas Eve. Several V1s found targets across Yorkshire and Lancashire – the nearest to Keld House landed at Pocklington. Suddenly there seemed less joy in celebrating the Christmas for which households had been given additional rations.

As always, at the hospital they laid on festive entertainment for their patients and were inviting the choir and clergy of their local church to attend on New Year's Eve for a watchnight service.

Although, following her grandparents' celebration, Rachel had been uneasy whenever she was alone with Hamish, he had apparently recovered his good humour towards her. He and Donald were planning to eventually turn Keld House into a small civilian hospital. They were including Rachel in any such discussions, but she had given them no indication that she intended to remain a part of the team. For the present she was staying only because Mike Preston had gone to a different post, and she hadn't the heart to leave them deprived of a further doctor.

Even while they continued to tend military personnel, she was looking ahead to a time when she could justify her impulse to leave. For the present, she could accept Hamish's assertion that they would be needed in their current capacity until most of their patients had received the necessary treatment. After that she could look forward to what she saw as her freedom.

And she did need to get away. Recognizing that she was fortunate that Hamish did not persist in trying to deepen their relationship hadn't removed the uncomfortable feeling he generated in her. And her discomfort was increasing because of the way her own emotions seemed to be altering. Rachel had always felt saddened that their differing expectations regarding their personal lives rendered their working together less congenial. She had developed her experience and her skills during her years at Keld House, and had become much more proficient in assisting in theatre. This was one aspect of her work which she would love to expand after the war, and she was willing to study further in order to become a surgeon. Over the years she had kept in touch with Shirley Trent, and envied her experience in assisting Archibald McIndoe, whose 'Guinea Pig Club' patients were proof of his advancing techniques in plastic surgery.

'I gather that Hamish is thinking of keeping your hospital going after hostilities end,' Bernard remarked one day when Rachel had called on them for tea. 'I dare say you'll be relieved that you've got a position ready made for you there, without starting afresh somewhere strange.'

Initially Rachel didn't know how to respond, but she decided to put them in the picture. 'Between ourselves, I'm not intending to stay on there once it's no longer a military hospital. Making changes to the set-up will be a good time to make changes of my own.'

Her reasons for wanting to get away were growing with her fresh consideration of her friendship with Hamish. She needed some distance between them again – to test whether she would miss him as much as she was beginning to suspect she might. The prospect of no longer seeing Hamish at work sometimes felt alarming.

'But where will you go?' asked Hedda. 'I hope that you will not choose somewhere too far from us.'

'I really don't know,' Rachel admitted. 'For the first time in my professional life, I don't seem able to look far ahead.'

'Any road, there's no saying quite when we'll have Hitler beat, is there?' said Bernard. 'Then there'll still be the Japanese to finish off.'

'Exactly,' said Rachel. 'Happen I'll need a bit of breathing space to think through what I truly want to do with my life.'

'And evidently that won't be with Hamish.' Bernard was disappointed. He had liked the young surgeon from their first introduction.

'And no other man either, is there, love?' asked his wife. She was too fond of Rachel to wish her to miss out on the joys of having the right partner.

Her granddaughter shrugged. 'I never meet anyone round here, do I?'

'Or don't believe they're good enough?' Bernard suggested.

Rachel grinned. 'It's never been that! It wasn't from choice that I used to feel unable to love Hamish in the way that he needed.'

'But he has helped you to overcome that feeling you had for so long – the emptiness that was caused by losing your twin,' Bernard continued.

'Actually, no. It was never Hamish who was responsible for that.'

She watched her grandparents exchange a puzzled glance, and felt surprised. Had Hedda Davidson never even suspected how much the meeting with Olav had done to heal that dreadful abyss in her life? Rachel only wished that there might have been something more substantial in that meeting, something that gave her reason to suppose she would even see Olav again, never name develop a deep relationship with him. Had there been anything of the kind, she wouldn't even be wondering if Hamish and she might have some kind of a future.

The closing months of the war allowed little time for looking towards her own possible plans. The wards at Keld House were constantly full, no sooner were patients discharged than further admissions arrived, bringing fresh injuries or medical conditions demanding immediate attention. Every doctor and nurse felt so harassed by such pressure that they were scarcely able to notice good news coming in from various parts of the battle in Europe. It was rapidly becoming evident that the approaching end to hostilities would produce little relief for those who were to tend the personnel who'd suffered in the fighting.

On rare visits home for a few hours' break, Rachel caught up on the news, especially relating to Scandinavia. During April she also learned from an injured coastal command pilot that 206 Squadron were working non-stop, hunting out

U-boats in the Kattegat and Skagerrak. One of his colleagues, arriving for treatment of injured fingers, brought word of what seemed to presage the end for Germany. He had seen an enormous amount of shipping, under escort of German fighters, crossing between the Danish and Swedish coasts heading towards Norway.

'We're positive it was a massive evacuation of enemy forces from Denmark,' he reported. This was confirmed on the following day, May 4th, when the remaining armies in north-west Germany and Denmark capitulated to the Allies. A day or so later, the Germans in Norway surrendered. Soon afterwards Allied ships were reported to be sailing into Oslo Fjord. The following day Winston Churchill announced that the war in Europe was over.

During the celebrations a military hospital was a good place to be, even if the heartfelt rejoicing had to be tempered by acknowledgement that some of their patients would never return to being the fit men who'd enlisted all those years previously. For a time, Rachel found her enthusiasm for the work they were doing was increasing. Any patients who weren't gravely ill were in good humour, and where visitors managed to travel to see them they came full of plans for civilian life.

Only the continued fighting in the Far East could diminish the general widespread relief, and most of the forces who were hospitalized assumed that the war out there would be over before anyone could send them to back up existing units.

Admissions to Keld House were beginning to ease again when Hamish called a meeting to outline further ideas concerning the future of the hospital. 'It won't be long now before our forces and the Americans have beaten the Japanese,' he told Rachel and Donald plus a couple of nursing sisters. 'As you probably know, this place has been requisitioned throughout the war. The position now is that the original owner has died, and his executors wish to sell. The sum they hope to realize sounds to me very reasonable, and I'm willing to invest in the place, to which end I've been speaking with a backer who would be interested in helping finance us at Keld House. If any of you wish to do likewise, we'd be delighted.'

'Forgive me, but I'm not certain I understand your purpose in wishing to acquire this place,' Donald began, looking somewhat bewildered.

Hamish smiled. 'Thought somebody might raise that. The fact is, details are beginning to circulate within our profession concerning our future once the war and its aftermath are truly over. There's plenty of speculation that there's going to be some kind of restructuring of all services connected with health.'

'Do you mean local doctors as well as hospitals?' Rachel asked. She couldn't believe her grandfather would wish to continue working if that should happen.

'The lot, so far as we can guess from what was first mentioned a couple of years ago. Which is why I feel compelled to put forward ideas for having an independent hospital here. One that'd be run by us, in ways we consider best.'

'For patients who can pay over the odds, you mean?' Rachel didn't like that idea at all.

'I'm not the first person to come up with such a prospect. It would mean we could invest in all the latest equipment, the best new medication.'

'Count me out,' Rachel snapped. 'I don't hold with any of this.'

'You could hear me out on all that I have in mind,' Hamish reproved.

'I've heard enough.'

'Why don't you listen?' Donald suggested gently. 'This could be good.'

'For the wrong people. The elite who have enough brass behind them to pay to have better service, even newer medicines. I don't think so. No, thank you.'

Frowning, Hamish gave Rachel a look, and sighed. 'For the rest of you who might be interested I've drafted out my early thinking on what the initial steps should be. There are copies here for you to study.' He wound up the meeting shortly afterwards, but invited those who were keen to know more to hang on so that he might answer further questions.

He caught Rachel up as she headed through the door. 'I might have guessed you would oppose whatever I suggested. It's all a part of your general dislike of me, isn't it?'

'I don't dislike you, Hamish, I never have. And I wouldn't let my personal emotions get in the way of a scheme that I considered good. Put simply, I loathe the idea of people having to depend on having plenty of brass in order to get the best health care available.'

'And you're quitting now, before you become contaminated by my ideas?' Hamish was looking upset.

Rachel smiled slightly. 'Only if you wish me to. Otherwise, I'll be here until this ceases to be a military hospital.'

'That's something,' he said glumly.

She nodded. 'But you have just helped me to decide what I shall be doing afterwards.'

The relief of having Hamish know what her intentions were was enormous. Rachel began to feel quite light-hearted about spending what might possibly be only a few more months at Keld House. She would have regrets about leaving, of course, when did any major change occur without creating them? This hospital had been the first where she had been given substantial responsibility and, because of the war, more authority than she'd have had elsewhere. But she would soon be free to work wherever she chose. And she would be free of Hamish.

She had wondered previously if getting away from him could be good, if only to test whether she cared more deeply for him than she'd believed. Today, she'd seen an aspect of Hamish that she hadn't known existed, and it proved that she'd no desire to become more closely involved with him. His basic ambitions had been a shock, and made her realize that he might have further motivations that she couldn't condone. The prospect of ending this chapter of her life seemed likely to become reality, and now with far fewer reservations. Rachel's spirits soared.

Her immediate reaction to Hamish's plans was to try

to discover what others in her profession knew about the proposed National Health Scheme. Bernard Davidson might know something about the rumours concerning the future for medicine in Britain. She would be careful not to alarm him – he might have heard nothing, and might be perturbed by a threat of potential changes to his practice.

There was one other factor to consider, and that was the confidentiality of what Hamish was planning. No one else at Keld House had mentioned the ideas he had proposed. She might not wish to participate in Hamish's concept, but she wouldn't create problems for him by having word get around.

Rachel also yearned to talk through some of her own future ideas. She would do so with Hedda and Bernard, rather than with her parents who might try to become too involved.

As it turned out, it was some time before she had the opportunity to join her grandparents for a chat. For weeks the scarce hours that she spent with her family were always in her old home, and general discussion then was centred on the ending of the war in Japan, and the appalling bombing which had brought enemy capitulation.

By the time she finally did see her grandparents on their own, Rachel was counting the weeks to leaving Keld House. The influx of patients at the end of fighting in the Far East was waning, and they were into the first peacetime spring of 1946. Bernard soon pre-empted her announcement of quitting by his own decision to retire.

'I'm long past the accepted age, and Hedda's determined to see more of me.'

'And enjoy having you with me,' his wife put in.

Rachel smiled. 'That's lovely, I'm very pleased for you both.'

'And there's a lot to be done here,' Bernard continued. 'Redecorating, and I'm going to have a good clear out. Make room for some of Hedda's things. She's making plans for sorting out the house over there.'

'Will Olav give you a hand? How is he?' asked Rachel.

Ever since Norway was freed, Rachel had hoped to receive a letter from Olav. When none had arrived she'd been disappointed, but had told herself that she wasn't the only one who needed to sort out their working life before considering anything else. Once when she'd asked if Hedda had heard from him there had been no word, but that was shortly after the Germans left. She must have received something since. Rachel yearned for any news of him, even second-hand.

Rachel watched Bernard and Hedda exchange a look. Both were frowning. Hedda sighed. 'I am sorry, I can tell you nothing about him. I have written to his old address, several times, and have tried to telephone the number I had before the war. I have also written to enquire of my old neighbours. They have not seen him at my house. I am afraid we have to conclude that Olav is missing.'

Fourteen

Rachel closed her eyes, terribly shaken, and failed to see the second, significant glance between her grandparents when they noticed her distress.

'How long . . . how long is it then since anything was heard of Olav?' she asked, and noticed how strain made her own voice sound unfamiliar.

'The last we heard was while you were recovering from that dreadful stabbing,' said Hedda.

'But that was ages and ages ago. And you hadn't told me he was missing!'

'We've only recently reached that conclusion, love,' Bernard said gently. 'All along we felt sure that the next thing we tried would locate him.'

'We knew how busy you have been, and did not wish to add to your troubles. In any case, it was just this week that my neighbours finally replied.'

'Even though he is family, we'd no reason to suppose you would be especially concerned,' Bernard told her.

'Or not for certain,' added Hedda. She only hoped that Rachel might begin to understand that she had only wished to spare her anxiety.

'But you say you're both going to Bergen to sort out the house? When exactly? Do you know?' At least between them they ought to be able to find out *something*.

'Actually, Bernard cannot come,' said Hedda. 'Or not for some long while at least.'

'Oh? There's nothing wrong with you, is there, Granddad?' Fresh alarm surged in to add weight to her panic about Olav.

'No, Rachel love, nothing like that. I'm as fit as any man my age. It's just that retirement's come upon me rather suddenly. There's a brilliant young doctor eager to take over my practice, exactly the calibre of man I had in mind. Before all this worry about Olav resurfaced I'd promised to be around for the first few weeks of his takeover. Hedda doesn't really want to delay going to Bergen, and I don't want her to.'

'I'll go with you. I've got to,' Rachel asserted. 'I haven't taken more than the odd day off in months. And if Hamish doesn't like it, I don't care. I came here today to tell you I shan't be at Keld House much longer.'

'Is it closing then?' Bernard wanted to know.

'As a military hospital, yes. Did I mention once that I had it in mind to leave? Hamish is intending to run it for private patients, especially if this National Health Service is introduced. I don't go along with his idea.'

'But what will you do?' her grandmother asked.

'Whatever I fancy when something turns up, I guess. Right now, that isn't top of my priorities.'

'So – changes all round, eh?' Bernard remarked eventually.

Rachel nodded, but she was more interested in asking when her grandmother intended sailing for Norway.

'The passage is booked – two passages actually. I had made reservations before things went into motion concerning your grandfather's practice. I should be delighted to have your company, Rachel Hedda, but it is to be next week.'

'Fine, fine. The sooner the better. And if Hamish protests, no matter.' Amid such intense concern for Olav's safety, she could not worry about anyone else's reactions.

'I am afraid that we are not exactly travelling aboard a luxury passenger ferry,' Hedda told her. 'I have a cabin reserved on one of the cargo vessels.'

'But it'll be infinitely better than our last crossing in this direction! Which port does it sail from?'

'Newcastle,' said Bernard. 'I mean to drive you there, unless your dad insists on doing so. He seems desperate to help.'

'He has already done a great deal,' Hedda told her. 'Once he learned of my intention, he made enquiries until he discovered that some cargo ships take a few passengers.'

The late spring day was cool as they clambered aboard – and blustery, tossing their hair and tugging at their scarves when they leaned on the rail to wave to Bernard.

'I can hardly bear to leave him, you know,' Hedda admitted. 'But I need to bring my old life to a conclusion – and while I still have energy for sorting everything at my house.'

He does seem rather forlorn, thought Rachel – a large man who somehow appeared *more* diminished by looking like a neglected bear. She gave him a further wave and blew him a kiss, then put her arm around Hedda's shoulders.

'We'll soon be back, Grandmother.'

'I do know that. And so does he. Security in each other is a massive blessing.'

And one for which I yearn, thought Rachel, as with a final wave Bernard turned away. She would give her right arm to believe that Olav might be there for her. Adjusting to news that he was missing wasn't at all easy. In fact, even thinking that she might not see him again seemed impossible. Whenever she attempted to discipline her mind towards acceptance of the facts as they appeared, her brain whirled out of control. But she hadn't needed his disappearance to convince her that Olav meant a very great deal to her. *He must be somewhere, he can't be dead, I would have known.*

Hedda was shivering. Rachel's role as her carer kicked in and, for a while at least, superseded anxiety about Olav. Until they reached Bergen there wasn't a thing they could do for him. And in the meantime, they must familiarize themselves with this vessel, discover what the routine on board would be, and all the while Rachel would, once again, keep an eye on her grandmother's condition. So far as she was aware, settling back into life with Bernard had helped to keep Hedda's diabetes stabilized, and Rachel did not mean to let it run out of control while they were making this trip.

Despite the cold, the sea was sunlit – if decidedly choppy. From on deck it all looked very pleasant as they left land behind. Ordinarily, Rachel would have relaxed in the knowledge that the threat of attack from German aircraft had long since been removed. But this journey was far from ordinary. She knew that unless Olav could be found, nothing would ever again feel right for her.

Their cabin was small and certainly spartan. But they laughed together on entering, comparing its facilities to the meagre features aboard that fishing boat.

'We surely had quite an experience, thanks to the famous Shetland Bus,' said Hedda. 'Although I do believe that I was more afraid afterwards, when we were in that aeroplane!'

'You didn't think you might fly across to Norway this visit then?' Rachel teased her.

'I decided I should wait a little, until commercial flights become more regular between these countries.' Rachel laughed disbelievingly. Hedda shrugged. 'If perhaps in future years Bernard will visit Norway with me, as he has promised, I *might* travel by plane. A very large aeroplane.'

'The RAF were very good to us,' Rachel reminded her.

'I would not deny that. But if I was destined to fly with them one more time, I fear that I should make my excuses to remain earthbound.'

The lightness of their conversation set the mood for the daylight hours of their voyage. Night-time for Rachel was less than happy, as anxiety about Olav kept her from sleeping.

Approaching Bergen from the sea, Rachel thought initially that very little had altered. She could see from way out that the many inlets of the fjord leading to Vagen, the main harbour, were surrounded by once familiar clusters of buildings that drew the eye inland towards the Floyen and Ulriken mountain peaks.

As the vessel prepared to dock fellow passengers began pointing, indicating the site where an important pontoon landing stage had been destroyed. And then Rachel saw that the Hakonshallen and the Rosenkrantz Tower both showed signs of partial destruction. She heard someone mention that the damage was caused when an ammunition ship exploded, and the unstable appearance of many of the old wooden buildings along the Bryggen suggested that they too had suffered.

At her side, Hedda said little, gasping occasionally as fresh evidence of the war's havoc came into sight, but refusing to give way to emotion. Rachel swallowed hard, resolving to avoid speaking of the damage unless Hedda said something. But all her grandmother did say as they stepped ashore was, 'It is good to be back, if only for a short visit.'

They found a taxi, and soon were rushing uphill towards Hedda's former home. They were met on its path by the neighbours from the next house who had been lighting fires to air the place. Both visibly aged, with their advanced years revealed in greater fragility, their welcome was nevertheless hearty, and came with insistence that Hedda and Rachel must come into their home to take tea.

'In one moment, thank you,' said Hedda, after giving each of them a hug. 'I wish first to see my old house.'

Despite the fires the place felt cold, and smelled slightly damp, neglected. Rachel was glad for her grandmother's sake that there was an alternative to sitting around there before those fires had taken some effect.

Hedda's friends spoke virtually no English, but Rachel was content to unwind for a few minutes while the other three chatted in their own language. She had slept so little since hearing Olav was missing that she was thankful to be allowed to escape conversation.

The time would come when she and Hedda must tackle the massive task of sorting through her grandmother's lifetime of possessions and selecting the few that might be shipped back to Yorkshire. Originally when this job had been planned, Rachel had visualized their having Olav's assistance, and indeed had expected that the pain of leaving items behind would have been eased by his willingness to accept some of them. And to accept the house, for Hedda had told Rachel that was her dearest wish.

It was, of course, for a reason far more serious than the fate of family belongings that Rachel was yearning for Olav. She couldn't stop thinking of the way that, from their previous meeting, she had sensed that he could become the one person most important in all the world to her.

As soon as they were inside her grandmother's house again Rachel noticed the disappointment in the elderly lady's eyes, and was unsurprised when told that her friends still had no news of Olav's whereabouts.

'The sole consolation is that they maintain nobody has ever declared him injured or, worse still, dead. Knowing our concern, they have scrutinised every report, although due to their age they could do no more than that.'

'And what can *we* do?' asked Rachel, trying to conceal her own distress. She was well aware that Hedda must be finding the whole purpose of this visit upsetting.

'Olav has friends, from his previous work within the transport systems. Some of them I have met, others are merely names mentioned. Tomorrow perhaps we may begin to contact them.'

Hedda seemed content to remain alone to begin salvaging from every room the things she wished to take to England. Rachel went into town, to the railway station. Hedda believed that someone in one of the offices there might know how to locate Olav's friend Roald Blystad. Despite her limited knowledge of the language, Rachel succeeded in tracing him to somewhere called Sandviken where he was establishing a private seaplane business. Lacking any idea about where Sandviken might be situated, Rachel returned to Hedda and explained what she'd discovered.

'Do you wish that we should go there together?' her grandmother asked, although she had only just come in from the market where she'd been buying food for their stay.

Seeing that Hedda had barely started on sorting out her old home, Rachel shook her head. 'If you show me on a map, I ought to be able to get there.'

Hedda did better than that. Going to telephone from her neighbours to Roald Blystad's number, she arranged for Rachel to call on him the next morning.

* * *

The sun glinted off the fjord and gleamed back from the paint of the tiny seaplane beside the jetty at Sandviken. Expecting Rachel, Roald emerged from his combined workshop and office and extended a strong hand to shake hers.

'My English is not ver' good,' he told her at once. 'I hope that you forgive—'

'Wait till you hear my struggle with your language! But I believe that my grandmother explained the reason why I am here,' Rachel interrupted.

'You wish to contact Olav Larsen, my old friend. Since speaking with your relative, I think some more. I regret to have no recent news, but when I last heard of Olav he was many miles inland, over near Rjukan.'

'How long would it take me to travel there?'

Roald was shaking his head. 'I am believing that is not a good thing to do. Not before knowing for certain that Olav is there. When I saw him the war still was on, and many things make him unhappy.'

'You're not saying . . . ?'

'That he would do a stupid thing? No, not at all. But I think he move from that place. If you could give me some time, I make the enquiries to other acquaintances.'

'Should I call on you again, tomorrow perhaps? We do not have much time in Bergen.'

'Tomorrow, yes. Same time as today.'

Hedda was pleased to have help back at the house, and they worked steadily during the rest of that day with breaks only to prepare and eat meals. Rachel was feeling despondent after finding out so little about Olav – and none of that concrete – but Hedda seemed more optimistic, hopeful that revisiting Roald would provide more information.

The following morning was cloudy and wet. 'A true Bergen day,' Hedda called it with a laugh. Rachel was thankful that her grandmother's knowledge of the Norwegian climate had ensured that they had travelled equipped with rainwear.

Meeting Roald again, Rachel instantly felt that her short

trip to Sandviken was worthwhile. Enquiring of other friends, he had heard that Olav was working in Voss.

'There is much reconstruction there, I fly to its lake quite often, but not today. I have a reservation to take clients elsewhere. There is a train from Bergen to Voss that you may take. A short journey only.'

'Thank you so much, that is wonderful. And how do I find Olav there?'

Roald sighed, shrugged. 'That I cannot tell you. He was doing reconstruction work, Voss was damaged sorely. Is only little town, you will find him.'

The train journey was through beautiful countryside enhanced by snow-topped mountains, but Rachel took in hardly anything of her surroundings. She was too anxious about her arrival in Voss and the problem of trying to locate Olav. Having come this far, she could not bear it if they failed to meet up; but without knowing the precise kind of work he might be doing, how could she find him?

The town was indeed reassuringly small, and Rachel decided to begin by enquiring at Fleischer's Hotel, the only one of any size that she could see near the centre of the place. She had chosen a good starting point. Although no longer resident there, Olav had hired a room immediately on his arrival. The staff remembered him, and the fact that he was employed on a nearby building site.

That didn't sound at all right for Olav, but it was her only clue, and Rachel was compelled to follow it up. She was still surprised when she found him laying bricks for what looked to be the beginning of a small house.

'You've taken some finding!' Rachel exclaimed, and waited for his reaction.

Olav turned extremely slowly to face her, he might have been fearful of having the truth deny what his ears had told him from her voice. 'Rachel! God, but this is wonderful!'

He set down the brick from one hand and his trowel from the other, and sped the few paces to hug her. His kisses covered her cheeks, her eyelids and then her mouth where they lingered, passionately. Dust from his face mingled with the rain and scratched at her lips, but she could not have enough of his kisses. When Olav paused to draw in air, Rachel sought his mouth again while she hugged him closer.

'How did you find me?' he asked at last, ignoring the laughter and remarks from his workmates who'd stopped to watch.

'With difficulty. You didn't wish to be found, did you?'

'By you, yes. *Now*. No one else mattered.'

'Not even Hedda?'

Olav sighed. 'How is she?'

'Concerned about you. Physically, she is well, much better than when you last saw her. Oh, there's so much to tell you.'

'But not here. You stay in Voss, yes?'

Rachel shook her head. 'In Bergen, of course.'

Olav hesitated, pondering. 'I must work the rest of today, but then no more. They employ me each day as it comes, you understand?'

'On a casual basis, you mean?'

'Casual, yes. I may finish this night. You meet me at dusk and we go for the train.'

The arrangement did not go as smoothly as he had made it sound. After meeting Olav at the building site they had to visit his lodgings, where Rachel waited again until he had showered and changed then collected his belongings.

During the train journey she filled him in on details of her return with Hedda, whose new life in Yorkshire with Bernard meant that the house in Bergen was to be Hedda's no longer. Rachel stopped short of revealing her grandmother's intention regarding her home. That suggestion was one Hedda would wish to make herself.

'And what about you?' Rachel asked him. 'Why didn't you come back to Bergen in 1945? Why go missing?'

She saw his eyes fill with tears and was alarmed. Olav sighed before beginning to speak. 'I needed to take myself away from the old life, needed to think. Even today I am hurting because of the way that . . . that *things* have been for me.'

'You don't have to talk about it if . . .'

'To *you*, I must. I need for you to understand how I was afraid that all my principles, my motivation, had been misconceived.'

'But the work you did, providing transport, that was good, surely?'

'I do not mean before the war. It was during it, and afterwards.' He paused, thinking deeply. 'You heard perhaps of the Norsk Hydro plant, and the heavy water produced there?'

'Weren't the Germans keen to obtain it? Afraid I never understood why.'

'The reason was the cause of my problem. Long before the plant was sabotaged, you see, I helped in preliminary work for our partisans. It seemed then that it could be only good to secure this heavy water for the Allies. Sadly, after months of struggle to keep it from German hands, most of the supplies were destroyed. Diabolically, this happened as it was being shipped by ferry and many civilian lives were lost.'

'I can see that would be upsetting. But why was the stuff so important, anyway?'

'You do not know? Since before the war it was discovered that this heavy water could be used to manufacture atomic weapons.'

'I see.'

Olav sighed again. 'And so we come to the chief cause of my own unease, the cause that made me to rethink the motives for my life. You have seen – we all saw – how serious it was to use that vile atomic bomb. And I . . . nothing could rid me of the knowledge that I had some small part in securing something that contributed to such a weapon. The fact that no such use has yet been made of the product from Norsk Hydro is of no consequence.'

'OK,' said Rachel slowly, trying to digest all that he was telling her. 'And is your present work helping? Have you reached any conclusion?'

At last, Olav smiled. 'But yes. Reconstruction is becoming

the antidote for me, as it was over in Rjukan near the Hydro plant when my feelings had so much rawness.'

'You're going to be a builder now, no more work on transport systems?'

He shook his head. 'You misunderstand me. Reconstructing is what I must do with my life, and in my old work that too might prove to be necessary. I am ready to go back, to be used in whatever purpose must benefit my country.'

He hadn't been entirely specific, but Rachel felt reassured. She could still recognise the Olav she knew.

'And what of yourself?' he asked eventually, taking her hand, smiling as their train rushed on through the darkness. 'Is your fine hospital looking to the future?'

'In a way. But without me.' She told him about Hamish's desire to turn it into a fee-paying hospital. 'That is not for me. But I'm afraid I don't quite know what is. To be honest, this trip with Grandmother is a bit of a relief, good reason not to decide quite yet about my next move.'

'But without resorting to a melodramatic disappearance in order to think matters through!' he exclaimed ruefully.

Rachel grinned. 'I don't suppose I have the guts to go off on my own in quite that way. And *my* war work wasn't that differently motivated from my normal occupation. Rightly or otherwise, medicine can generally claim to have moral justification.'

All serious reflection ceased the moment Hedda met them at her door. Incoherent with delight, she hugged Olav and kissed him on both cheeks, while the two of them chattered excitedly in their own language. Rachel stood beside them, smiling, until her grandmother eventually recovered to realize that she hadn't yet invited them into the house.

It was too late at night to do more than rejoice together over being reunited. All three were exhausted, especially Olav who had laboured hard for hours before travelling back to Bergen. When he explained that he no longer had a home of his own, Hedda made up a bed for him. With promises that they would talk in the morning, he gratefully went off to sleep.

The following day was bright, sunny and dry, but with a

cool breeze. Sitting with the two women, Olav gave Hedda an edited version of the circumstances keeping him away from Bergen, and then suggested Rachel should walk with him. She expected they would wander through the city centre towards the harbour, but instead he began walking her uphill, leaving behind most of the houses, to stroll between trees, heading in the direction of Mount Floyen.

When they gained the summit at last he stood all but motionless, his head alone moving as he scanned the entire horizon with its many hills and glinting arms of the fjord. The wind was tossing his hair, reminding Rachel of the photograph she treasured, but this was a different Olav, matured by experience, a man who smiled less readily. She yearned to restore his happiness.

His arm went around her shoulders, he drew her close against his side, and she felt his kiss in her hair. Gazing downhill, nearer to the city itself, they noticed little evidence of war damage.

'If you don't look too keenly,' she said, 'you can believe nothing has changed here.'

Olav's laugh was rueful. 'I guess that might apply to me. Perhaps Bergen and I might belong together. If I have earned the right to return.'

'Someone thinks you might belong. Has Hedda spoken to you, about the house?'

'No. What about the house?'

'She wants you to have it, has planned that all along. Since deciding to go back to Grandfather, anyway.'

'But that is all wrong. I am not her closest family, you are. You and your mother.'

'You will see what Grandmother says.'

Rachel needed no house to make her completely happy. She felt complete this morning – Olav was at her side, his arm warming her, his breath more evident than the breeze about their heads. Her continuing happiness was rather less certain, despite the appearance of all being well with the city below them.

She hadn't known how much she cared. Only witnessing

the war damage in Bergen had revealed her own, intense concern for this place which was such a part of her heritage. With each hour she understood more of Olav's need to participate in reconstruction. Perhaps no action of theirs might entirely put right the harm that their generation had done here; they could only attempt to improve present circumstances.

'What happened to the people who once lived here, Olav? The Jewish people forced into leaving, others who lost their homes. How many struggled to oppose the German occupation and didn't survive? And what of the people who are left? The facilities they must have – replacement of all that is essential to make Bergen viable again, vibrant? If schools need rebuilding, they'll want new teachers.'

'And *doctors*, have you considered that, my Rachel?'

'I haven't dared to.'

'Not . . . dared?'

She couldn't explain that her longing to remain in Bergen depended entirely upon his wishing her to be with him.

At the house Hedda was waiting impatiently, uneasy because she hadn't yet told Olav of her decision regarding its future ownership. He had for so long been accustomed to being self-reliant, she suspected he wouldn't readily accept anything from her. There was this new strangeness, too, the tendency to *reflect*, far more evident in him than ever in the past. She could even believe that he might decide not to settle in her city.

Hedda was unable to delay one moment before discovering if he meant to ruin all her plans. 'I want you to have this place, Olav,' she began as he came in through the doorway. 'I have a home in Yorkshire, and a husband who needs me. I shall not be entirely happy to leave my birthplace, but shall feel easier if I know you could make it your home.'

Olav gazed all around him, smiling slightly. 'If I cannot revert to keeping an eye on you once more, second best might be caring for the home you loved.'

Hedda looked at him uncertainly. 'You do understand you would own this place, not merely cherish it on my behalf?'

'Whatever you say, and bless you. Thank you a hundred

times, for giving me a place where I can belong.' But belonging meant more than just possessing a house.

'We must drink to that,' said Hedda, going through to the kitchen to get the aquavit she had purchased that morning.

Glad to be alone with her, Olav turned to Rachel. 'Suddenly I have a future to offer, a home, and a loving heart. I may work once more on transport systems, make them my route to reconstruction. Would you consider sharing my life in this home which, I suspect, should really be yours?'

Rachel smiled, kissed him. 'You did say doctors could be useful in Bergen.' Living with this man, loving him, her work would be with his people, helping them to rebuild their lives. And building their own future. Together.

1